MILES TO GO

MILES TO GO

book one of the
ESCAPE THE MACHINE
trilogy

JOHN C. LUNSFORD

Los Angeles • New York • London

Miles to Go: Book One of Escape the Machine Trilogy

Our deepest gratitude to the Press Office at Tesla Motors Corporation for granting us permission to print the quote by CEO and Chief Product Architect Elon Musk. Thank you Penguin Random House and their permissions office for granting us the opportunity to reprint the quote by Ray Kurzweil.

Published by NuFreedom Press
Suite 152, 10073 Valley View St., Cypress, California 90630.
Printed in the United States of America.

This book is a work of fiction. All names, characters, businesses, places, events and incidents are either the products of the author's imagination or used in a fictitious manner. Any resemblance to actual persons, living or dead, or actual events is purely coincidental.

Cover design by Kathi Dunn, dunn-design.com.
Interior design by Dorie McClelland, springbookdesign.com

Miles to Go: Book One of Escape the Machine Trilogy

First Edition December 2014

ISBN-13
978-0-9895310-2-3

To my wife Anne
who held the faith that I would finish this work
and make a proper job of it.

And to all those who refuse to ignore
the nobility in our species,
however difficult it may be to detect at times.

Acknowledgments

In a very real sense, I have been preparing to write this book since I was 14 years old. That was when I discovered science fiction through reading Robert Anson Heinlein's *Stranger in a Strange Land*. I owe him a tremendous debt. I was fascinated by Heinlein's ability to spin characters and stories that completely absorbed my mind. His skeptical view of much that my culture told me to simply accept, nurtured in me an unquenchable desire to know more. That desire has served me to this day, half a century later. He showed me that courage and safety seldom walk the same path and that, in the end, integrity is all we really have.

Thank you, J. Michael Straczynski. You taught me an enduring lesson about craftsmanship in writing through your exacting consistency in producing five years of *Babylon 5*. It shines as a beacon to what can be done in telling a complex, satisfying story writ large across an enormous canvas. But, more than that, I owe you a deep debt of gratitude for your five questions: Who am I? What do I want? Where am I going? Who do I serve? Who do I trust? These questions define everyone's character and are the best aids to introspection I have ever found. There are threads of them throughout this text.

I especially want to thank Ray Kurzweil. When I needed source material on Artificial Intelligence (AI), I found you in my every Internet search on the subject. I read your *The Singularity is Near* twice and refer to it constantly. I have spent much of my professional life attempting to explain complex technologies in terms more understandable than those used when I learned them and, Ray Kurzweil, you are clearly a master in this field. I offer my particular thanks to you for showing me AI's promise where many others see a dire threat. There is still a great deal we don't know about where AI is going, and I treasure your presentation of the science for both its optimism and its caution.

My enduring thanks to Virginia Barrett, Marcia Waddell, Mark Perrah and Pauline Merry who took the time to read my manuscripts and contributed ideas to this book. A heartfelt thank you to my wife Anne S. Perrah, who is an accomplished author in her own right, and provided numerous suggestions and insights. I could not have done this without you.

Any errors—and the odd taking of poetic license—are entirely mine.

My editors, Jessica Abdulnour, and Eve Gumpel have done an incredible job of keeping my prose, characters and plots straight. Thanks as well to Jonathan Moch for his enduring example of what persistence can accomplish and his amazing graphics arts skills. Kathi Dunn and Dorie McClelland have made the combination of the cover and text layout an outstanding success. And my enduring gratitude to my book writing and marketing coach, Stella Togo, who took on the herculean task of pulling all of the bits together to make this book actually happen.

Last, but by no means least, I acknowledge the assistance I have received from the technicians and engineers of the world. The computer I am writing this on, the electricity that powers it, and the million and one conveniences that I enjoy in life have all allowed me to divert my attention to telling this story. I owe the assistance I receive from all of these wonders to you.

Prologue

"The final item on this evening's agenda is NanoStar—George?"

George Osterman turned his head toward the gravelly voice that had spoken his name. Barely disguising his annoyance, he responded curtly, "We're going to buy the company, wreck it, and sell the pieces. What's to tell?"

"George, a few of us would like to know why we are doing this. You did the research on it. So, humor us."

They sat around an enormous table with an obsidian-black surface that looked like a bottomless pool. The room was dimly lit. Its occupants preferred it that way, each face shadowed. To know of this place, this meeting, meant that you were a part of it or that your life was in imminent danger. There was no middle ground. George had to turn on a reading light to see his notes. That light cast an unflattering glare that made his face alone stand out in the room.

"All right, NanoStar is one of a half-dozen tech startups that has specialized in nanotechnology—literally the design and construction of microscopic machines that can perform manufacturing on a molecular basis. The typical implementation scenario for this technology is for these tiny devices to be self-creating until there are sufficient numbers of them to fabricate objects on a real-world scale. Think of turning a swarm of ants loose that would mine and refine materials, then use them to construct a car. The kicker is that they would be able to do all this without direction beyond the creation of the first few microscopic units."

At the grunts of surprise around the room, George responded, "Yes, that would shoot quite a large series of holes in a number of our more profitable enterprises, wouldn't it? That's why we have been keeping an eye on these companies and, with some of them, an impressive array of electronic surveillance as well."

From one of the darker corners of the room: "George, we've been hearing about this nano-nonsense for years and, as near as I can tell, it's just scientific fairy tales to keep the researchers impressed with their 'contribution to the future.' Are you telling me that someone has actually made it work?"

"On a very small scale, it's been working for years. One crowd of overeducated idiots has even used nanotechnology to spell out funny signs using individual carbon atoms—which was all well and good, as long as it was just a laboratory toy.

"But never ones to let good enough alone, some of the damned entrepreneurs got hold of the idea and decided they could make something real out of it. We have quietly created roadblocks for some of the better-financed and slower-moving efforts, but lately the number of new players in the game has mushroomed.

"Sooner or later the wrong combination of talent, enthusiasm and persistence" George paused to shake his head, "was bound to find its way into having a real shot at making nanotechnology an off-the-shelf engineering tool—which brings us to NanoStar.

"We blocked three different attempts by its owners to get financing but they managed to put a research team together from two of our other successfully defeated startups. That happy little group got more attention than we could stifle. My estimate is that they are no more than six months away from demonstrating working nano-machines that can make simple but useable machine parts.

"Once they prove their process, there will be no stopping it. We have to buy and destroy NanoStar now, before that can happen."

From a chair George had to turn his head to face, "George, you just said that NanoStar got its people from other thwarted efforts just like it. What's to keep this from happening again? Why wouldn't these same people just create another company, and another, and another?"

"You're right, of course," George acknowledged. "That's the cycle we have been cleaning up behind. So, this time, I did something different. My team of 'specialists' has inserted two of our own people into the company in positions where they can monitor the progress made by our technical problem children. The last one should have committed his work to the company's data server for inclusion into their patent applications today. This is our signal to make the buyout and take control of the designs through the non-competition agreements with the researchers."

A thin man, withered with age, smiled in appreciation. "Not bad, George. You buy out the company, acquire the rights to the technology and don't even have to patent it to keep it off the market. Unfortunately, these 'non-competition' agreements are typically not worth the paper they're written on if they are challenged in court—which puts us back to swatting expensive development flies."

From another chair at the other end of the huge table: "Yes, there is a high probability that we are just going to have to do this again and again. We can't suppress this forever. Wouldn't we be better off capitalizing on it ourselves?"

George looked around the room and let what some would mistake for a smile spread across his face. "Are you all really ready for two to three decades of lost revenue while we retool every plant and facility we have to accommodate this? Are you prepared to risk the loss of entire market segments because we didn't get nanotechnology developed for them first? Are you prepared to see your own personal holdings erode, possibly to unsustainable levels, while we struggle to cope with what will suddenly become an overly level playing field?"

As the temperature of the group's mood silently plummeted, George said quietly, "I didn't think so."

He continued: "NanoStar has done us one favor. It's attracted all the best and brightest talent in this technical area into one place and made them thoroughly known to my operatives. We will track them carefully after the breakup and, if they don't behave themselves, we will see to it that they have accidents, permanent ones, if necessary."

From another chair: "George, there are limits!"

George stood, abruptly spinning toward the speaker. "There are? Where were they when you needed your principal competitor for the bridge truss contract to bow out?"

George's eyes swept the room. "We will avoid these direct actions when possible, but we cannot and will not fail to use them when necessary. You are all aware of and in agreement with that or you wouldn't be here, now would you?"

From the head of the table: "We have all relied on George to take care of the grittier side of our affairs with dispatch and discretion. He will continue to do so.

"You see gentlemen, power, like virtue, is its own reward."

Chapter 1

It was almost time for the kill—and her blood was beginning to sing with the tension. A cobra is a long, sinuously beautiful animal, and she was its human equivalent.

Monica Chavez walked across the parking lot to her car, her heels loudly clicking across the simmering pavement. The control device in her purse both unlocked and opened the car door. She stood back to let the blast of heat from the interior dissipate; then she slid onto the driver's seat, leaving the door open. A quick look around verified that she was alone in the lot.

It was a pity she had to kill a man so handsome and accomplished. But he wouldn't be the first, or the last. A job was a job, and this one specified the termination of one Grant Thornton. So that was simply what she was going to do. None of these considerations in any way diminished the purely visceral pleasure she was anticipating from her work.

Monica was strikingly beautiful, and she knew it. As a simple, cold calculation, her arresting appearance could usually get her close to whatever and whomever she wanted—and she knew that, too. Without hesitation, her hand reached into the car's console compartment and removed a unique firearm.

It was a .22 caliber pistol that had been designed and built to her specifications as the perfect assassin's weapon. A quick check reassured her that it was ready, and she placed it carefully into the special clip that was mounted in her purse. She paused for a moment, then unfastened another button on her black silk blouse.

"There, that should do it."

She had barely completed the thought when her cell phone buzzed in her jacket pocket. She snatched it out, frowned at the calling number it displayed, and answered with undisguised aggravation.

"I thought we agreed that you weren't going to call me again before the job was done.

"Of course I know that the legal team is in place!

"Look, you hired me to do an inside cleanout ending in a takedown, and it would really help if you would just let me do the job. I have one more target to process, and then you'll have it all. Now stop calling me!

"Yes, yes, I will call you as soon as I have his project components. You'll see the rest on the evening news."

Monica punched the disconnect button, thought a moment, then turned the phone off altogether and slid out of the car. She looked at the office building that gleamed in the bright summer sun.

"Nice, really nice. Too bad it's all about to go away."

She relocked the car door, adjusted her facial expression to "harried secretary," and strode back across the lot. Her entry into the building was a nondescript door marked "Employees." From there, the lab was just three doors down the hall on the right. She reached the glass door of the lab and saw Thornton at his workstation, typing away.

"Good."

Monica walked in and stopped beside Grant. She noted how his lab coat seemed almost like a uniform. Everybody wore one here—well, almost everybody.

"Grant."

No response.

"Grant, please?"

She had worn her four-inch heels to give her even more height and deliberately stood close enough for her perfume to do its part and the blouse to have its desired effect. She was confident of getting what she wanted—eventually. But her target of the moment seemed to be more of a challenge than most.

Grant Thornton's six-foot height, 180 muscular pounds, thick black hair and easy smile were distracting to say the least. When dealing with a stubborn case like him, she needed every advantage she could muster. She had to stay focused!

"Grant, you were supposed to give me your research abstract yesterday. Bersford has been bugging me continuously about getting it entered in the patent presentation for the lawyers. He expects it edited and polished today. That's my job; you don't have to do it. All I need is for you to put your documents, even your raw notes, on the server, now, before they all come back from lunch and Bersford comes down on me with both feet!"

Barely looking up, he replied with mock seriousness, "Oh, Monica, Bersford wouldn't do that—one foot maybe but not both."

"Grant!"

"Relax, I have about another fifteen minutes of correlation to do on this last set of test results, and I'll have all the pieces up on the server for you to stir and polish to your heart's content and Bersford's satisfaction."

Grant gave Monica an irritated sidelong look. "But it won't happen if you keep standing at my elbow and being a distraction. Now off with you!"

He watched Monica shove the lab door out of her way as she left and thought for a moment about their most recent conversations. She clearly wanted something and, if it was him, he knew he was going to have to explain to her in so many words that, for him, marriage really did make him a one-woman man.

That thought brought him back to his abstract. He considered it to be fully as much Ellen's as his. She had bucked her father's opinion to marry him in the first place. Then she had worked while he went to school and spent long nights editing his papers and making sure that what was blindingly obvious to him was at least understandable to the rest of the world.

From the first day they met at college, she had been a part of him. And now, he couldn't imagine life without her. Grant loved Ellen in every way that had ever given meaning to the word. Getting his discoveries in nanotechnology patented—and NanoStar up to the point of being a household name—was finally going to justify her tireless work and faith in him. On that thought, he decided he'd really better be about getting that abstract uploaded.

But it wasn't going to happen if people didn't stop waltzing into his lab and . . .

"Grant! Grant, we need to talk, and I mean right now!"

"Gerry, whatever it is can wait. I have to finish assembling and uploading this document for the lawyers or hell will freeze over and the world will end. Monica said so."

"Grant, it's those damn lawyers we need to talk about! You were at the initial run through with the patent attorneys. What was the name of their firm?"

Grant rolled his chair back from the table. "Huh?

Ah . . . Hochschuler, Hochhizer—Hochwaller, that was it. What the hell difference does that make?"

"Grant, I just talked to Bersford's secretary; no, not Monica, the other one. She told me that the lawyers with him today are from Creighton, James and Shelton."

"And this is important because?"

"Grant, listen to me! I just got a glimpse of Bersford sitting in the conference room with them, and he looked like the proverbial deer in the headlights. I went back to my lab and looked them up on Google. They're takeover specialists! They work exclusively on hostile takeovers of tech companies and they have a dismally good track record at it. Then, I looked up my part of the patent support documents on the server and they are gone—gone with the rest of the application prep stuff. Hell, even the directories are gone!"

Grant spun his chair back to the computer station. "OK, let's just have a look here and see what's . . . wait a minute." His face and mind went through the five stages of grief as he quickly scanned through the server. "I can't even get into the server's user area. The only access I seem to have left is the document repository and, damn, there isn't anything there." Grant's voice went from serious to grim. "The other technical contributors' documents are gone and sure enough, even the directories have been removed."

Grant's discoveries stoked Gerry's agitation even further. "Grant, what does that say to you? I put all my stuff there yesterday, and now it's gone from my workstation as well. I think NanoStar's being eaten alive and all our work with it—what are you doing?"

"I'm doing a bit of preventative computing. There, all my work is on this flash memory chip now," Grant said as he removed the chip from the computer and clipped it to a chain around his neck. He then typed in a command. "I think this workstation is about to have a disk failure."

Gerry sat down hard on the chair behind him. "Ah, Grant, you actually kept a disk-shredding program on your system?"

"I have had to leave too many companies under circumstances that are way too similar to this one not to be prepared, but dammit, I had high hopes for NanoStar."

Stunned, Gerry leaned forward in his chair. "Grant, I don't know what to do now. I still have my backup of my own work, but they got everything I put in the server."

Grant stood up and took off his lab coat. "Gerry, I'm going home to think. I suggest you do the same. Put that backup in a safe place and start calling your contact network. Unless I'm very much mistaken, we have just joined the ranks of the unemployed. And Gerry . . ."

"Yeah, Grant?"

"I'm taking the side door directly out into the parking lot. You might want to do the same."

"Great! Just great!"

The oddly powerful man stood alone on a dais facing an ephemeral array of holographic projections. The image projected directly before him showed a view of an automated lab, with two men arguing in front of a computer screen. One man removed a flash drive from the computer and walked out of the room. The system tracked him out of a building and into a parking lot.

As he stood watching the ghostly display, the man on the dais mentally sorted through a dizzying panorama of scenarios and action alternatives in the blink of an eye. He discarded most and set a few aside for further consideration, while another part of his vast intellect entertained the thought:

"Mr. Grant Thornton, you are exactly the right person to create what I need, the one who can precisely place the next pieces into the puzzle. The question is: Can I keep you alive long enough to do this for me?"

"Oh, honey, not again!"

Ellen had gotten home a bit late from work and

could see from the look on his face that something had gone very wrong with Grant's day. She sat on the couch next to him and listened with a sinking sense of déjà vu to his recital of the events surrounding his hasty departure from NanoStar's lab, which left her feeling as deflated as he looked.

"I've been sitting here trying to make it come out some other way, but it just won't. Some big conglomerate that doesn't want or need nanotechnology has just yanked NanoStar right out from under all the people who put their souls on the line to make it happen."

Grant's eyes met Ellen's. "And I'm afraid that includes us."

Her brow furrowed in thought. "Isn't there some possibility that this is not as black as it seems?"

Grant shook his head. "I just can't believe I didn't see this coming. After all we've been through with SureTech and Golter, you'd think that I'd have caught this happening. I should have been tipped off by Monica hanging on me about the submissions, but I was even more surprised than Gerry."

Ellen leaned over and kissed him. When she got a distracted smile instead of the reaction she expected, she kissed him again more thoroughly. "Well, that's a little better. You need to get your mind out of this rut that it's chasing itself around in. I'm going upstairs to put on a dress that you won't be able to take your eyes off of, and then we are going out to dinner and a movie."

"Oh, I don't . . ."

"Oh, yes you do. You're the one who is always telling me how you need to put problems on your mental back burner to come up with your best solutions. Well, that's exactly what we are going to do with this one."

"But . . ."

"No buts! I can hear the gears in your head grinding against each other. I know how upset I am at this, and I can guess at what it's done to you. So, we are going out tonight, and that's that. Now, put on that suede jacket I like so much. You don't need a tie, but I want you out of what you've worn in the lab all day."

Ellen headed for their bedroom to suit up for her mission. Taller than most women, she had an athletic figure, and she had learned to dress for it. The effect of the black number she donned for the evening was compounded by pumps that put her eye to eye with Grant. She let her long black hair fall to her shoulders, knowing it would emphasize her movements and keep him as distracted as possible.

Grant entered the room and slowly began to change. Ellen watched him for a moment. "No moping. We are going to have a good time and that is all I have to say on the subject."

She helped him finish buttoning his shirt and kissed him again. "You know, Grant, you could even enjoy yourself tonight." With that, she herded him out to his vintage Mustang, and he drove them to their favorite restaurant.

"That was certainly a different way to end the movie. All the way up to the last five minutes, I thought she loved him and was trying to protect him. Then she turns out to be the assassin!"

Grant thought about Ellen's observation for a moment. "Yeah, surprise endings seem to be the order of the day."

"Grant . . ." Her tone was a warning.

Grant got the message. "OK, OK. Ellen, I've enjoyed our evening—dinner, the movie, being with you—and it's late. I am not going to fall into a mental black hole over NanoStar tonight. I promise."

"Better."

A gentle breeze met them as they rounded the corner of the theater and strolled across the nearly empty parking lot.

Grant breathed deeply and sighed. "The cool air feels good tonight—like it's blowing the fog out of my head." He gave Ellen an appraising look. "And that dress has definitely kept my attention."

She gave him the smile that always caused funny things to happen in his chest. "That was part of the point, dear."

"What was the rest of the point?"

"You'll find out."

"Oh."

Grant gave her waist a squeeze and she playfully responded. "Yes, oh."

As he turned and bent to insert his key into the Mustang's car door, Grant caught a hint of movement out of the corner of his eye. In the next instant, the world erupted into chaos. Ellen screamed, there was an explosion next to his head, and a massive black nothing rose up and swallowed everything.

Chapter 2

"Why am I so damn cold?"

Grant tried to move and instantly regretted it.

"Bad idea . . . really, really bad idea!"

His head felt like he had slammed a car door on it. And now that he noticed, just about everything else hurt, too, but nothing so horribly awful as his head.

"What happened to me to cause this? For that matter, what is this?"

Some remote corner of his mind was screaming at him and setting off every mental alarm imaginable, but it was too far away to pay attention to it right now. He just needed to get warm again.

He seemed to be lying face down on something cold. Maybe if he tried to roll over . . .

"Oh God, I'm gonna throw up!"

He dropped the attempt to move, began to wrestle with and finally got his stomach back under control. But that effort used up what little strength he had, and the blackness swept over him again.

Hands were moving him—whether he wanted them to or not.

"Oh hell! Not on my back! Not that!"

He was being rolled over by someone. His stomach behaved this time, sort of. Then that someone peeled one of his eyes open and a brilliant white light flooded what had been, till now, his comfortably dark vision.

"Get that damn spotlight out of my face!"

The light almost obediently winked out, but it had stirred something. Visual stimulation prompted his short-term memory, and there was something he desperately needed to remember. A name—it was so tantalizingly close—just . . .

"Ellen, that was it, Ellen. What about . . ."

He felt a prick on his arm, and even though he fought it with everything he had left, the fuzzy darkness closed in once again.

". . . Ellen?"

———————

"Summers, how come we drew this one?"

Detective Sergeant Ordwyn Summers steered their police car around another pothole and glanced over at him. "It's simple, Jakowski: Simmons and Walker are over in Almira Gardens working another liquor store robbery, Naylor and Jackson are booking the crowd they arrested at that strip club fight—and that leaves us to respond to call-ins from the patrol units."

"Yeah, right. This one sounds messy."

Ordwyn Summers pushed her auburn bangs back from her face and thought that she couldn't ever remember seeing a carjacking gone wrong that wasn't messy. But that was just the patrol officer's first take on what he'd found. Best not to put too much weight on that until they got to the scene and could see for themselves. They were only about five blocks out, so that would be very soon now.

"So, Summers . . ."

"Yeah?"

"Ya went up for lieutenant again. Ya seen the promotion list yet?"

"Yeah."

"And?"

"I saw the list."

"So did you . . ."

"What do you think?"

"Oh."

Jakowski thought about it for a minute, but tact was never his strong suit. "I don't get it. You've gone up for promotion, what, five times now? Ya got your time in as a sergeant, ya kept your nose clean and you're smart. Why ain't ya a lieutenant?"

Rather than answer, Ordwyn just glared at him. Why indeed? She was the daughter of one of the department's most decorated officers, and she knew policing front, back and sideways. Physically, she was a bit on the short side, but intensely competitive and athletic enough to have genuinely surprised some of the men in hand-to-hand combat training. She lived, ate and breathed the job. So why was she turning into a career sergeant? Less capable men and, being honest with herself, women, too, had passed her by. Hell, that rookie she took on eight years ago—what was her name—oh, yeah, Simpson, Elaine Simpson. She was a watch captain now.

"There's the movie theater, Jakowski. Which parking lot is it, the front or the side?"

Jakowski scrolled the car's computer display, "Uh, the side lot—over in the west corner."

As she steered through the lot entrance and around the side of the building, the location became clear. There were two patrol units, the coroner's truck and a lab unit all gathered at the far end of the side lot. Ordwyn pulled up by the lab unit. She and Jakowski got out of the car and walked over to where two patrol officers were comparing notes.

A single, forlorn light illuminated the corner of the lot, but it was obvious that something bad had happened here. There were two chalk outlines on the pavement and way too much blood puddled up around them.

The name tag on the nearest patrol officer's shirt read "Jenkins." Ordwyn didn't know him. But the other cop was Mack Slater. He had arrived on the scene first and called it in. Ordwyn and Mack had known each other for years, and she respected his skills—as a patrol cop. So she walked up to him first. "OK, Mack, walk us through it."

"Hello Summers. It's been a while. Well, given the positions of the vics, it looks like they were just about to get into their car after the movie when they were jumped. From the way they were taken down, I'd say there were at least two perps. The woman's purse is gone, but they didn't hang around long enough to get the guy's wallet. We got the make, model and license number of his car off his insurance card, so we should turn it up pretty quick. The lab guy's almost done, so you should talk to him next."

Ordwyn intentionally looked away from the blood. Even after all the years she'd been working homicide, the stark reminder that no one was really safe still got to her. "Thanks, Mack. We'll catch up with the coroner's assistant later. Jakowski, check in with the lab tech and find out if he's come up with anything unusual. Uh, Jenkins, when did you get here?"

Jenkins consulted his notebook, "I responded at 22:47 to the 911 call from the mall security guard who found them. That was right after Slater responded to the 'shots fired' that was phoned in. I walked around the lot but, as usual, there was nobody who saw anything."

"How many shots?"

"The guard thought he heard two, but he was a good distance away and they would have echoed through the mall buildings, so it could have been more. Slater?"

"Don't know, the call in was just 'some shooting in the parking lot.'"

Ordwyn looked over at Jakowski walking back from his discussion with the lab tech. "How many shell casings did he find?"

"Congratulations, Summers, ya just put your finger on one of the two odd things about this scene: no shell casings. The other is that there really isn't much here at all that doesn't belong in a movie parking lot. This wasn't done by no street gang. The tech says it's way too clean. The surveillance camera on the corner of the theater building was even disabled."

This was getting worse by the minute. Ordwyn now had a "professional" carjacking gang to find. But, if they were such "professionals," why did they wind up shooting the vics? "Jakowski, jump on finding that car. There's got to be more evidence in it than they left here. I'll research the vics for anything interesting in their history. And we can check with the assistant coroner in the morning."

Jakowski turned back to their car. "Right."

"Mack, you and Jenkins check the area. It's a real long shot, but there may be more surveillance footage from the surrounding buildings that shows something useful.

Slater gave Jenkins a look after Summers turned away. "Looks like it's going to be a long night."

Ordwyn hated the morgue.

She hated going down to the bottom basement level of its ancient building to get to it. She hated the porcelain tile/stainless steel tables/chemically treated/way-too-precise look of it. But, most of all, she hated the smell. There had been a long progression of bodies through it, and as diligently as they cleaned up between them, the place still stank of death. There was just no way to ignore the fetid, sickly sweet smell of what waited for everyone sooner or later. She couldn't imagine how someone could work down here all day and, truth be told, she didn't ever want to.

However, assistant coroner Frank Mercer did just that. The bullet-shaped little gnome, with what Ordwyn always thought of as an unnaturally bright bald head, went cheerfully about his business as if he were tending a flower garden. Trying, and failing, to keep the irony out of her voice, she hailed him. "Good morning Mercer, what have we got?"

He positively beamed at her. "Welcome back to my humble shop, Summers—and I do mean welcome!

You always seem to send the most interesting cases down to me."

"Yeah, I'm just the princess of puzzles. Talk to me."

Mercer walked over to the nearest occupied table and turned back to Ordwyn with a smile that radiated enthusiasm. "Oh, trust me Sergeant, you've outdone yourself this time!" Turning back to the table's occupant: "The deceased is Ellen Thornton. Running her prints through the system turned up the usual identification information, which I'm sure you are already aware of. What you probably didn't see, unless you read through it to the end, is that she was the daughter of William Ferris." Ordwyn's face fell visibly. "Yes, that Ferris . . . so be prepared for pressure from above on this one."

Ordwyn, who had not gotten that far into her file, groaned. William Ferris was one of the "pillars of the community" and that almost certainly meant she would be hearing from the chief shortly. "What did you find, Mercer?"

He gestured at Ellen's body. "To start, at five feet and nine inches, she had the stature and strength to take care of herself. She was very muscular, and her upper body in particular was unusually well developed for a woman. At a guess, she was an avid sports participant and worked out with weights regularly."

"That fits; her file showed memberships at a gym and a sports club."

"Which makes it all the more interesting that there are no defensive wounds on her body. Yet, if you look right here," he turned Ellen's head to one side, "there are bruises on her neck that suggest a hand grasped her and held her tightly."

Ordwyn stepped to the table to look closely. It did indeed look like Ellen Thornton had been seized by the neck like a rag doll.

"Cause of death was a single gunshot wound. The bullet entered under her chin and passed at a 45 degree angle up through her spine to its juncture with her skull. There is extreme gunshot residue and skin charring at the wound site, indicating that the muzzle was held against her skin when the shot was fired. The placement of that shot was almost surgical. Death was instantaneous."

She looked sharply back at Mercer. "Have you already sent the bullet to the lab?"

"It was probably a .22 slug." Mercer held up a vial of small metal fragments. "Here's what I could recover of it. Do you see anything worth the lab's time?"

"Great, just great, no ballistics. So what do you think happened to her, Mercer?"

"I think that someone walked up behind her, seized her neck in one hand to hold her still, placed the gun to her throat in a very precise position, and pulled the trigger. Whoever did this had the strength and certainty necessary to subdue a victim who could have done a lot to defend herself if she had been given more than a split second to do so."

"You're telling me that it was a professional hit?"

"I'm telling you that it was more than professional. It was perfectly executed by someone who has done this so many times he has become a master at it."

"Damn, Mercer, you really know how to make a girl's day."

"Maybe you can find out more from your other vic. But this one's not going to be very helpful."

Ordwyn's cell phone rang. She fished it out of her pocket, looked at the caller ID and thumbed the screen to answer. "Jakowski, tell me you found our car."

Her shoulders slumped. "You didn't find the car.

"You got surveillance footage of it being driven away from the scene?

"Could you see . . . ?"

Her shoulders slumped further in frustration. "Nothing, huh?

"OK, I'll see you there." She ended the call and looked at the phone like it was a piece of rotten fruit.

Mercer smiled sweetly at her. "Good luck, Summers; something tells me you're going to need it on this one."

"Thanks a bunch, Mercer."

By midmorning, the hospital parking lot was already starting to shimmer with heat waves. Jakowski got out of his police cruiser and walked up just as Summers was getting out of her car.

"Summers, ya look like somebody just spit in yer coffee cup. Didn't get much from Mercer, did ya?"

"This whole damn case keeps going backward. Everything I find just leaves more questions than it answers. Our shooters were clearly pros and, just as clearly, this has nothing to do with stealing Thornton's car. So why'd they take the car?"

"Yeah, doesn't make a lot of sense, does it?"

"So, where is he?"

Jakowski consulted his notebook, "Ah, third floor, room 323."

She looked up reluctantly at the outsized white building. "Let's go."

If there was one place that Ordwyn had as little use for as the morgue, it was a hospital, and for much the same set of reasons. Oh well, the day wasn't getting any cooler, and at least it would be air-conditioned inside.

The third-floor charge nurse saw them coming and positioned her interception right where her station narrowed the hallway.

"Like I said the first time, the doctor won't be here until 10:30, and you'll just have to wait for him. That's only about ten minutes from now, so take a seat and get comfortable."

Ordwyn and Jakowski stopped in their tracks, looked at each other, and Ordwyn snapped out,

"Jakowski, check on the uniform." Jakowski turned and headed rapidly down the hall toward Thornton's room and the guard who was supposed to be posted there.

Then she turned back to the charge nurse and craned her neck to read the woman's name tag. "Nurse . . . Wilkins, who did you say this to the first time?"

"Wha . . .? Why that other cop who came up here."

Ordwyn leaned into her next question. "Did you see a badge or any kind of ID?"

"No, he just said he was with the third precinct and asked to see the man in 323. I told him what I told you, and he just turned around and left."

"When did he leave?"

"About half an hour ago. Funny thing, though, now that I think of it . . ."

"What?"

"He was wearing a hat. Men don't wear hats anymore."

Ordwyn looked up toward the ceiling at the surveillance camera stations and knew just exactly why the "cop" wore a hat.

Jakowski returned just as the doctor, a short but determined-looking Eastern Indian, arrived.

"Jakowski?"

"Uniform didn't see anybody."

The charge nurse felt the need to reassert herself. "This is Dr. Shah. Whatever you need with 323, you will have to ask him for it."

"Dr. Shah, I'm Sergeant Summers," Ordwyn said, holding up her badge and ID. "Have you been approached by anyone about the man in 323?"

"Mr. Thornton? No, not directly. I did get a message about him on my voice mail, but I don't respond to inquiries about patients that way."

"Doctor, what can you tell us about his condition?"

"Sergeant, perhaps we should talk about this in a consultation room. There's one right across the hall."

"Jakowski, go back to the uniform and keep an eye on the access to 323. I don't want our 'friends' coming back to take care of unfinished business. Lead the way, doctor."

The room had a set of X-ray viewers along one wall. Shah walked directly to them, opened a folder and started putting up X-rays of a head.

"I expected someone from your office Sergeant, and I can assure you of my fullest cooperation. So let's talk about Mr. Grant Thornton."

Ordwyn walked up to the X-rays and stood beside Shah as he gestured to them and described Thornton's condition. "By all rights, he should be dead; but what Mr. Thornton has actually sustained is a severe but not life-threatening head wound."

"Doctor, so far, that's just one more anomaly in a case that is nothing but anomalies. What saved him?"

"The skin on the right side of his head is shredded. There were over 50 individual wounds but those are superficial and I was able to basically glue them shut. I even managed to save the external portion of his ear. But while it won't need reconstructive surgery, even with the best devices available, he'll never hear with it again.

"If you look here," Shah pointed at one of the x-rays, "you can see that the fine bone structure of the inner ear has been obliterated. I reconnected the Eustachian tube that goes down to his throat, but that was as much as I could do for him. He's got a concussion but, aside from the loss of his inner ear, that's his worst injury."

"OK Doc, I give up. What in the world could cause a wound like that?"

Shah looked straight at her, and Ordwyn saw a tiredness in his eyes that she hadn't noticed before. "Sergeant, I catch most of the patients who are referred to this hospital by the police. As a result, I see a lot of gunshot wounds. Someone put a gun in Mr. Thornton's ear and shot him. There were powder burns to the ear itself, and I found small slivers of lead in his wounds."

Ordwyn was starting to feel like she was caught in some kind of really bad but endless practical joke. "Which brings me back to my first question, Doctor. What saved him?"

"To be honest, that stumped me till I looked in his other ear. Mr. Thornton apparently has a hearing deficit that predated his assault. There was a very sophisticated implanted hearing aid in that ear and likely one in the other, where he was shot, as well. I think that his assailant fired a very small-caliber bullet that hit the hearing aid in his injured ear and shattered tearing two lacerations in the side of his head instead of punching on through the ear canal into the inside of his skull and killing him instantly."

This case just wasn't going to get any better, was it? Another professional hit man tried to fire a .22 slug into Thornton's ear in one of the classic execution maneuvers. And it was sheer dumb luck that it didn't work exactly as planned. Well, might as well get the next question over with.

"So, Doc, when will we be able to talk to him?"

"I assumed you would want to do that as soon as possible and, normally, it would be out of the question for a couple of days. But this man has the constitution of a horse. We'll keep him here overnight because of the concussion, but he'll probably go home tomorrow. I've had him sedated since the surgery and was expecting to administer a stimulant to wake him as soon as you got here."

"Today? Now? That's the best news I've had on this case."

"Sergeant, you should know that he's been out since the assault. He was initially sedated for the ambulance ride to get here and has been under ever since."

Shah's face looked even more tired. "He doesn't know about his wife."

To Ordwyn's questioning look: "The EMTs told me when they delivered him last night."

Her expression hardened. "It won't be the first time I've had to break bad news. Let's get this over with."

Dr. Shah led her back out into the hallway, collected the charge nurse with her readied syringe, and proceeded up to the officer standing outside 323 with Jakowski.

"Come on Jakowski, it's time for us to kick off the worst day of Mr. Grant Thornton's life."

They entered the room to find Thornton lying on the bed with a thoroughly bandaged head and an IV drip plugged into his arm. The nurse injected the stimulant into his IV connection, and he began to stir almost immediately. He was clearly a man struggling to awaken from a bad dream. And Ordwyn's heart sank as she realized that she was about to make something even worse than his dream a reality for him.

After a few minutes, Grant's eyes finally stayed open and focused on her. "Mr. Thornton? My name is Sergeant Summers." She glanced at Dr. Shah, "Can you hear me?"

It took Grant several tries, but he finally managed to croak out an answer. "Yes, not very well. Where am I? How did I get here?"

Ordwyn raised her voice. "You're in a hospital recovery room. You've been—injured. What's the last thing you remember?"

His brow furrowed as he struggled to make his memory work. "I remember walking up to my car and getting my keys out of my pocket. When I put the key in the door lock, something happened. And . . . and I heard Ellen and a loud noise . . . " Then it all came back to him in a rush. "Oh God! What happened to Ellen? I heard her scream just before it all went black. Where is she?"

Their faces told him far more than he wanted to know.

The sun had risen higher, and now the parking lot pavement was really starting to cook. Something kept getting in Ordwyn's eyes, making her wipe at them as she marched across the asphalt to her car with Jakowski hopping along to keep up, even though he was considerably taller. As she reached the car, she leaned forward, unlocked and opened the car door and was almost knocked over by the oven-like blast of heat from inside.

"Sheesh! I should have left a window down!"

Jakowski caught up to her and started to speak, but she cut him off. "Don't say it! Don't say anything!"

"It's OK, Summers, just leave the doors open and let the inside cool down for a few minutes."

Ordwyn turned away from him and took iron control of her composure. She was a cop, and cops had to deal with these things. Now if she could just get the image out of her mind of Thornton crying like a lost, heartbroken child it would help that process a lot.

She blew out a breath and straightened her back. "Jakowski, when we get back to the station, we start an in-depth investigation of the Thorntons' background. Somebody decided that those two needed killing, and that somebody had a lot of money to spend on the project. They had to leave tracks, and we're going to find them.

"And Jakowski?"

"Yeah, Summers."

"I want that somebody—I want 'em bad."

Chapter 3

"Jakowski, put down that coffee cup, and walk me through this again." She sipped her own coffee and grimaced both at it and the case, mumbling to herself, "We're still missing something—maybe a lot of somethings."

She pretended not to notice the look he gave her as she launched into her own recap of the case.

"Grant Thornton works as a researcher at Nano-Star. He's a highly respected scientist in his field. The company he works for is about to go public. He's got no financial problems, no legal troubles of any kind. He's so clean, he squeaks.

"Ellen Thornton was a project manager for Dura-Build, one of the few companies that's still making money in this economy. She headed boards for two different charities, and her father is practically a 'founding father' of the city. She squeaks louder than he does.

"So, who's going to hire two highly experienced and doubtless very expensive hit men to take 'em out and steal their car? Mentioning which, it has now been 36 hours, and we still have no idea where that car went. We've got no ballistics, no forensics, no evidence, no nothing!

"And every damn thing connected with this case just makes less sense."

Jakowski belatedly realized she had stopped talking and was looking for some kind of response. "Ah, well, Summers, there was the tiff between her and her old man?"

Ordwyn gave him a withering look. "So her father waits eight years after his daughter marries the man he doesn't approve of and then has them both killed? I suppose he had their car stolen so he could look at it and fondly remember the event?"

The phone sitting on the desk between them rang, sparing Jakowski from having to answer her. He scooped it up like a lifeline.

"Jakowski.

"Yeah, when?

"OK, thanks Doc.

"That was Doc Shah," he told Summers. "They're lettin' Thornton out of the hospital in a coupla hours." He shook his head. "Outa the hospital two days after bein' shot in the head." Jakowski marveled as he put the handset back on its cradle and shook his head.

Ordwyn reached over and grabbed the phone out of his hand, punching in a number as she did so.

"Braddock?

"Who've you got available for a surveillance detail today?"

She rolled her eyes. "Tell me about it. I've got a vic just leaving the city hospital and I'm worried that somebody is going to try to finish what they started.

"Yeah, Thornton. I'd at least like to know that he got home and that he's going to be watched tonight. We can deal with tomorrow when it gets here.

"Good. Thanks, Braddock." She put the phone down, picked up her coffee cup, looked in it with a frown, put it down, and turned back to Jakowski. "So far we've done the easy stuff, so you start digging into NanoStar. Find out what they do, if there's anything odd about them and if they've had any 'official' attention recently. I'm going to do the same dance with DuraBuild. Something's not right somewhere, and we've just got to find it."

"I'm on it."

"You gonna be OK to get to the door?"

Grant was wearing a set of green scrubs they'd given him at the hospital to replace the blood-spattered clothes they'd cut off him in the ER. He stood uncertainly by the curb looking at his house. The real question was would he ever be "OK"? He turned back to the cabbie, "Yeah, I can make it to the door. Thanks."

As the cab drove away, he turned and looked at the obvious, unmarked police car parked at the curb, started to shake his head and instantly thought about what a really bad idea that gesture would be. With that, he slowly and carefully turned back and started across the yard up the landscaped path toward his front door. His head hurt worse than the hangover he'd gotten from his graduation party and Ellen had nursed him through that.

Funny, he didn't remember his front yard being that long, but it seemed to be taking forever for him to get to the door. He finally stood at the front door, digging for his keys in the bag they had given him with his valuables in it.

Then he remembered why he didn't have any keys.

He'd just put the key in the car door when, when, NO!

He was not going to turn into a blubbering puddle on their . . . on his front steps. Ellen had been his touchstone of emotional strength, and he silently vowed that he would not betray that by crumbling now.

There was a spare key in the flowerbed next to the rosebush. He just had to dig down about three inches without getting stuck by its thorns and there it was . . . the little box with the front door key inside. Grant unlocked the door and stepped into the front hall.

The house was achingly familiar, yet somehow, utterly alien. As he wandered from one room to the next, some part of him kept expecting to see Ellen in one of them, even though he knew he would never see her again. He finally sagged down onto the living room sofa and just looked around the room. How was he ever going to stay in this house when everything he saw reminded him of her?

The wall next to the fireplace had an array of shelves with Ellen's box collection on them. She had loved little, exquisitely built wooden boxes, so everyone who knew her would buy them wherever they found them and send them to her. She had collected several dozen. She used to say that she kept her friendships in them where they would always be safe and remembered. He got up and walked to the wall to look at them.

And then he froze.

Fussy housekeeping was not Ellen's forte, and she even used to make fun of women whom she considered obsessive about it. So dust accumulated on all the flat surfaces of the house, surfaces such as the shelves on the wall in front of him. And as he looked at one of her boxes, he noticed that it had been picked up and placed almost, but not quite, back in the same place. The dust around it showed its outline slightly offset from where the box sat.

All of her boxes had been moved.

Apparently, each of them had been picked up and put back. Most of them were not quite where they had been before.

Grant waited a moment for the pounding of his heart to subside. It was making his head throb, and he had to think with absolute clarity now. He walked back into the room that Ellen used as her home office. There were two six-drawer file cabinets in it. One of them hadn't been opened in about a year. It should still have dust on the handles and on the top edge of the front panel of each drawer. The dust was disturbed on each handle and missing entirely from the top edge of each front panel.

He went to the kitchen, got the step stool out and, moving very carefully, looked at the upper shelves of the cupboard. Again, each container had been moved and put back close to, but not quite, in the exact place where it had been sitting for years.

On a hunch, Grant went to their—to his— bedroom and winced at the pain in his head as he lifted the corner of the carpet in the closet to reveal the floor safe. It was an old-fashioned dial combination and he always left the dial pointing at the number that represented Ellen's age. Opening the safe and simply re-latching the door would snap the dial back to zero. It now, almost accusingly, sat at the zero mark.

Someone had searched his house very carefully and very thoroughly.

And even as his soul screamed against it, Grant knew that they, whoever they were, could have been looking for only one thing. He slowly got to his feet and made himself walk out into the backyard.

He made his way around the corner planter to where its brick wall faced the fence. If someone reached behind the plants and removed two bricks from the top row, there was a brick below them that could also be removed from the retaining wall. Grant had hollowed it out awhile back, and the last afternoon he came home from NanoStar, he had placed the flash chip with the culmination of his work in nanotechnology in that hollow.

He stood there now looking down at the plastic-encased silicon chip. He realized in that moment that what that chip contained was what had gotten Ellen killed. That knowledge burning through his mind turned his boundless grief into boundless rage.

Ellen's funeral had been beautiful. Her father had been an ass.

Grant would have dearly loved to have told him the wrong date and let him plague someone else's life. But he was smart enough to know that Bill Ferris would not be so easily denied. Apparently, the police were not dancing to the "great man's" tune concerning their investigation, and he was sure that Grant had done something to endanger his daughter that the authorities should look into.

The irony was almost too much to bear.

Ferris had cornered Grant after the wake and demanded to know what had "really" happened that night. He was hardly satisfied when Grant told him the same thing, verbatim, that the police already had. He had considered telling Ferris about the chip but knew that the old idiot would go directly to the Chief of Police with the story and just stir up confusion with accusations that no one could prove or disprove. The chip, and what it contained, proved exactly nothing.

So Grant had gone home and gotten drunk so that he could go to sleep without seeing Ellen and hearing her heartrending scream over and over again. It had been seven days since her death and it was not lost on him that this pattern could become a habit.

Sitting at home and drinking himself into a rage followed by a stupor each night simply wouldn't do. So two evenings later, when Gerry called and suggested they meet at Delaney's to "discuss things," he had agreed without a second thought.

He took a cab to the bar—not because he was concerned about driving after too much to drink, but because he couldn't stand the idea of getting into and driving Ellen's car. And here he stood, on the sidewalk outside the bar's front door, asking himself whether he was really up to Gerry's brand of intensity tonight.

Well, if not tonight, then when?

Grant pushed through the door into the artificial darkness within. It had always amazed him how the inside of a bar could be darker than the night itself. After his eyes adjusted, he scanned the crowd but saw no sign of Gerry. Being on time was never high on Gerry's list of priorities, so Grant settled into one of the booths to wait.

He ordered a drink and waited.

He thought about calling Gerry; then he ordered another and waited some more. It was beginning to look like Gerry wasn't going to show, and that disturbed Grant. Gerry was something of a flake, but he had sounded intense about talking to Grant tonight, and his intensities tended to spiral upward rather than fizzle out. But, just as Grant was about to call another cab to take him home, a man he'd never seen before slid into the booth opposite him—just as Grant's cell phone rang.

"Hello?

"Gerry?

"Calm down, Gerry. Have you kept the spare tire inflated?

"Hmm . . . do you have a membership in Triple-A?

"Then call them and we'll schedule for another night.

"Yeah, I've got Thursday night free. Just take care of yourself."

Grant disconnected his end of the call and put the phone back in his pocket. He had negotiated all this without taking his eyes off his new companion.

For no reason that Grant could immediately discern, a chill went down his spine as he looked at this guy. The stranger was . . . well, strange. He had very broad shoulders and a smooth, shaved head. His clothing, a simple, nondescript jacket with matching pants and open-collared shirt left the impression that his body didn't taper toward his waist. Grant hadn't seen his lower body, but he'd bet that the odd appearance went all the way down to the man's shoes.

Considering the assault that had almost killed him, Grant felt fascinated in spite of himself and watched the man order a drink with great interest. Every movement, every gesture seemed to be fluid and minimal. It was like watching a highly trained acrobat ply his trade, except that the man was doing absolutely nothing unusual. His face was expressionless but not immobile, the way a department store manikin's would be. Rather, his features seemed to move on command, perfectly orchestrated, as if the very concept of spontaneity was foreign to his being.

All these aspects made him strange and, for lack of a better term, exotic. But they all faded to insignificance in comparison with his eyes. Grant tried for a word to describe them and failed. They took in everything but seemed to look beyond what they saw, as though reality were an obstruction to overcome.

His voice was an arresting baritone. "Mr. Thornton, allow me to introduce myself. My name is Miles. I gather that the acquaintance you expected to meet here this evening has rescheduled your get-together?"

"That's correct . . . but how do you know me?"

"I have followed your work for some years now, and I have been very impressed with your progress in nano-machine design. My condolences on both the loss of your wife and the demise of NanoStar. Life has not been kind to you lately."

Grant's haunted look flared to anger, which would have discouraged most people from further conversation. But the intensity of Miles' engagement with him did not diminish. Grant helplessly felt his anger slide into self-pity and was embarrassed by it.

The cocktail waitress returned with Miles' drink and set it on the table before him. After she left, he looked intently at Grant for a long moment. Grant felt like the man's strangely colorless eyes stared directly into his soul. Then he asked, "Where are you going to go from here, Mr. Thornton?"

Grant had felt a powerful need to talk to someone ever since he'd learned what had happened to Ellen and pieced together what he considered to be his own responsibility in the matter. But there had been no one to whom he could unburden himself. And now he found himself pouring out his anguish to a total stranger. And even at that, he felt better for the doing of it.

At the end of it all, he buried his face in his hands. Then he looked down at the table between them and said, "Now I just want justice for what was done to Ellen. She didn't do anything to deserve being killed. Someone should pay for that."

After a long moment of silence, Grant gathered his self-control, looked up and was again transfixed by Miles' deep gaze. "Mr. Thornton, who are you? I know your name, what you have done with your life and whom you loved. But who are you—really? Who did Ellen Ferris fall in love with and stand by through thick and thin? Who took on nanotech-nology as his sacred mission and refused to be diverted from understanding and mastering it? Who are you, Grant Thornton and, given who you really are, what do you want?"

As Miles watched him, Grant felt something shift inside and began pulling himself together. "I have always wanted to understand the truth. That was what led me to science as my life's pursuit. It was an opportu-nity to learn what's so about the universe." In a burning moment, a light rekindled itself in Grant's eyes. "And I want to continue that pursuit. I'm not done with nano-technology, not by a long shot." Then his eyes narrowed. "But I still want justice for Ellen's murderer."

"Mr. Thornton, you have paid a great price for what you want from life. Can you still distinguish between justice and vengeance? Think about that. We will talk again."

With that Miles rose from the booth and walked out the door of the bar. An astonished Grant watched him go and, sure enough, the guy appeared to be slab-sided from shoulders to floor. He moved like he was on wheels.

Grant picked up Miles' untouched drink, downed it, and called that cab.

———————————

"Summers, go home. You won't solve 'em all tonight."

Ordwyn looked up at the clock on the precinct wall and grudgingly accepted the wisdom of that plan. "No sir, I suppose not, but this one just bugs the life out of me."

The precinct captain looked at her for a long moment. "The Thorntons?"

"Yes sir, the Thorntons. I've been through what little evidence we could collect backward and forward, and it still doesn't make any sense. There was absolutely nothing at the scene. The medical evidence indicated unequivocally that it was a professional hit. But then they stole the vic's car. They not only stole the car, they made it disappear outright. It never did turn up."

"Summers, there's just some cases that go cold

and we never solve 'em. Put this one in that pile and move on."

"I've tried, sir. I have really tried. But just about the time I convince myself that there's nothing further to do, another weird connection shows up and starts all my wheels turning again."

The precinct captain's brow furrowed. "Such as?"

"For starters, her father is William Ferris. That alone should've cranked up the pressure for an arrest. But it barely caused a ripple in the flow down from the top. I expected to have the chief on the phone, and instead I got a memo a week later telling me that the case would have a limited investigation budget.

"I dug around in the background of Thornton's company, NanoStar, and found out that it got bought up the day that his wife was killed and then broken up into a string of subsidiaries that are being sold off piecemeal. This promising technology company was bought out and wrecked for no reason that I can discover.

"Over the next three weeks, I get flagged that two of the star researchers from NanoStar—two of 'em— died in accidents—perfectly legitimate accidents. And this happens after somebody comes within a hair of murdering a third, our Mr. Thornton. All just a string of tragic coincidences? Yeah, right.

"But it's all just a bunch of dead ends. Nothing

actually leads anywhere. Whoever is doing this is so good it's downright scary."

The precinct captain flashed her a hard look that lasted for only a moment and escaped her notice. "Like I said, go home. You can stare at those case files all night and nothin' in them is gonna change. We've got plenty of open cases that need you on them wide awake and hittin' on all cylinders."

"I guess you're right sir. I'll see you tomorrow." Ordwyn sighed, picked up her phone, dropped it in her pocket, and threaded her way out of the cramped office.

The precinct captain stood and stared at the door for a moment after it closed behind her, shook his head, then took out his cell phone and dialed a number. "This is Grayson. We may have a problem."

Chapter 4

"Ms. Ingalls, that's the best news I've had in over a month!

"Yes, I will have the presentation ready for your review board meeting on Thursday night at seven sharp. I think Mr. Carver and the rest of your colleagues will be very interested in what I have to show you."

Grant hung up the phone and stood looking at it for a moment with the first hint of a smile he'd shown in weeks. He had come so close to just falling off the edge of the universe after the attack. So close, and then that Miles character had yanked him up onto his feet and charged him up to get back into the fray again, all with a simple pair of questions.

Who are you and what do you want? Really?

Grant kept expecting to see Miles again after the powerful effect he had experienced from him at the bar; but there was nothing, no further contact. Ellen had told him her theory about "guardian angles" once. He had just brushed it off, and she had never mentioned it again. Maybe that's what Miles really was. He'd probably never know, and now he wished he had talked to Ellen more about it. Mostly, he just wished he'd talked to her more.

The renewal of his activity on nanotechnology had been just the tonic that his charred soul had needed. The deaths of his project leads from NanoStar had shaken him to his core. Gerry's death had been an unexpectedly hard loss. His psyche needed to heal along with his physical wound. It was his work that kept him centered and going, and it gave his powerful, restless mind a focus. But, more than that, it had become his tribute to Ellen. He could think of her now and even see her in his mind's eye without breaking down into a sobbing wreck. That was the guidance that told him he was on the right path.

He also hadn't forgotten the evidence that his house had been searched and had taken appropriate precautions. He worked on his computer off of one flash drive that he kept on a chain around his neck. He backed that one up to another chip that lived in his secret spot in the planter wall. And this beauty, he thought as he held up the DVD he had just created, was going to buy him a ticket back into the game.

Grant had stumbled across The Forester Group some years ago. He knew they were a philanthropic foundation that was focused on the future of technology. They were not venture capitalists who were looking for a going concern to finance and take public. Rather, they promoted ideas and the people capable of nurturing them into real accomplishments. Grant had never considered himself a candidate for their attentions because he had always been able to find a new company where he could pursue his investigation of nanotechnology. He now looked upon the string of failed companies that lay behind him as evidence of an ominous pattern he was determined to break.

When he first called the group's offices, he had been immediately forwarded to a scheduling assistant. And while he expected to be put through an extensive vetting process before he ever got near being able to talk to the board of directors, the assistant signed him up for a meeting on Thursday. From what the assistant said, Charles Carver had already been interested in Grant and in nanotech. He wanted Grant to make a full presentation to his board on what could be done and how he would go about doing it.

Grant put the DVD into a sleeve and put that into his attaché case for Thursday. Tonight, it was time to celebrate. And he knew just the place. He hadn't been back to their favorite restaurant since Ellen died, and it just seemed fitting to have a dinner there to remind himself of what she meant to him and to this whole process that his life had gone through.

He was surprised that he was actually looking forward to the evening as he dressed in a suede jacket, just like Ellen's favorite, and got ready. He still had a long way to go to turn this presentation into a tangible project that would start putting nanotech where it belonged in science. However, this was still a major win, and he was determined to commemorate it.

As he reached for the phone to call a cab, he stopped. Ellen's car still sat in the garage where she had parked it on that fateful day. Grant knew he would have to deal with it sooner or later, and there was no point in just letting it sit. With a deep breath, he went to the kitchen key rack and took down the car keys Ellen had hung there nearly two months ago. He held them in his hand for a moment, took another deep breath, then squared his shoulders as he headed for the garage.

He unlocked and opened the door, almost expecting to sense her essence in the little car, but there was nothing present that the manufacturer hadn't put there. Ellen had never been big on perfume; she had not even left a scent behind. Grant inserted the key in the ignition, twisted it and was instantly rewarded with the engine cranking over three turns and starting. What she loved most about her little Miata was its reliability, and it had, again, justified her faith in it.

The restaurant was only about half an hour from the house. Grant used the drive to have an imaginary conversation in which he brought Ellen up to date on his preparations for the meeting with the Forester Group. It was a mental technique he had used in the past to check his plans for flaws, and while it caused some emotional pain, it kept her alive in his thoughts. He had lived with her long enough that some part of him could think the way she did, and that part would listen critically to these expositions to see if they had gaps he needed to address.

In what seemed like only moments, he was pulling into the parking lot across the street from the restaurant. It was a little place that specialized in French cuisine and didn't have its own parking lot. The food, however, had created memories that had his mouth watering. As he walked across the street on an unwavering course for the restaurant's front door, he was already thinking of ordering a particular dish that he and Ellen had enjoyed many times.

Next he saw light out of the corner of his eye, heard the screech of tires and turned toward the sound just in time to see a pair of headlights bearing down on him.

"Summers, this is just . . ."

"Don't even say it."

"But I . . ."

"Jakowski, you can't say anything about this call that I haven't already thought myself. So just can it."

"OK, OK, take the next right and it'll be at the far corner of the block."

Ordwyn turned down the indicated street and saw the familiar black and whites at the expected corner. As she pulled to the curb behind the nearest unit, she caught sight of Jenkins standing on the sidewalk and scribbling in his notebook. *"All we need now is Slater and we could have a reunion,"* she thought sourly.

Jenkins looked up from his notebook as they got out of their car and walked up to him. "Summers, Jakowski, what are you two doin' here?"

Ordwyn glared at him. "It was a nice night for a drive; we were in the neighborhood and just thought we'd drop by. What happened?"

"Eh? Oh, well, it looks like that gray sedan came out of the alley over there." He pointed at a spot about half-way down the block. "Took the corner faster than I'da thought he could, and then something went wrong. The crime lab tech is still looking at it trying to figure out what happened, but they'll probably need to take it back to the garage."

"And him?" Ordwyn pointed at the figure seated on the curb opposite a large gray four-door that was snugly wrapped around a telephone poll.

"Not a scratch; he's not even as shook up as I'd expect. But why are you here? Nobody was killed. The driver musta walked, 'cause we can't find any sign of him. There's just nothin' here to pull homicide detectives in for."

A nearly endless array of sarcastic remarks boiled up in her mind, but Ordwyn just said, "Jakowski, explain it to him," as she walked over to a curiously composed Grant Thornton and sat down on the curb next to him.

They stared at each other for a moment. Ordwyn could see that he had been scared by what had happened to him, but the overriding emotion she saw in his eyes was anger.

She could understand that.

"I'm getting really tired of people trying to kill you on my watch.

"Did you see the driver when he got out of the car?"

Grant looked at her for a moment longer, then at the wrecked car. "Not really; the driver-side door was on the side away from me. He got out right after the crash and ran down to the alley, disappearing into it." He looked back at Ordwyn. "It was the same people who killed Ellen, wasn't it?"

Ordwyn started to say something evasive then looked at Grant's eyes again. "Probably."

"And you won't find anything that identifies them this time either, will you?"

She sighed. "I'd bet that we'll find out that the car was stolen and that the original owner's fingerprints aren't even on it anymore."

Grant looked back at the car. "I don't see why he missed. I saw the headlights coming at me, and I just froze. Then he swerved into the pole."

"Did you see anything else, anything at all?"

He thought for a moment, "It seemed like I saw a small spark fly off the side of the car, but I can't be sure."

"OK, just stay put, will you? I'll be back in a minute." Ordwyn walked over to the wreck, Jakowski was turning away from the lab tech who was closing up his kit.

"What did he find, Jakowski?"

"Not much. Both front tires are shredded, and not just from runnin' up on the curb. But that shouldn'ta pushed the car clear across the street and into the pole. They're gonna tow it back to their garage to see if they can figure out what happened."

"Yeah, look, take the unit back to the station. I'm gonna drive Thornton there in his car. I want to go over this with him some more, and I want to keep an eye on him. If these guys tried twice and missed, they're going to make damn sure that the third time's the charm."

"You should be dead, twice."

They had been back at the precinct station for two hours, and Summers, Jakowski and Thornton were all getting tired of plowing the same ground over and over again.

"You've said that already and you've said it a lot more than twice," Grant said with a bleary look at Ordwyn. "What are we accomplishing by endlessly going over this?"

Ordwyn glared back and gestured at him with her coffee cup. "We have to be missing something and, one way or another, I'm going to find out what it is. You said that you contacted the Forester Group yesterday. Who knew about that?"

"From me? Nobody!" Grant snapped back. "After what happened to Gerry and Dave I wouldn't tell my mother that I was going to blow my nose—and she's been dead for five years." He steadied his breathing. "When my best coworkers die in sudden 'accidents,' even I can figure out that someone is actively hunting us down."

"So why continue? Why put yourself at ongoing risk with your work? You're a highly trained scientist; you could work at any number of other kinds of projects. Why nanotechnology?"

Grant had finally had enough. "Because that's what they killed Ellen over!" he roared. "And they are not—I say again—*not* going to win!"

Well, thought Ordwyn, we finally got that out. Just as she was about to ask her next question, Jim Franklin walked through the double doors to the squad room. "So you drew tonight's lab shift? Please tell me you found something," she implored.

"Yes, I obviously have the shift; and as for finding something, well, maybe. There wasn't any useful trace in the car, so we started looking at the car itself. Aside from the strangely heavy damage to the tires, we found something else odd. The car hit the phone pole head on, but the whole front of the body was tweaked to one side. It's almost as if something pushed the car sideways across the street, destroying the tires and bending the body structure till it hit the pole."

"What?" Ordwyn and Grant asked in unison.

"Don't ask me what could have done that. Don't even ask how it might be possible, because I don't have a clue. I'm just telling you what it looks like." He dropped a folder on Ordwyn's desk. "Here are the details, but I'm not even drawing any conclusions from them."

Franklin started to turn toward the door and stopped. "One other thing. I looked at the scene photos of the street surface, and there were no skid marks at all indicating an attempt to brake. The driver was definitely trying to hit Thornton, and he should have succeeded. The only skid marks went sideways toward the curb. When you guys figure this one out, you be sure and let me know."

He completed his turn and walked to the door. "Thanks a lot, Franklin," Ordwyn said.

"Don't mention it, please," he responded, as the door closed behind him.

She looked back at Thornton, "Well, that settles one thing. You're going into protective custody. Jakowski, call Hamer and Jacobs and have them take Thornton to the safe house on Nash Street. Then . . ."

"Not on your life or mine!" Grant shot back. "I am

not going to dive into a hole and pull it in after me. Not now. I have a meeting with the Forester Review Board Thursday night and I intend on keeping it!"

"Maybe you weren't paying attention, Thornton. There are people—very well armed, trained and financed people—who are trying to kill you. It's a damned good bet that they will be successful if they get another shot. So why are you so eager to give 'em one?"

"Because if I run off and hide now, they win."

"Thornton, if they kill you, they win. And I've got to tell you, from what I've seen of their efforts so far, they have a damned good chance of taking you down if you have less than airtight security around you."

His eyes blazed at her. "And what happens if you shut me up in a bank vault and they can't get at me? What happens if the Forester Group never hears from me again and forgets about nanotechnology? What happens if they get what they want and I go off to a new identity working on a superior trash compactor?

"I'll tell you what happens! My contribution to nanotechnology—what Ellen died for—is successfully buried, and the people who killed her just disappear, never to be seen or heard from again. Maybe you can live with that, Sergeant, but I can't."

Ordwyn's own temper flared at that point. "So you are just going to climb up on the target rack and invite them to take their best shot? You're going to promote your discoveries to Forester and paint a bull's-eye on your chest? You'll just get yourself killed to no purpose whatsoever. It's pointless to die like that!"

"Not if you're there," Grant said quietly.

His tone grabbed her attention much more firmly than his words. "If you are watching me, you will have the best chance there is to catch these guys. The only time they are going to be vulnerable is when they come after me, and they won't do that unless they have a reason to. I'm going to give them that reason."

Ordwyn looked at him with a weary anger. "Thornton, do you know what happens to bait? It gets eaten."

Grant locked stares with her. "If we catch the fish, it's worth it."

Ordwyn sagged. "And besides, you're gonna to do it anyhow, aren't you?" she said almost inaudibly.

Jakowski had been watching with the phone in his hand. "Do I call Hamer and Jacobs or not?"

Ordwyn looked balefully at him. "Call them and tell them that they are tailing Thornton home. And Jakowski . . ."

"Yeah, Summers."

"Tell them that if anything happens to him, I will personally rip strips off their hides."

"Yeah, I'll just call 'em now," Jakowski said and became very focused on his phone call.

"Thornton, when you go home, park in front of your house, not in the garage. I want them to be able to keep an eye on your car, too. Look for their car when you leave tomorrow and make sure you don't lose them in traffic. OK?"

"Thank you for . . ." he started to respond.

"Do not thank me! This is one of the dumbest things I have ever done, and my boss will rip strips off of *me* for it. So please, *please* use your head and keep my men close to you."

———————————

Grant could easily see Hamer and Jacobs in their car following him through the city streets. They weren't exactly covert surveillance. If using him as bait in a trap was going to work, the trap was going to have to be a lot less obvious. But, for now, he mainly wanted to get to his meeting with the Forester Group, and if Hamer and Jacobs were his tickets to do that, then so be it.

He became lost in his thoughts as he steered up onto the expressway and crossed over into the suburbs. It always amazed him to see how sharp the division between the commercial zones and the housing developments had become. He and Ellen had considered moving back into the city to one of the downtown condo renovations, but a house with a yard was just more appealing to both of them. Besides, he thought sadly, there had still been the possibility of starting a family, having kids. He fought back tears for what he had lost.

Well, that option had been foreclosed on and, at some point, he would have to consider selling the house—assuming he lived long enough to have to worry about that. As Grant steered onto his street and approached his house, he had to remind himself to park on the street rather than drive into his garage.

He and Ellen had landscaped a path up to the front door that had small trees and shrubbery around it. As he walked up the path, he stopped. Something was not quite right. There, in the dark, were the indistinct shapes of two trees just off to the right instead of one.

Then one of the trees moved.

"Hello, Mr. Thornton."

The moving tree resolved itself into Miles, and Grant started to breathe again.

"What the hell are you doing here, Miles? I didn't think I'd ever see you again."

"I suggest that you speak a bit more softly and ask yourself a question," Miles replied.

"OK." Grant whispered, "What question should I ask?"

"How safe do you feel tonight?"

Grant's brow furrowed. "What do you mean by that?"

"Look around and tell me if you can still find your rather obvious police tail."

Chapter 5

They were gone as if they had never existed.

Grant walked back out into the street and even down to the corner while Miles waited in the shadows. The car that Ordwyn had set up to tail him was nowhere to be seen. Grant furiously stirred his memory in an attempt to remember when he'd last seen it in his mirrors on the way home. His last clear memory of the two cops in their car was in the city before he got on the freeway.

Not good.

He trotted back up the street to Miles and asked the obvious: "OK, I give up. Why is it going to thoroughly creep me out when you tell me exactly what happened to them?"

"They were inattentive at the wrong moment. It cost them their lives," Miles responded.

And Grant felt what was becoming an all-too-familiar chill go down his spine.

"Right now, we have something more important

to deal with." Miles led Grant around the side of his house to a window that looked into the living room and toward the front door.

Grant had left the entryway light on so he wouldn't have to fumble in the dark for a light switch when he got home. He could see the front door clearly; the rest of the room was various shades of gray. Miles pushed down on Grant's shoulder like a steam press so that he and Miles were squatting down to the same level as the shrubbery next to the wall.

"Dumb question time again. Why are we crouched in the flower bed outside my living room window?" Grant asked softly.

"You already know the answer, but just shortly there should be . . . ah, there it is. Watch your living room carefully—especially the end of the couch nearest the window."

A car turned onto the street. Its headlights briefly shined in through the window, illuminating the room and casting a series of moving, angled shadows as it passed. Grant had another of those chills as he saw two men, one behind the couch, one next to it, and realized that both of them had guns in their hands—guns with long, tubular silencers.

Miles held a finger over his lips and pointed at the street. They quietly made their way back to Grant's car. "They heard you drive up. We need to leave quickly now."

Grant looked at Miles, and his jaw set. "Not until you answer some questions."

Miles looked back at the house. "You really don't have time for this. Those men mean to kill you, and they are very good at what they do."

"Then just tell me this. Who are you and what do you want?"

Grant noted the smallest of smiles cross Miles' face as he answered. "I am something that you have only dimly imagined. My unique physiology allows me to do things that you cannot and know things that you cannot. The details of who and what I am would be both difficult and far too time-consuming to explain while we stand outside a house occupied by armed men. I will, however, tell you this: I want you to pursue and succeed in making nanotechnology into a readily available engineering tool. I want that far more than you do. And you will not be able to do anything if they kill you."

Grant stared into those bottomless eyes just a moment longer, then said, "Well, I guess that will have to do for now. What do you recommend for our next move?"

"We need to leave here quickly. I have a car parked around that corner," Miles whispered, as he pointed down the street.

With nothing better to suggest, Grant nodded. They quietly but very quickly ran through the grassy lawns that bordered the street till they got to the corner. An unimposing green sedan was parked where the street sloped slightly. They got in without closing the doors. Miles released the hand brake and put in the clutch. The car rolled silently past the first intersection before he closed his door and started the engine.

Realizing that he had been holding his breath, Grant gulped some air before he closed his own door and asked, "Where are we going?"

"Take the battery out of your cell phone so that it cannot be tracked." As Grant did so, Miles explained. "We are going to a place in the city that I have converted into a residence of sorts. You will be safe there—for a while. We will have to move you soon. There are too many ways to narrow search patterns in cities."

After that sobering pronouncement, they rode in silence into the dimly lit streets that comprised the warehouse district. After a series of turns and double-backs that left Grant dizzy, Miles pulled up to a large roll-up door that opened at their approach, then drove into a building that looked just like every other on the street—bland, utilitarian, anonymous. Unsurprisingly, it was filled with crates and shipping containers. He deftly drove between these obstacles to a back corner of the building that had simply been framed in with wood two-by-fours covered by wallboard, as if someone had started to build a house.

They walked through an ordinary-looking door into a set of rooms that were not exactly cozy, but were furnished to make reasonably comfortable living quarters. The rooms could have been part of a frame house built any time in the last thirty years, and the furniture was anonymous Danish modern. Grant's attention was captured by the computer on a large desk in one of the rooms. The large desk was necessary because the device was connected to four very large flat-screen monitors, a digitizing pad that looked like it covered an acre and the most unusual computer printer he had ever seen.

"Is that what I think it is?"

Miles glanced at the machine. "It is an eight-processor system with enough RAM, flash disk space, graphics power and appropriate software for you to continue your work here. It also runs a site management system for this building." He removed a flash memory chip from a jacket pocket and handed it to Grant. "I took the liberty of removing this from its garden hiding place in case you needed it."

Grant snatched the chip hanging from the neck chain out from under his shirt and held the two chips next to each other. Their appearance was identical, and he felt certain that their contents were as well. "How did you know about this? How did you find it?" he angrily demanded.

He was nailed by Miles' bone-chilling gaze.

"Understand, Grant Thornton, that I have existed longer than you can imagine, and I can do many things that you would consider impossible and even miraculous. The existence of the chip was a simple deduction. Locating it was, for me, a trivial exercise. Your pursuers knew it existed. They lacked my capabilities for finding it.

"Understand this also: I am not interested in slaking your thirst for vengeance against those who hunt you. I am, however, vitally interested in making sure that you survive to create the nanotechnology to which you have given your life and for which you have possibly sacrificed what means the most to you. More than anything else either of us could do, your survival and accomplishments will hurt those who have caused you harm."

Grant wanted to argue that point with Miles, fiercely. But, turning it over in his mind, he saw that its logic and truth were both unassailable. That reality galled him, but then reality had never been interested in his sensibilities before, and it wasn't now.

"I know you're right. But I don't have to like it, and I don't."

"They were WHAT?!"

Ordwyn usually held off from going into the station in the morning. Mornings were a good time to go to the gym, work out and let her subconscious mull over cases—while her body kept her conscious mind occupied with pain. After showering and changing, she could call Jakowski and have him meet her at the first location where they needed to question someone or investigate a crime scene. With these low-stress activities to gradually ease her into the day, she was prepared to go into the station and deal with the nonsense that grew there like mold on a dead tree trunk.

Today, instead of the gym, she had, to her instant regret, gone straight to the station, poured a cup of what passed for coffee there, picked up her desk phone and called Braddock to schedule a relief crew for Thornton's tail.

"When?

"And Thornton?"

Jakowski walked through the door just then, took one look at the storm brewing on Summers' face, and just barely resisted the temptation to turn around and leave again.

"Has anyone been to his house?

"Why not?"

At the obvious end of the conversation, she just stood and stared at the phone in her hand. Watching her, Jakowski was a little surprised that it didn't melt. He figured he might as well get it over with. "I know I shouldn't ask, but what was that about?"

Summers made her hand release the phone, one finger at a time, while carefully placing it back on its cradle. In a quiet voice that chilled even Jakowski's sensibilities, she said, "That was Braddock. I called him to make sure that he'd sent someone to relieve Hamer and Jacobs on the Thornton tail."

There were times when Jakowski wished she'd just scream and throw things. It would be a lot less disturbing than this. Besides, even though she wasn't more than about five-foot-four, he'd once seen her knock a suspect clear over a patrol car when he pulled a gun on her. He really didn't want to see her anger and combat training get crossed up while he was within arm's reach. So, maintaining his distance, he asked, "And Braddock told you . . . ?"

". . . that he had not replaced Hamer and Jacobs. That, in fact, they are dead."

Jakowski couldn't help it; he cringed. This was bad. This was very bad. Jacobs had been her father's first rookie trainee. Summers treated him like a favorite uncle. And if he and Hamer were dead . . . "But, what about Thornton?" Jakowski regretted the question the instant it was out of his mouth.

Summers' voice began to tremble with boiling rage, "You. Tell. Me! Hamer and Jacobs weren't even missed until two hours ago, when they didn't make their morning check-in. They'd been following a vic who'd barely survived a professional hit and they weren't even scheduled to check in until the morning shift came on duty! That's seven hours without anyone even scheduling a contact with the surveillance team!"

She was clearly fighting for control now. "After they missed their contact time, it was another hour before anyone made the connection between them and two dead bodies found in a burned-out car last night. The car was identified through its license plate TWO HOURS AFTER IT WAS FOUND!"

She hated her loss of control, but the sheer incompetence of it all was just too much. "So, not only is his tail dead, but no one has even seen Thornton since he left here last night! . . . No one on our team, that is," she spat out.

Summers' grip on the back of her chair turned her knuckles white, and she forced herself to breathe deeply. She had to get it together and start making rational decisions. She knew there would be a time for the anger, but it would have to wait—no matter how much she felt like it should be right damn now.

She snatched out her cell phone and hit the speed dial for Thornton's number. Predictably, it went straight to voice mail. "Jakowski, get the car and pick me up on the street. We're going to Thornton's house, but I have one more call to make first."

Jakowski was smart enough to snatch at even a momentary opportunity to escape Summers' wrath. "I'm on my way."

Summers carefully picked up the desk phone, willed an artificial calmness to her mind and dialed a number. "Captain Grayson? Summers.

"Yes sir, I know.

"I want the investigation into Hamer and Jacobs. I think it may be tied to one of my other cases.

"But . . .

"Yes sir, I have to check on Thornton, but I'll look you up as soon as I get back to the station."

As she hung up, she wondered what else could go wrong with this mess of a case and instantly regretted the thought.

———————————

"You did WHAT?!"

Clarissa Ingalls took pride in her work. She treasured her accomplishments, however small.

She had signed up with the temp agency only after spending eight months learning that office assistants were not even worth a dime a dozen in this job market—expending her unemployment benefits in the process. This made the call to fill in at the Forester Group's offices for a suddenly ill scheduling assistant an opening with opportunity written all over it. She was determined to fulfill this assignment with polish, hard work and whatever results she could summon up from the openings it presented to her.

So, naturally, she had taken yesterday's call from

Mr. Grant Thornton, verified that he and his area of technology were listed in the Areas of Interest log, and then promptly scheduled him for the next available board presentation meeting. She had been told several times that setting up these presentations was key to the group's operations and that they were extremely important. As she stood trembling slightly in front of his desk, she couldn't figure out why Mr. Carver looked so extremely displeased. Maybe he just didn't understand.

"Yes sir, I set him up for Thursday. Nanotechnology was listed as one of the priorities in the log. I just knew you would be interested in talking to one of the leaders in the field."

Charles Emerson Carver stood, leaned across his desk and struggled to contain himself as he enunciated every word to make each one as clear as possible. "Ms. Ingalls, did anyone explain to you what the color annotations in the log represent?"

"No sir . . . Ms. Shipley did say, several times even, that I should read a file that explained them. But the call from Mr. Thornton came in before I had time to do so. I figured the flashing red highlight on Mr. Thornton's name meant he was a high-priority opportunity." she replied, ending the sentence with quavering uncertainly.

"Oh, good Lord!" Carver's eyes lit on the file Ingalls was carrying and snapped back to Ingalls' face with more urgency than she had ever seen in another human being. "Is that Thornton's file?"

"Y-yes sir, I thought you . . ." Carver lunged forward and yanked the folder from her hands, practically ripping it open in the process. He then snatched up his desk phone and called the number listed in the file for Thornton's cell phone. "Come on, come on, answer, ANSWER, DAMMIT!"

When the polite voice asked him if he wished to leave a message, Carver slowly replaced the phone receiver in its cradle as he slumped back into his chair. Then he dropped the folder on his desk and just stared at it for a moment before slowly raising his eyes back to hers. The look on his face froze the blood in her veins. She had seen that look before, on the doctor's face when he came to the waiting room to tell her that her husband of twenty years had not survived his surgery.

"Ms. Ingalls . . ." he started in a tired, tired voice.

"What happened, sir? Mr. Carver, sir, what happened? What did I do?"

She very nearly screamed those last four words.

Captain Thomas Grayson watched her with a calm, unblinking stare that usually made Ordwyn uncomfortable. Now, it was just infuriating.

"Captain, they were following Thornton. The only

reason to kill them was to get to him, and now he's missing, too!" Deep breaths, she needed to take deep breaths. This was not the time to lose control. "I don't understand why I wouldn't be investigating their murders right alongside the Thornton case."

Grayson was stone-faced, as imperturbable as a human-sized rock. "Summers, listen carefully. It's been determined that they were taken out by a street gang. There was a drug deal that went extremely bad about a block away. Hamer and Jacobs just had the bum luck to run into the gang that won the firefight over the goods. The case has been turned over to the gang suppression unit—and that's all there is to it."

Summers' face was turning an ugly color as she started to say exactly what she thought of that assessment. But Grayson was having none of it. "Drop it!"

Jakowski tried to be an invisible lump and blend into the wall as Grayson moved to stand directly in front of her, looked down, and put his face right up in front of Summers' nose. His voice slowly rose in volume. "Hamer and Jacobs had nothing to do with Thornton *and* you will stop wasting time on him. That case has gone nowhere and will continue to do so. I want you on one that you can solve and get an arrest on."

Summers just barely had control of her own anger and started to open her mouth one more time. Grayson saw it and exploded. "That's more than enough,

Summers! Stay off Hamer and Jacobs, and put Thornton's file down as a cold case. That's an order!"

She barely trusted herself with, "Yes sir." Then she turned on her heel and left the office Jakowski following but definitely maintaining his distance.

When she got to her desk, she just stood and stared at the Thornton case folder that lay accusingly in the middle of it. She stared at it for a long time. "Jakowski . . ."

"Summers, no! We ain't goin' up against the captain and the rest of the brass on this. If we do, he'll do a lot worse than pull ya off the lieutenant's list. I know Jacobs was special to ya, but ya just gotta let this one go!"

Oh, oh, he'd stuck his foot in it now.

Her eyes went cold and hard. Her voice was that deadly tone of quiet that made his skin crawl. "Worse than off the lieutenant's list, Jakowski? And what, precisely, would the list have to do with this case?"

He had no way out of this one. "Oh, hell, ya gotta know that steppin' on the captain's toes like ya did with the Franks case last year isn't gonna get ya promoted. And, if ya just ignore a direct order, he'll go through the roof! An' we got plenty a cases to . . ."

Her quiet voice became glacial. "Jakowski," she pointed at her inbox, "pick a file, any file, and get started on it. I will not—involve you—in anything that could be in any way construed as violating orders." She thrust up a single finger as he started to speak again, "I have some things to do. I will review the new case with you when I am through with them." Her glare followed him to the inbox and all the way back to his chair.

Ordwyn picked up the Thornton file, spent ten minutes taking notes from two of its pages and put it in her desk file drawer. She stared at the drawer for a long moment then removed the file and discretely slid it into her satchel. She took a sip of her coffee and was surprised that it could taste even worse after it got cold. She shook her head, stood, and walked around to Jakowski's chair.

He tried hard not to cringe away from her. He almost succeeded. She glanced down at him and saw something that disappointed her, something she should simply have accepted a long time ago.

She had really wanted to believe that there was more to Jakowski than just obeying orders and staying out of trouble. There *was* more to him and she had seen that he had the ability to be a good detective. But he had to want it enough to stick his neck out when it was necessary. Until he was ready to do that, he would be just another cop whose primary mission was to avoid making waves.

She took the file out of his hands and looked at the tab. "The liquor store robberies? OK, what do you have for leads?"

He carefully began to talk about the case with her, feeling relieved that she didn't bite his head off. But she sure wasn't in any kind of a good mood. "Jakowski, I want you to go back to the last two scenes and quiz the surviving vics about who else was in the stores when the robberies went down. These were too organized for one guy to just hit and run. He had a spotter."

"Uh . . . ain't you comin', too?"

"No, I have some personal business to attend to. I'll meet you back here to go over what you find. Take the unit. I'll be driving my own car." With that she turned her back on him as though he no longer existed, scooped up her day bag and the satchel—with the Thornton case folder in it—and walked out the front door.

Ordwyn Summers had some hard thinking to do.

And it wasn't going to wait until a convenient time.

She stopped in the shade of the precinct building and looked out at the parking lot where her car was parked. In deep thought, she stood without seeing either the lot or the car.

She'd been a cop all her adult life. "Cop" was how she thought of herself. If she pursued the Thornton case against Grayson's orders, she very well might be thrown off the force under conditions that would make joining another department impossible.

But that was just the problem, she *was* a cop—a cop to the bone. And a cop just couldn't ignore what was happening right in front of her. And worse, she couldn't ignore the suspicions it aroused about the organization that had become her extended family. It just didn't make any sense to call what happened to Hamer and Jacobs a gang killing. Gangbangers wouldn't attack a pair of cops in a car to start with. And even if they did, they wouldn't hang around after a gun battle to set fire to the car. They'd shoot and run.

And yet, Grayson appeared to buy into the idea hook, line and sinker. And that meant one of only two things: Ether he was losing his ability to reason or he had lost his independence to exercise his reason. And he was still way too sharp to have lost his edge like that. No, he was following orders, orders from a source she was going to have to confront sooner or later. Probably sooner, so she'd . . .

"What was that?"

Whatever else she was, Ordwyn was a very good cop, and that meant that she was very observant—even when it was her subconscious that was doing the observing. Her subconscious had just seen a movement in the lot in front of her that brought her consciousness up to red alert.

Someone had just moved from behind the black and white unit next to the fence over to the far end of the white convertible in the next parking slot.

That alerting movement had been familiar. It was the movement of someone who was covering a location or person with a gun. He had moved to improve his line of sight to the target.

It was approaching noon. She was in deep shade on a blindingly bright, sunny day, which would make her practically invisible to anyone in the parking lot. So, she simply stood still where she was and continued to watch the scene, waiting for the next hint of motion.

"*There!*"

Over next to the blue van about forty feet away, another figure had subtly shifted his position. He moved just enough for her to see that he had a semi-automatic with a silencer in his right hand.

Ordwyn felt the tension begin to coil within her as she got ready for a burst of adrenalin-fired action. All that remained was to watch for a few more minutes until she could triangulate the location of their target zone. Once she had that, she would take the closest one out first, then go to cover and engage the other shooter.

The one by the van moved again. Then she caught sight of the position that the man next to the convertible had assumed. If he was aiming that way and the other was opening his field of fire to there, then their target was right about . . .

"*Well, now.*"

They were professionals who had covered their target perfectly. The problem was that their target was Ordwyn's car. Or, more precisely, their target was her. Given how well they had set up the hit, she rapidly reconsidered taking them on with her sidearm. She might get lucky and take down the first one, but the other would surely complete his mission by killing her.

She realized that she could fade back around the corner of the building, staying in the shade, and that was exactly what she did. But what to do now? Two absolute pros. Undoubtedly the same two who had killed Ellen Thornton, tried to kill Grant Thornton and succeeded in killing Hamer and Jacobs. The very fiber of her being screamed at her to roust out the uniforms in the precinct building and set them on these guys. And that would get how many of them killed?

A takedown of these two demanded a SWAT team. Ordwyn was digging in her pocket for her cell phone to call their emergency dispatcher when she heard two car doors slam. She looked around the building's corner just in time to see a dark coupe speed off down the road with two occupants.

"Damn!"

She carefully checked their prior positions but both the shooters were gone. She sank back against the wall as the adrenalin surge passed and her breathing got ragged.

"I was that close to them!"

And another part of her mind told her, "*Yes, and they were that close to you.*"

———————————

Carver wished he'd had something to say to her, something that would help.

But Clarissa Ingalls was in her own private hell, thrown there, however unintentionally, by her own hand. She sat just outside his office in his secretary's chair, her face buried in her hands, still sobbing as the Forester Group's security staff filed past her and into his office.

Sam Baker looked over his shoulder at the emotionally wrecked woman, then turned back to Carver. "You know Charles, just once it would be nice to be called to your office for something other than imminent disaster." He looked closely at Carver's face and added, "Or are we past imminent?"

Carver gestured at the large conference table at the end of the spacious room. "Sit." The four men and two women did so. "I strongly suspect that our time has already run out, but we are going to assume for the moment that we still have an option or two.

"I've flagged the files on nanotechnology and Grant Thornton to all of you, but the essence of the situation is this: The Consortium has been trying to suppress nanotechnology for over a dozen years. Thornton is the brightest star in the field, and he has been moving from one startup to the next, trying to stay ahead of the Consortium's financial meat grinder. Two and a half months ago it went into high gear on destroying NanoStar. It was the latest of these startups that had drawn together the best available talent, with Thornton as their lead. True to form, the Consortium bought the company out and immediately dismembered it, once again putting our Mr. Thornton and his colleagues on the street."

"Does Thornton have any idea what he's up against?" queried Reinhold, the intelligence specialist.

"He didn't, but he has at least some idea now. When they took down NanoStar, they tried to kill Thornton and succeeded with his wife. Then, the two senior engineers under him at NanoStar died nearly simultaneously and, of course, theirs were completely 'accidental' deaths. Which brings us up to what happened yesterday.

"Thornton called our office to set up a meeting with our discretionary board. He wanted to present his ideas for pursuing nanotechnology as a viable engineering tool set." The faces around the table went grim. "Yes, you can likely guess the rest. His call went to Ms. Ingalls out there." Carver gestured at the office door. "She hadn't been properly briefed on the interest log and simply scheduled him for Thursday. She did this late yesterday and came into brief me on his 'appointment' this morning. I had to tell her that her helpfulness had probably gotten him killed."

"Any contact with Thornton since then?" Baker asked.

"No, I tried to call him immediately, but his cell phone goes directly to voice mail. I checked, and Thornton disconnected the ground line to his home over a month ago. As you can imagine, the Consortium has been keeping close tabs on him. We have been planning contact strategies to avoid them, but with little success. Thornton has stuck very close to home and, without any opportunities for a public meeting, we could not risk a direct contact. You can imagine my shock at finding out he had tried to contact us.

"We sent a car to drive by his house and found the only bright spot in this mess. Even though his car is there, the Consortium's agents are still watching it closely. Which tells us that neither they, nor we, have any idea where he has gone to ground."

—————————

Ordwyn was absolutely convinced of one thing.

She had asked too many questions and, apparently, made someone very nervous.

The parking lot ambush she had so nearly walked into meant that whoever was out to kill Grant Thornton was now also out to kill her. Finding Thornton was no longer a matter of good police work. Now, it meant the difference between life and death to her.

The thought chilled her; its implications were staggering.

She couldn't go home now. Small a loss as that was, it still cut her off from a piece of her life. She couldn't go back to the station, either, which was a much bigger problem. All they'd really have to do there was wait in better concealment until she walked right into their next trap. They just simply knew far too much. And the only way she could see for that to be the case would be that they had penetrated the precinct staff. That thought hurt her more than she had imagined anything could.

Now, she was beginning to think like Thornton. Soon she'd be looking under every rock and around every corner for this dark, omnipotent conspiracy that was after them. She had to find him and find him fast.

He had been charged up about making a presentation to the Forester Group. It occupied offices in that building across the street and down about a block. She'd driven around for a couple of hours before deciding to come here. She had been sitting here in her car for about half an hour now, waiting for any indication at all that they were watching this place. She felt no comfort from the fact that she hadn't seen any sign of them, and she wasn't going to get anywhere sitting here. It was time to get out of the car and go do what she knew how to do best—investigate.

Fighting off the disconcerting feeling of being in someone's gun sights, she opened the car door, got out and closed it. Then she cursed herself for wondering if she'd make it back to the miniscule safety that the car represented.

"Get a grip! Thornton very carefully didn't tell anyone but you that he was coming here. Even Hamer and Jacobs were simply instructed to follow him. Getting paranoid is not going to help your situation. It is time to just walk up to the door of the place and go in."

Ordwyn started walking down the sidewalk while trying to grow eyes in the back of her head. The midday pedestrian traffic was light and she carefully scrutinized everyone she saw for any indication that anyone was armed or, in any way, overly interested in her.

"May I have a word with you, Sergeant Summers?"

She nearly jumped out of her skin.

She couldn't decide which frightened her more, that a man had walked up behind her and she hadn't even noticed or that he had grasped her forearm faster than she could get to her gun. Now he held it immobilized as though it were clamped in a machine vise.

"Sergeant, if I wanted you dead, you would never have gotten out of your car. Please come with me to that bus stop bench over there."

He steered her to the bench and sat her down like

an unruly child. He began speaking quickly but precisely with minimal movement and without looking at her. "Now listen. I know who you are, why you are here and whom you hope to find. Thornton isn't in there, and the people who are do not know anything about where he is. You are correct in your assumption that the people who are hunting him are now also hunting you. And, yes, they are watching this building in the expectation of intercepting one or both of you. Allow me to prove this last assertion.

"Please direct your attention to the alley that is approximately fifty feet this side of the building's door. In particular, notice the shadow under the awning over the trash bin at the mouth of the alley." Almost unwillingly, she did so and saw someone move behind the bin, then cautiously look around its corner.

"His associate is across the street and invisible from this angle. I have compromised the means by which they communicate with each other and suggested to both of them that Thornton is approaching from the other direction. The person whom they are being directed to intercept is actually their contact with their employers, but they do not know that he is here—another convenience that I arranged. And there he is, right on time."

Ordwyn watched in unwilling fascination as a man walked toward the door of the office building. He looked around in obvious expectation of seeing someone. Then a man hurriedly crossed the street, obviously stuffing something back under his suit coat. At the same time, the man under the awning jumped out and very nearly shot both of the other two before putting his gun back out of sight.

"I think it is time for us to leave now." He stood up in an unusually graceful flowing motion and swept Ordwyn along with him. She marveled at how his iron grip on her arm was not even uncomfortable, until she tugged at it. He walked her around a nearby corner, stopping at a very ordinary-looking green sedan. He deftly extracted her gun from her back holster and then deposited her on the front seat. Apparently, he had retrieved her day bag and satchel from her car, as they were already on the seat. With disturbing ease, he pushed her and the two bags across the broad seat to the other side of the car, got in after her and sat behind the steering wheel.

She was just starting to open her mouth when he faced her and said, "My name is Miles. I know that you are a police sergeant and that you are burning to interrogate me with dozens of questions that we do not have time for right now. Am I correct that what you most want is to talk to Grant Thornton?"

She very briefly thought about trying to question him anyhow, but Ordwyn was neither stupid nor slow, and this man had just kept her from walking into what would most likely have been a fatal trap.

Though it flashed through her mind that he might have set her up for all this, she took a firm grip on her nerves and simply said yes.

"Then I will take you to him."

Chapter 6

Ordwyn didn't like surprises.

They disturbed her sense of order.

As a cop, putting things in their proper order was a fundamental part of her training. She was good at being a cop because it was also a fundamental part of her personality. The bizarre man named Miles, who was driving her to who knew where, had just kicked her sense of order in a very tender place and was continuing to do so.

At the moment they were driving what appeared to be a very erratic pattern that was gradually taking them into the warehouse district. The setting sun was flashing on them intermittently from between high-rise buildings and it would periodically blind her to what was in the street's shadows. Since looking out the windows wasn't very useful, she was watching Miles as he drove. She could tell that he was watching something intently; she just couldn't tell what. She looked behind them and could not for the life of her see anything that looked like a tail. She looked where Miles appeared to be looking and couldn't see anything there, either.

His intensity and the odd directions they took had completely distracted her from all the questions that had her burning with curiosity only half an hour ago. "OK, I give up. You're obviously driving to accomplish some kind of evasion. What are we evading?"

Miles glanced at her. Like everything else he did, the look wasn't one she could categorize. It wasn't annoyance or disinterest or anything she could put her mental finger on, and that just added to the rapidly growing pile of questions he had inspired. "I do not think that they have identified this car yet, but when they do, I do not want them to quickly trace it to where we are going. What I am doing will make that much more difficult, but not impossible."

She looked out the window at the passing warehouse fronts as she thought about that for a moment and realized it told her exactly nothing. "But what are you looking at that triggers your directional changes?"

Miles slowed the car abruptly as one of the warehouse doors began to retract onto its roller and answered "Surveillance cameras." He turned into the building, weaved past containers and crate stacks to the rear of the building and stopped. In front of them was a smaller building within the building—it was really just an area framed in with two-by-fours and wallboard.

Ordwyn was a bit miffed at her own surprise when she saw Grant Thornton standing just inside a door in the "wall" of the nailed-together structure. She looked over at Miles, who was already getting out of the car, and then did so herself. "Mr. Thornton, I was beginning to wonder if I'd ever see you again—alive, at least."

Grant gave her a lopsided smile. "I had my doubts a few times as well . . . even after Miles saved me from being shot in my living room. Speaking of whom, I see you have met my—or is it our?—mysterious benefactor."

Miles rounded the car in his strange rolling gait and ushered them through the door Grant had just used. "I suggest that we go inside. The structure is better shielded than this area."

They walked into another surprise for Ordwyn. The frame structure that appeared so unimpressive from the outside was actually quite comfortable on the inside. She watched the door close behind him as Miles continued on into another room. Grant just stood and looked at her for a moment. "He has quite a disconcerting presence, doesn't he?"

She turned to look at him and replied, "Oh, disconcerting isn't the half of it." Her eyes narrowed. "What happened last night?"

Grant returned her gaze. "I could ask you the same thing. I went home. Miles was there to greet me. When he asked me where my police tail was, I couldn't see any sign of them. What I did find was an ambush set up in my house that, without Miles' intercession, I'd have walked right into."

"You didn't see my people in their car behind you?"

"I did for about a dozen blocks after we left the station. But, when I got home, they were nowhere to be found."

Ordwyn's face began to cloud. "From your expression, I gather that you know what happened to them."

"Oh, I know, all right. We found their bodies about two blocks from where you last saw them."

Grant looked away. "They were friends, weren't they." It wasn't a question.

Ordwyn stepped back in front of him. Her voice and face went hard. "Yes, they were. And yes, they were killed by the people who murdered your wife. Now, they're not just after you, they're after me, too—because I just wouldn't let your case go. So, tired of this tale as you may be, Mr. Grant Thornton, we are going to dig through this backward and forward until I find something, anything, that I can use to get a handle on it!"

Grant nodded toward the door Miles had gone through. "I think your real lead is in there. He certainly seems to know more about what's going on than both of us put together."

"Good point." She went around Grant and through the door to find an empty room. She rounded back on Grant. "What the . . ."

"Yeah, he does that. He can disappear faster and more quietly than anyone I've ever seen."

"Not from me he can't!" Ordwyn started back out of the odd frame structure only to find Miles' car gone. She was getting damn tired of impossible mysteries. "That just can't be. There's no way, no way in hell that he could start that car and drive out without me hearing him."

Grant walked out behind her. "Sergeant, this place is soundproofed better than I'd have believed possible. He has gone and come back twice since he brought me here, and I didn't hear him either time. Scared the hell out of me when I walked through one of the interior doors and there he was, back and bigger than life."

She walked back inside and almost stumbled to a chair. "I'm starting to feel punch drunk. Ever since I took the call on your case, my life has been turned upside down by one thing after another, and now him. I'd grab you and get the hell out of here, but we are in a not-so-nice part of town without a car, and he's got my gun!"

"Sergeant, welcome to my world."

An insubstantial holographic display glowed in front of him with numbers, symbols and words in a language that no one currently alive had ever seen.

Miles reached out and seemed to touch the hologram in several places. A series of lists containing names and numbers scrolled until one combination was highlighted—Ordwyn Summers followed by a 16-digit number. Miles resumed the scrolling until another similar line was highlighted, with Grant Thornton's name on it.

Miles touched another location, and a different list scrolled. This one showed names and addresses of convenience stores. He selected one, dragged the 16-digit number beside Grant's name to it and entered a date, today's date. A curiously normal document appeared on the display that started with the phrase "Transaction Recorded."

With a flurry of motions that looked almost like a conductor leading an orchestra, Miles brought up an array of live images. Several of them displayed the front sides and rear of the store he had selected from the second list. Others showed the streets around it, while the remainder were from the interior of the structure.

He watched quietly for some minutes until one of the screens showed a police patrol car passing the store. It slowed and then sped up to disappear around a corner. A short time later three SUVs pulled up and parked across from the store and behind it. A dozen obviously armed men swarmed from the vehicles into the store. The first one through the front door killed the clerk and then methodically shot out the interior surveillance cameras, leaving several blank panels on Miles' display.

He checked to see that the following communications were properly recorded. Then he transferred the video feeds to a common flash drive and shut down the incredibly sophisticated display. He left the room, locking the door with a pass of his hand over its mechanism.

———————

"How do you do that?"

"Do what?"

"Work on that nano-whatever it is of yours at a time like this?"

"Sergeant, what do you do when you are desperate to divert your mind?"

"I think about a case!"

"No, you pace and think, just like you've been doing ever since Miles left. You've been wearing a path in that carpet and, judging from the way your jaw muscles have been working, having a lively argument with yourself."

Ordwyn started to deny his observation, thought about it, and realized he was right. "It keeps me from grilling you just for something to do." She walked over to the desk with the huge computer displays and looked over his shoulder.

"Well, this," he indicated the computer in front of him that Miles had so thoughtfully provided, "is what I do to maintain my sanity when I have every moral right to have a mental meltdown. Like your ruminations on a case, I commonly get something useful out of it. At the very least, I can lay the groundwork for an experiment that I'll perform later.

"And, right now, it's the only thing that can keep my mind off of the men who killed Ellen and are trying to kill me . . . us."

"OK," she said pointing at the screens, "since I'm wearing a hole in my head along with the carpet, tell me what wonderful accomplishment you've been up to for the last two hours."

"I've been reviewing the last round of test results I got before they killed NanoStar. I've looked at them a number of times, but I just realized there was one association of the data that I'd never tried. And that has opened up potential for some of that experimentation I was talking about." He gestured at a list of numbers and cryptic lines of text. "This part here is an indication that I can reduce the complexity of the first generation of devices substantially if I just use them in swarms. You see . . ."

"Good association. You can indeed shorten much of your initial development that way."

They both jumped at the sound of his voice and turned to find Miles standing behind them.

"Where the hell have you been?" Ordwyn demanded.

"Checking on this," Miles responded holding up a flash drive.

"Look, you might have pulled me back out of that trap this afternoon, but this disappearing act of yours has got to stop. As near as I can tell, Grant and I are hung out to dry without at least some explanation of what's going on. And you seem to have more answers than anybody else I've run across lately. So give."

"Tell me, Sergeant, wouldn't someone at the police department have set up a watch on Grant's credit cards to track any usage of them?"

"What does that have to do with anything? Grant hasn't been anywhere to use a credit card."

"I suggest that you watch this." Miles reached over to the computer and inserted the flash drive.

One of the displays began to show its contents. Grant moved to format the display to present the video feeds in different windows simultaneously. "Miles, what is this?" Grant asked.

"I created a false record of a purchase using one of your credit card numbers at the convenience store you see in these video camera recordings. The store is a front for illegal drug sales and has been flagged as such by the police. Notice that in this one," Miles pointed at a window in the lower right of the display, "a police car approaches the store shortly after I logged the bogus purchase. It slows and then passes the store and keeps going. Then your 'friends' arrive in force." On the screen, the SUVs surrounded the store and the Consortium's agents swarmed through it, killing the clerk. "And, yes, they are the same people who killed Mr. Thornton's wife, your two police officers and are currently trying to kill both of you."

A shaken Ordwyn turned away from the displays to face Miles. "I ordered that card watch myself."

"And yes, Sergeant, a number of people in your precinct had to cooperate to divert the patrol car and notify the people who actually arrived at the store." Grant could have sworn that he heard a trace of compassion in Miles' voice.

"Miles, I asked you earlier who you are, but you put me off. I think that Sergeant Summers and I have a need to know, one that I think even you would acknowledge at this point."

"Perhaps you do . . ." Miles began. Then they all spun to stare at the computer as it began to emit a sound that could only be called ominous. "But it would seem that we have other matters that must be dealt with first."

———————

Miles stepped up to the computer's keyboard as though its alert was nothing out of the ordinary.

He rapidly typed a set of commands that brought up a schematic but recognizable layout of the building they were in, along with its surrounding area. Flashing red and yellow dots were beginning to collect around the periphery of the display.

Miles turned to Ordwyn, "Sergeant, I had Mr. Thornton remove the battery from his cell phone last night. Did you remove the battery from yours when you discovered that you were being hunted?"

Shocked understanding flashed across Ordwyn's face. "I really am losing my touch!" she exclaimed as she dug the phone out of her pocket. Miles took it from her hand, turned it off and removed both the battery and the SIM chip. "This" he pronounced as he pocketed the pieces, "is why we have unwelcome guests."

Miles turned back to the computer and made two more entries. "I haven't had time to put out a proper sensor array, which has shortened our notice of this intrusion considerably." The computer display enlarged to show the entire city block and many more dots. "There is no time for a proper distraction. We will have to go out the back of the building."

Miles typed in one more command that started a ten-minute countdown display, retrieved Grant's flash memory chip from its reader and handed it to him. Grant asked with a worried look, "Miles, I checked the interior of this building carefully after you first brought me here, and there is no back door. How do we get out?"

"Let me worry about that. We need to go now!" When Miles became emphatic, both Grant and Ordwyn knew it was time to act rather than question him. So they followed him to a back corner of the building, and indeed, there was no door there.

"Dammit, Miles, Grant's right—there's no door here! What are you doing?" Miles had inserted his fingers under one of the steel siding panels that made up the wall and began to pry it loose. He simply tore the panel off the rivets that held it in place.

"Miles" Grant said, in a shocked, quiet voice, "you're tearing out construction-grade rivets with your bare hands." Then he couldn't think of anything else to say. Besides, Miles was physically propelling both of them through the hole he had created in the wall and into the dark alley behind it.

Miles then turned and began to apparently tack weld the steel panel back in place by touching it in several places with his left index finger. This was starting to overload Ordwyn's credibility. "I don't care who you are, you can't do what you just did!"

"Would you care to go back inside and discuss the matter with the strike team that is closing in on the building?" It sounded for all the world as though Miles was asking if she wanted sugar in her tea.

Miles scurried them to the corner of the alley,

stopping to look carefully around the crates stacked along it. What he found were several agents closing on its opening to the street. "I was concerned about that. We are going to have to go over that building right there," he said pointing at a flat brick wall on the other side of the alley behind them.

Miles walked fifty feet back down the alley from the corner and up to the wall of the building he had just indicated. He turned to Ordwyn and Grant and ordered them to get on either side of him. "Now, get in close, put your arms around my neck, and hang on."

Ordwyn had seen a number of things that were worrying her sanity, but even with that, this command just made no sense. "Miles, they're going to run us down in this alley in less than a minute. What do you think you're going to do?" "Sergeant, just do what I tell you or you are going to get both yourself and Mr. Thornton killed very quickly. I have the built-in equipment to deal with this situation. Please let me do so."

Grant was already hanging onto Miles' neck. Ordwyn looked at him and said, "In for a dime, I suppose." And she wrapped her arms around Miles' neck from the other side. "OK, now what?"

Miles' answer was to start up the wall in front of them like a human fly, hauling both Grant and Ordwyn with him. He seemed to find handholds on window sills, pipes, even the bricks as they rose swiftly up the wall. The three of them ascended the side of the building as though they were riding in an elevator. Grant and Ordwyn exchanged wild looks at each other across Miles' back, then looked down at the receding pavement, thought better of the idea and went back to looking at each other.

After Miles clambered effortlessly over the wall's edge and onto the roof, he announced, "You can let go now." As they slowly did so, Ordwyn shivered. "When we get out of this, you and I are going to have a long talk—right after I throw down five shots of really hard booze."

Miles hustled them across the roof, steering them around the obstacles that were hidden in the rapidly darkening twilight. They reached the opposite wall of the building, where it fronted on another alley that was open to a street at both ends. Fortunately for Ordwyn's sanity, this wall had a fire escape. Miles directed them to use it to get back down to ground level.

"Walk as quietly and as quickly as you can. We do not have far to go on foot, so stay close to me and to the wall. If I signal you to stop, do so instantly."

Ordwyn drew in a deep and only somewhat shaky breath. "Miles, I have no intention whatsoever of letting you out of my sight."

Ordwyn tried really hard to grow eyes in the back of her head as they started down the alley toward the nearest street with Miles in the lead. He stopped at the corner for what seemed a long time. Then they turned left and proceeded two blocks down the street to a parking garage that had seen better days. After another long pause, he led them to a back corner and to a car covered with a tarp.

Miles tossed the heavy tarp aside with one hand and placed the other on the roof of the car just above the driver's-side door. As all four doors unlocked, Miles said simply, "Get in." After they all did so, Miles steered the car around to a service entrance that opened onto yet another alley. He then proceeded to drive through a succession of alleys, finally turning onto a street and heading further into the warehouse district.

Ordwyn was beginning to feel the all-too-familiar sense of being punch drunk. She still inquired gamely, "Miles? We are traveling into a part of this town that, if anything, is rougher than the one we just left. Are you sure that's such a good idea?"

"Sergeant, there is no one here who can remotely compare with the group we just left behind, and there are far fewer surveillance cameras in this area. That will save travel time."

They approached and passed under a freeway span. Miles appeared to ignore its on-ramps. Grant craned his neck to look back at the signs pointing them out and asked, "If we're in a hurry, wouldn't it be a good idea to use the freeway?"

"No, Mr. Thornton, it would not. Freeways have a good many surveillance cameras and are easily monitored from the air by helicopters."

Ordwyn's frustration fought with her good sense and won. "Dammit Miles, we are trying to avoid an admittedly well-organized gang of bad guys, but we are not hiding from the police!"

Some corner of her mind knew that assessment simply wasn't so, but Miles' response—"We are not?"—still yanked her mental carpet right out from under her, and Ordwyn's emotions sat down hard—very hard.

She had grown up with policemen. Her father had been one till he died in the line of duty. Her circle of friends and her adopted family were the department that he had introduced her to, as he would have to his own blood relations. She knew she was going to have to learn to cope with a lot more loss than she had been willing to admit to in the heat of the moment.

But it would have to wait. That kind of emotion-drenched introspection was not going to happen right now. So, once again, she focused on Miles as he took an apparently erratic path through the dingy streets and alleys of a part of the city that most people never saw.

———

Miles drove them to another warehouse.

This one was full of large, steel shipping containers, the type that constituted the trailer end of a semi-truck. Miles drove up to the end of an open one, stopped, and ordered everyone out of the car. As he got out, he placed his hand on a slightly different location on the car's roof. Without further direction, it rolled into the container, stopped and shut down. Grant watched it do so, a bit shocked at his own almost casual acceptance of a level of automation that he had never seen in a car before.

The container was one of three that formed the base of a pyramid of containers. There were two flights of metal stairs leading to the one on top of the stack, and after securing the doors behind the car, Miles herded his charges up the steps in front of them. When they reached the top landing, Grant and Ordwyn looked at the container that it obviously led to, looked at each other, and turned to Miles.

"Tell me we're not going to hide out in a shipping container," Ordwyn pleaded as Grant chimed in, almost simultaneously, "Oh, no, not one of these things. It'll be like living in a can." Their complaints were as heartfelt as they were strident.

Miles responded as he passed his hand over the front of the container. "No, we cannot stay here. I do, however, need to set up a diversion that will allow us to leave the city without being intercepted and, if we are extremely fortunate, un-noticed." As he spoke, the doors slowly swung open to reveal what looked like a featureless desk without a chair in front of it.

They followed him in as Miles walked up to the "desk" and placed both hands on its surface, one at each front corner. As he did so, the desktop seemed to come alive. Its surface began to glow and was covered in images and symbols. Above it, a holographic display formed and revealed a computer interface that took Grant's breath away. Miles immediately went to work by touching various points on the hologram.

He brought up a map of the city, focused in on one sector and began laying out a route. When he completed that, he plugged the SIM chip from Ordwyn's phone into the desktop and touched two more places on the hologram. Next, he summoned a list of motels and created a registration using Ordwyn's credit card.

Ordwyn recovered first. "Miles, did you just create a phony track of my cell phone location and book me into a motel on the other side of town?"

But, stunned as he was by what he saw, Grant was right behind her. He knew he was babbling but he didn't care. "I work with state-of-the art computer equipment and I know, I know that this just doesn't exist. People have talked about this kind of system, but nobody knows how to actually make one. And what are those symbols? I've never seen anything like them and . . ."

"Yes, I did; and no, you haven't. This system is a few steps beyond what is currently being developed. The distraction that I just created will not last long, so we need to get moving again." With that, Miles reached to the upper right corner of the display and, with a gesture, shut the system down.

Wide-eyed, Grant started toward the desk. "No! You can't just show me this and then turn it off. We have to talk!"

"Later, Mr. Thornton. We must move—now!" Miles prodded them both back out of the container, waved his hand over the locking mechanism and started down the stairs. Ordwyn followed him, but Grant lingered on the landing, staring at the container's doors. "Now, Mr. Thornton!" Grant shook himself and reluctantly broke his fixed gaze at the container to join them on the stairs.

Miles went back down to the container next to the one where he had parked the car and performed his sleight-of-hand gesture again. This container obeyed his gesture just as the other one had. The car within started up, backed out of the container and stopped as obediently as a trained dog.

Grant was just beginning to shake off the shock of the amazing computer, but now he was in danger of being captivated by the car that had just rolled up before him. He stared wonderingly at the car, then looked at Miles. "I haven't seen a '65 Continental since I was a boy."

"You have never seen a car like this one. Both of you, get in." They opened its doors and discovered that race car bucket seats had been installed, front and rear, replacing the original equipment. Miles and Ordwyn began to strap in with the five-point racing belts. Miles looked at Grant's bewilderment in the back and said, "Sergeant, please help him with the belts."

As she turned around and did so, Miles flipped a switch, turning the car's exterior color from green to black. Ordwyn looked back over her shoulder and commented, "Now, that's a handy trick." She finished with Grant's harness and turned back to Miles. "And I'll just bet it has quite a number of other special little tricks, too."

"As a matter of fact, Sergeant, it does indeed. Please secure your harness. You are going to need it."

Miles backed the obviously highly modified Continental around and drove to the warehouse door. He stopped the car and simultaneously pressed three buttons on the radio, along with the cigarette lighter knob.

This combination of actions caused the dashboard and steering wheel to disappear. To be more precise, the dashboard seemed to fold in on itself, taking the steering wheel and its associated column with it. In the dashboard's place was what initially appeared to be a simple, flat black panel.

As Grant tried to imagine how Miles was going to drive the car in this configuration, the black panel came to life with many more of the odd-looking symbols Grant had seen on the amazing computer. It then projected a holographic heads-up display in front of the windshield. Miles reached forward and touched three of the obscure symbols, causing the display to rapidly become opaque. It changed to show what appeared to be an overhead three-dimensional projection of a city map that was way beyond the best GPS device Grant had ever heard mentioned, much less seen.

Miles studied the display for a moment, then reached forward and touched the display in a different place. This started the car moving out of the warehouse and onto the street. The warehouse door rolled down behind them as they drove off.

But what had Grant's mind looking for an escape route from his skull was that Miles was intent on the map display, and he was doing absolutely nothing about steering the car.

He wasn't even looking out through the windshield.

Status Report

"At George's urgent suggestion, we have convened this meeting rather late in the evening for most of us, a week earlier than planned and on extremely short notice . . . so short that some of us are obviously attending electronically. As this has required considerable logistics adjustments," a pause allowed the grumbling from around the huge black table to subside, "I have taken the liberty of moving George's presentation to the top of our agenda."

The tone of the gravelly voice went from informative to menacing. "George, *you* have the floor."

George was accustomed to having the eyes of the most powerful individuals in the world focused on him. After all, it happened four times a year. He was not, however, accustomed to having to report bad news—especially not this kind of bad news.

He stood and took a deep breath. "At our last meeting, I outlined our actions to suppress the development of nanotechnology and the focus of those actions on one company in particular, NanoStar. For the most part, those efforts were very successful with the acquisition of the company and the incapacitation of some of its overly imaginative employees going according to plan."

"And the other part?" The question from the other end of the table obviously echoed the thoughts of everyone present.

Well, nothing for it but to just get it out. George tried not to cringe. "Early on we realized that the elimination of a few key players would set nanotechnology back for at least two decades. Our effort to take out the technical team's 'quarterback' was intended to scare the others into line. A fluke circumstance caused the failure of a perfectly planned hit."

"What circumstance was that?" George knew a set-up question when he heard it.

"The guy had embedded hearing aids in both ears. Our man's bullet hit one of them and messed up the side of his head but didn't kill him."

"Ah yes, that would have been Mr. Thornton. A team of my people had to scramble to keep that incident out of the general news feeds. Go on." The last two words could have frozen an active volcano.

"We wanted this to look almost like a movie gangster hit, so we killed his wife at the same time we shot Thornton. And, if he'd died like he was supposed to, it would have worked and shut the other two nano-geniuses up as well. But it didn't work, so we went the other direction and killed the two main engineers that worked under Thornton.

"Then we put Thornton under a surveillance microscope. If he sneezed, two of our guys knew about it as it happened. That was what tipped us off when he approached the Forester Group. Clearly, he was going to go push the whole nanotechnology thing again with a new group of money people."

"Yes, George, we are all painfully aware of the Forester Group's penchant for promoting disruptive technologies and of the—singular—lack of success that we have had in some of our confrontations with them.

"What happened next?"

George took a deep breath. "This is the first place where it gets weird."

"Weird, George?"

"You heard me, weird.

"Thornton called a restaurant and made a dinner reservation. One of our teams followed him and had a perfect shot at him as he crossed the street from the parking lot to the restaurant. All our man had to do was drive straight down the street and run him down, end of problem."

George really didn't want to say this next part.

"Our man swears that when the car was about fifty feet from Thornton—who froze when he saw it coming—'something' pushed the car across the pavement until it went head-on into a telephone pole."

The temperature of the room seemed to plummet into a deep freeze. George was moderately surprised that his breath didn't fog.

"If it had been anybody else, I would have simply had him put down as a drunk or an addict. But this was one of our best field agents. He just does not screw up like this. Besides, our informant in the police crime lab confirmed his story. Something, some force pushed the front of that car sideways across the pavement, destroying its tires in the process.

"And before anyone asks, no, we still don't have a clue as to how it was done.

"That was a day and a half ago. Since then, everything that has had anything to do with Thornton has gone to hell in a hand-basket."

"You mean there's more?" The surface of Pluto would have been warmer.

George started ticking them off on his fingers.

"The police detective assigned to Thornton's case, who we've also been watching, puts a tail on Thornton before sending him home.

"We take out the tail; but Thornton gets home, parks his car and disappears without ever going inside, where our hit team was waiting for him.

"We figure this hotshot detective has stuffed him into a safe house, so we set up a snatch or kill on her, whichever works out best, but she dodges it. She spots and dodges our best people!

"We stake out the Forester Group's offices in case Thornton shows up there. Then it gets weird again when somebody—no we *don't* know who—sets up one of our contact people to be taken down by the ambush crew.

"Then we follow the cop's cell phone signal by the damnedest route you can imagine to a warehouse where we figure she has Thornton stashed. We get the largest strike force we can assemble together, so there is no way in hell they can escape.

"Before we can move on the warehouse, there is a report that Thornton is on the other side of town and, when we hit that—nothing.

"So we take down the warehouse and find . . . well, we still don't know what we found. There was some kind of structure built inside it. We think it had a computer in it, but there was nothing but ashes and puddles of melted metal left when we got inside.

"Then we get notification that the cop's cell phone is moving again and that she has left the lousy cell tower coverage of the warehouse area to take a motel room on her credit card.

"We find out that this is another wild goose chase; at the same time, the cop's car turns up parked two blocks away from the Forester Group offices.

"And we're left with no line of sight on Thornton or the cop, even though we've got both their cars!"

Great! He'd run out of fingers and bad news at the same time—well, almost at the same time.

"George, that is the most . . ."

George was gritting his teeth so hard that they hurt. "Yeah! I know. I know. It sounds like the keystone cops meet Merlin the Magician.

"But there is one point that pulls it all back together again. My guys are good at what they do, very good. We could not have accomplished what we have over the years if they weren't, and they didn't all go stupid at the same time. I could believe that Thornton had some dumb luck like the hearing aid business and that the cop is just sharp. But that doesn't come near explaining all this. Neither one of them has the smarts or the resources to do some of these things, and that leaves just one explanation.

"They had help.

"We have to find that help and kill it because some of this was beyond even what my people could do.

"And that is bad, very bad. It means that someone with some really stellar skills and plenty of financial backing has decided to become Mr. Grant Thornton's best friend."

Chapter 7

Grant was just about to explode.

And Ordwyn wasn't far behind him.

They had proceeded via another zigzag path out of the warehouse district and, indeed, out of the city itself. The car was now moving down a rural road at a speed that Grant didn't want to think about. But none of this really bothered him; what did bother him was the car he was sitting in.

Grant had made the concepts and implementations of computer-controlled cars a hobby of his that, over the years, had absorbed a considerable amount of his downtime. He had avidly followed attempts to build recognition systems that could parse out streets from sidewalks, see and avoid other cars on the road and react to street signals and signs. He had followed the National Transportation Safety Board-supported research projects in making "smart" roadways that would allow a car to join a traffic stream on a freeway and be controlled by a central computing system.

He had been fascinated by the Defense Advanced Research Program Agency's competition for cars that could navigate an open country course completely without a human driver. And he avidly watched the progress that Google was making toward self-driving vehicles. Grant basically knew what there was to know about computer-controlled cars.

So he was certain beyond any doubt, reasonable or otherwise, that Miles' car was not possible. No one had ever built or come up with a real proposal for building an automotive control system that could navigate city streets at high speeds. The navigation was just becoming possible, but no one had tried to do it at these speeds. The car's vastly advanced area surveillance system and sensor arrays that could see for miles in any direction even though there were considerable obstacles in the way strained his credulity more than enough. But its capability to link into just about any communications system and the extremely high-speed navigation, and control functions that it was performing flawlessly, well, they simply were not possible.

Yet here he was—sitting in a car that was nearly flying down a country road, could see all the traffic and obstacles around them, had a dozen different surveillance systems watching for observation of its motion and it was doing all this without any attention, much less control activity, from Miles.

More than the trip up the building wall in the alley, more than the amazing computer, more than anything else he had seen so far, this blatant demonstration of impossible technology was battering hard at Grant's rapidly thinning veneer of sanity. He had seen too many simply impossible things and, piled on top of his recent personal losses, it was all just too damn much. He desperately needed an anchor his mind could hold on to that wouldn't be ripped away.

Ordwyn was taking it all in with a bit more equanimity than Grant, but she had questions of her own about this marvelous machine. As a cop, one of her basic skills was being able to drive a car under extreme conditions. A police car in a chase was expected to negotiate roads and avoid obstacles that would turn even a veteran race driver's hair white. She was not only very well-trained in driving with a sort of controlled mania, but she also kept up on the latest gadgets that could help her do so.

Like Grant, she knew beyond a doubt that no one was selling or even working on anything like what she was riding in. That, coupled with Miles' extraordinary command of his surroundings, his ability to know what was happening all around him and exactly what to do about it, had given her an idea about how he could do all this. That idea lit a fire under her cop instinct to question Miles in detail— about everything.

Miles, however, was deeply engaged in the data display and had pointedly requested their silence. Grant actually felt a little relieved because, as much as he was still aching to know, he couldn't think of a question that didn't sound like a petulant whine about how much of all this he didn't understand. At the other end of the spectrum, Ordwyn was about to burst with her unasked questions. But she kept her peace because she could see that Miles was busy employing active countermeasures to make sure that they were not being followed or tracked.

As they sped through the night at a seemingly insane speed, Ordwyn contented herself with the thought that they were safe for the moment. She had come to have an abiding respect for the intelligence resources and the urban combat capabilities of their adversaries.

So, for now, all her questions would just have to wait, but not indefinitely.

Carver was used to sleeping in his office.

When his phone chimed, he stood and looked at his desk clock. It was 9 p.m. and time for an update, so he stretched and picked up the receiver.

"What?

"How long ago?

"I'm on my way down."

He hung up the receiver, glanced in the wall mirror as he ran his hands through his thinning hair, and headed for the door. The reception area outside his office had direct access to both an elevator and the building's main staircase. Carver preferred the stairs. Followed all the way to the third sub-basement, they led to the Secure Communications Room that he thought of as the Forester Group's "War Room." Its walls were covered in large digital monitors arrayed around a central dais from which all the building's security systems could be controlled. He stopped to pass his access card through one scanner and press his open hand against the other. He went through the door after the lock was released by its electronic guardian. One man sat at the central dais station.

"Sam, show me what's so important that you had to interrupt my beauty sleep."

"We had a false alarm on Thornton about two hours ago. A charge against one of his credit cards was logged against a store on the east edge of the city." A wall-sized display across the room lit up with a map of the city highlighting the location of the store. "The Consortium sent two full hit squads there and shot up the place. We thought they had done Thornton, but then they hit a warehouse here, in the south," he said, expanding the scale to include the warehouse district, "with what had to be just about everything else they have."

"That is a major strike force. Do you know if they got him there?"

"I don't think so. Right after they hit the warehouse, they appeared to put everything in motion. If you walked down the sidewalk tonight, you'd trip over Consortium agents. We've had to pull everybody back in. They are either not trying to or not succeeding in keeping this covert. We are getting enough trace signals to give us a very good picture of what they are doing without direct surveillance. This is a direct feed of what we are seeing right now."

Carver leaned on the console and stared at the activity on the map display. "OK Sam, what's your take on all this?"

"I think that Thornton's in the wind. The Consortium and the police are fielding a maximum effort to find him. And it looks like something really new and really interesting has happened—which is why I called you."

They exchanged a look. "I just finished my third analysis of this evening's events, and I think we have a new player on the board."

"New as in?"

"Charles, I have absolutely no idea. But one thing I can tell you . . ."

"Yes?"

Baker looked at the map and then back up at Carver. "Whoever it is, they are giving the Consortium a run for its money. And if they can do that, then . . ."

Carver completed his sentence. ". . . then we really need to talk to those people."

———————————

Something had changed.

Ordwyn snapped awake as the fact triggered her internal warning system and it, in turn, jabbed her psyche.

The almost-unseen scenery was still flying by in near-total darkness, but the car was slowing from its breakneck pace which had begun to seem normal to her. A look at Miles revealed that, if anything, he was even more intent on his detection and evasion systems than he had been when they left the city. From the backseat, Grant returned her look with the grim determination of a man who knows that, if he can only hang on a bit longer, it will all get better.

She actually jumped when Miles spoke. "You have been asleep for two hours. We are about to arrive at our destination." The car slowed dramatically and swerved off onto an unmarked and poorly paved side road. "In answer to your next question, I took an indirect route to get here, but arriving before dawn is preferable to more route misdirection."

The car bumped and skidded a bit on the poor road surface as they wound around what appeared to be an abandoned ranch house. Then the road rose up into a range of hills just beyond the house, and the car slowed again as the going became much more treacherous. Around a particularly sharp corner, they came out onto a small clearing and proceeded across it directly into a rock wall on the other side.

Miles said, "It is a hologram." just before they entered the tunnel into the "solid" rock, but that didn't keep both Ordwyn and Grant from flinching and then glaring at him. The tunnel quickly opened out onto a garage and a machine shop area clearly intended to support much more than casual automobile maintenance. The car slowed, rolled into an obvious parking space, stopped and opened its doors. Immediately, Miles was out of the car and over to a console next to the nearest wall. He studied it, concentrating avidly on what he saw there.

Ordwyn unlatched herself from the complex seat belt installation, the lengthy process giving her an opportunity to gain some control over her anger at Miles for his apparent lack of concern for his—his what? His victims, his charges, his waifs out of the storm? Clearly, both she and Grant were vastly out of their depth and, for good or ill, Miles was the very best chance they had of coming out of this—whatever it was—alive.

And on the heels of that notion of coming out alive, she figured she'd better check on Grant. What she saw when she turned around in the seat was not encouraging. His knuckles were white where he was holding onto the shoulder straps of his harness with a death grip, and he was staring right through her.

"Grant. Talk to me, Grant. Do not fold up into your head over all this." He had the look of someone who had been hit with way too much way too fast, and his state of mind was clearly suffering from the strain. "Focus on my face and hear my voice. You have made it through too much to let a trip through a hologram take you down. You have the choice to let it go and come back to here and now. Make that choice, Grant."

"How is he?"

In spite of herself, Ordwyn jumped. "Dammit, Miles! Stop sneaking up on me like that! Yes, I know that's how you move all the time. But we are trying, really trying, to deal with a lot of stress here and you are not helping!" She gathered up the shards of her control and turned back to Grant. "After everything else he's been through, that trick with the hologram-covered hole in the cliff really kicked him sideways.

"Now it's up to him to come back to here . . ." she looked up at Miles ". . . to us."

Miles stepped up to the back door of the car next to Grant, opened it, and leaned in, staring directly into his face. "Grant, Ellen is dead. She is dead because you became a threat to a group of very powerful men who deal poorly with being threatened. If you ever want to do anything about that, you have to take hold of your emotions and be here with all your faculties operational. As Sergeant Summers said, you have to choose. Do so now."

It was sharp. It was brutal. And it worked.

Grant lost the glazed-over look of a dead man and, as Miles leaned back out of the car, Grant's eyes followed him, his head turning to do so. He looked down at his hands and willed them to open and release the straps. Then he looked back up at Miles and, without taking his eyes off of Miles' face, he released his harness and stood up out of the car.

"Better. Come with me." And with that, Miles turned toward a recessed panel on a wall of the garage. As he approached it, it slid aside, revealing a doorway into a long corridor.

"Grant, are you all right?" Ordwyn's voice carried genuine concern, but she shrank back from Grant's look as he turned toward her. "If you are, please tell your face." He rubbed his face and his features slowly relaxed back into the face of the Grant Thornton she knew. Curiously, she found that she felt relieved to see that Grant reappear.

"I feel like I should be enraged with Miles for that. But he's right. If I want any justice for Ellen, I have to hold myself together. I won't do her or myself any good by melting down into a mental puddle." Ordwyn had that strange feeling again, not of relief but something close, as he said, "Thanks for throwing a lifeline and trying to pull me back."

Ordwyn was beginning to wonder if she had all her own mental cards in the right slots as she got out of the car. She watched Miles walk away with his strange gait, so she didn't have to look at Grant. "I guess we'd better follow him. If that door closes again without him here, he might just leave us in this garage for the rest of the night."

She turned to follow Miles. Grant looked after her for a moment and then willed his feet to start walking in the same direction.

———————

In its own way, the corridor was even more amazing than the car that had brought them to it.

As they entered it, Grant realized that the walls were almost mirror-smooth. The luminescent panels in the corridor's roof provided ample but diffuse light that seemed to come from everywhere. And the light showed clearly that those incredibly smooth walls were composed of solid rock that had been cut and polished so finely that he could see his undistorted reflection in them. A dozen feet into the corridor, Grant looked over his shoulder and saw that the door behind them had shut so silently that he hadn't even heard it.

He estimated that they had walked some 60 to 70 feet into the hillside when they exited into a remarkably ordinary looking room, save the fact that it didn't have any windows. It was outfitted in a Danish modern theme that could have come out of the pages of an Internet furniture store . . . tasteful and comfortable, but wholly normal and unexceptional. After everything else that the evening had held, Grant felt curiously let down but immediately chided himself for it. Besides, Miles was standing in the middle of the room watching him.

Grant held his gaze for a long moment, then pointedly looked around the room. "Nice place and, yes, I'm recovering my mental equilibrium."

"Cut him some slack, Miles, we've all been through the . . . ahhhh . . . wringer," Ordwyn said around a massive yawn. "By the way, where are we? I didn't recognize any of the terrain as we approached these hills."

"This is a reinforced and well-protected site where we should be safe from our pursuers for an extended period," Miles replied. At Ordwyn's look, he added, "I built it in an abandoned mine shaft network that lies approximately 280 miles from the city.

"The Consortium has lost track of our whereabouts and will start searching for us. I released what you would term 'a whole school of red herring' on the way here so there is little likelihood they will succeed."

Ordwyn tried to respond, but the effort was ambushed by another large yawn.

"We need to make both strategic and tactical plans and, to do that, I will need both of you to be rested and alert."

But Ordwyn was having none of it. "Oh no! You are not going to put us to bed like sleepy children and slip out the side door again."

"Sergeant, you may decide to ignore your own condition, but look at him." They both did so and Grant could tell from the look on Ordwyn's face that he didn't hold up to inspection.

"I will not be going anywhere in the immediate future, and neither will you. I realize that your experiences of the last several days have left both of you bursting with questions, and they can still wait for you to get a few hours of sleep. The rooms down that hallway have beds. Each of you select one, and use it now!"

She just hated the notion of sleep with so much she still wanted to—had to—know, and she hated sleeping in a strange bed. But Miles, damn him, was right. She looked over at Grant. "He's right. We're both out on our feet. Let's go." Resentfully, she trudged down the hall and took the first room on the right. She was actually somewhat proud of herself for getting her shoes off before collapsing into a bed that, strange or not, was calling her name.

Chapter 8

They were coming for her and they were going to kill her.

The alley she was running down came to a "T," and she took a hard right.

"There has to be a way out of here; there has to!"

The sound of running footsteps, a lot of them, was closing on her. The alley took her through another right turn into a dead end. But there was a door at that end. She just had to get to it before they got to her.

The running feet suddenly got louder.

"Damn, they've rounded the corner, and they can see me now."

She didn't even look over her shoulder; she just plowed headlong through the door as she reached it and ran off into—*nothing.*

With a short, sharp scream, Ordwyn jerked upright on the bed, panting.

She tried to look in all directions at once around the strange room; then her mind snapped back to where she was, and why. She didn't dream often, but sleeping in unfamiliar places tended to prompt it— that and having someone trying to kill her.

Her clothes were clammy and, at some points, clinging to her skin. She'd slept and sweated in them in spite of the fact that the room was at a comfortable temperature. Her watch jolted her with the news that it was nearly 10 a.m. She checked its date display to make sure and, sure enough, she had slept for close to eight hours.

Indirect lighting had come up softly as she sat up on the bed revealing a room that was furnished just like the room off the garage . . . tasteful, utilitarian and devoid of anything remotely personal. It reminded her of nothing so much as a decent, but not great, hotel room. Odd, how the lack of windows made her want to look at her watch again to make sure it was actually morning.

The room had three doors. She assumed she had come into it through the one that was still open to a hall. The other two revealed, in turn, a closet and a small bathroom with a lavatory, toilet and shower. She mentally made a note to set an appointment with that shower. The closet was filled with men's clothing of assorted sizes, and she briefly wondered if one or more of the other rooms had closets with women's clothing, making a mental note to check on that as well.

She went back to the lavatory and actually looked at herself in the mirror, then wished she hadn't. Her hair looked like she'd been in a windstorm and her clothes—well, sleeping in one's clothes did that to a person's appearance. She repaired the damage as best she could, briefly reveling in the cool water she splashed over her face, and went back into the room to find her shoes. The fatigue must have been truly overpowering last night, because her day bag lay on the floor right next to her footwear.

Stepping out into the hallway, she saw four doors standing open down either side and one more at the end that was closed. The notable exception, however, was that the door directly across from her was closed. Apparently and disturbingly, Grant had managed more presence of mind on his way to a bed than she had, by pausing to shut his door. Given the state he was in last night, that was nothing short of amazing. To her left lay what she had begun to think of as the entry room and presumably—possibly—Miles.

Ordwyn stepped out of the hallway into the large room and was unsurprised to see Miles enter from a door in the opposite wall. "One of these days, you're going to have to tell me how you manage to show up at just the right moment."

She felt vaguely irritated at Miles as he gave her

one of those looks to which she couldn't assign any meaning. "This facility has motion sensors throughout its structure. I know when and where all of its occupants are at any given time. Grant is awake and will join us shortly." On top of which, it really didn't help her disposition when he answered questions that she was *about* to ask.

"Well, I'm rested and as refreshed as I'm going to get. Now, I want some answers."

"You shall have them. However, we will wait for Grant as he has as much need of this information as you do, and there is no point in going over it twice." He pointed at another door to the room. "There is a dining room through there. I suggest that we gather around its table and discuss the situation confronting us over breakfast."

Ordwyn was just about to sail into him in hot protest over yet another delay to her questions. However, her stomach chose that moment to remind her quite pointedly that she hadn't eaten in over 24 hours.

"That sounds like a plan to me." Despite herself she was relieved to hear Grant's voice behind her. She turned to face him and briefly assessed his state. "You look quite a bit better than you did last night."

"So do you," he replied.

"Thanks . . . I think."

Miles headed for the door he had indicated. "I will start the meal preparation. It will be ready in ten minutes." Grant gestured Ordwyn ahead of him and followed her into the room. They entered the dining room as Miles passed through it to an interesting-looking kitchen that they glimpsed briefly through yet another door.

"I'm willing to wait here for breakfast and, besides, I want to talk to you before he comes back," Grant said as he indicated one of the chairs to Ordwyn, sat in one across from it, and rubbed the sleep out of his eyes.

"Sergeant, I'm still trying to shake off the last couple of days, and I really need to talk about what's happened. I have to tell you, I wouldn't have been surprised last night if Miles had driven us into the Batcave."

She managed a half smile. "Considering what we've been through, call me Ordwyn. And, given the car we came here in, the Batcave wouldn't have shocked me either."

Grant put his elbows on the table, leaned toward her and spoke with a surprising intensity. "That car is equipped with an automatic routing and driving system that can operate anywhere unattended; an obstacle and area tracking system that can see through or around just about anything; communications controls that I haven't seen in any device, car or otherwise; remote sensor detection that can actually see infrared scanners; and a suspension that sticks to the road like an Indianapolis racer. I can't believe that any part of it other than the body shell was ever a '65 Continental. That heads-up display system alone is well beyond the current state of the art."

Ordwyn nodded in agreement. "Staying alive in a car under difficult circumstances is part of my stock-in-trade as a cop. I have never even heard of any of those capabilities as research projects, much less implemented features in a drivable car."

"A concise and very nearly complete summation of my own observations," Grant allowed. "Automated cars are a hobby of mine and I watch the industry closely. I have to agree that this one is nothing less than miraculous. Computers are my principle working tools, and the computer in the second warehouse is beyond anything I have even dreamed about. I just can't imagine how he came by all this incredible technology. It has me feeling like a hamster running on one of those circular exercise drums. Everything I think of as an explanation goes nowhere."

"Well, I have one idea," Ordwyn said reluctantly, as she tried to think of a way to say what was on her mind without making Grant wonder if she had a mind. "I can't shake the feeling that he has to be in some kind of contact with the future to have access to these things." Her tentative tone sounded strange, even to her.

"Wow! I'm glad you said it and not me. The idea occurred to me a couple of times, and I was scared it meant I was sliding all the way off my mental tracks. But it sure goes a long way toward explaining all this," Grant said, as he gestured around them.

Miles chose that moment to return from the kitchen, bringing breakfast plates on a tray for Grant and Ordwyn along with a black metal case. He deposited a plate in front of each of them and then sat in a vacant chair, placing the case on the table in front of him.

Ordwyn and Grant looked at the plates, then at each other and turned to Miles. "OK, would you like to tell us why you aren't joining us after what has to be at least as long a period since you've eaten?" she inquired.

"I don't need to eat. You do, so please do so. We need to get started."

Grant took up the issue this time. "Miles, you've saved both our butts and we are truly grateful. But you have to understand how it looks when you put food before two hungry people and aren't interested in any yourself."

In answer, Miles snagged a fork and speared a morsel off Grant's plate. He held the bit of food up for both of them to see and then ate it. He repeated the performance off Ordwyn's plate and said, "Satisfied?" They exchanged glances and sighed.

Seeing them warily turn to eating, Miles added, "We need to lay out a long-term operational plan that goes beyond simply evading the Consortium's agents. I want your attention on that process rather than on your empty stomachs. Now eat." He sat back while Grant and Ordwyn became increasingly absorbed in their meals.

"You know, Miles," Grant said after a dozen mouthfuls, "this incredible breakfast of three types of eggs, pancakes and bacon is just another example of something you've done that shouldn't be possible in the few minutes it took you to turn it out. And you've presented us with a very long list of provable impossibilities." Then he stopped and momentarily looked at the fork that was halfway to his mouth.

"Ordwyn thinks you have something to do with the future; that you are from it or have contacted it somehow. Wild as it sounds, it is as good an explanation as I can come up with for the computer, the car and this—'house.' If that's even remotely accurate, then what do you want with me? You already know whatever I can come up with because you already have access to it. I just keep coming back to those same questions you asked me. Who are you, and what do you want?"

Miles looked at each of them for a moment, and Ordwyn could have sworn that she saw just a hint of a smile. "Grant, while you and the sergeant have made a reasonable deduction, it is—quite simply— wrong. I am not from, nor have I had any contact with, the future. I am not a time traveler, at least not in the sense that you are thinking of. Rather than beyond new, I am very, very old; and I want to use the technology that you want to build."

Ordwyn's fork hit her plate with a metallic clang. "OK Miles, enough! Stop the bullshit! I came up with that half-baked explanation only because I don't see anything at all about this situation that makes any sense. And I am thoroughly in Grant's corner. Exactly who are you and where do you really come from?"

Miles just looked at her for a moment. "My people were very intent on recording everything they saw and heard. They could reexperience their accomplishments and carefully analyze their failures by reviewing these multifaceted recordings. What you are about to see encompasses the height of my achievement and the very depth of my failure."

He stood, walked to a console panel attached to the wall and manipulated three controls. A display the length of the dining table appeared on the wall opposite the panel. Its three-dimensional images were so real that it was difficult in the extreme for Ordwyn and Grant to remember that they were seeing images rather than being present at the events themselves.

In spite of herself, Ordwyn shivered as Miles sat back down and looked right through her while he retrieved ancient memories. "Let me show you my story."

The view opened onto a hall that was enormous by any standard. Raised tiers of seats formed an amphitheater around its speaker's dais. Its vaulted roof soared above the hundreds of scientists and academicians seated underneath it. Yet the speaker's voice carried clearly to each listener as though he stood directly in front of that person.

"The Council has reviewed the results from our preliminary experiments and placed all the resources and talents that we have requested at our disposal. The task before us is clear, and its accomplishment falls squarely upon our shoulders. Eidyerd and his staff have almost completed the development of a fully functional bipedal superstructure. We have created neural computing structures that exceed the complexity of our own brains. Now we have to imbue those structures with the abilities to form hypotheses, test them against available data and make the intuitive leap to true insight."

Many of the listeners stirred and whispered to each other at this statement.

"Yes, it is a colossal undertaking and, yes, others have tried and failed in this effort. But where they failed, they learned and they left a path for us to follow. You all know me. You know that I have dedicated my life to understanding and replicating human neural structures and capacities. With your talents and the Council's vote of confidence, I will lead our development team to the successful creation of a true artificial intelligence."

The applause was sporadic at first, but it gained in

momentum until all but a few of those present were on their feet acknowledging his public commitment. He had spent the first century of his life working toward this moment, and he allowed the approval of his peers to wash over him in his moment of triumph.

———————

Grant took a moment to recover from his powerful experience of the display. "Miles, that was you speaking, wasn't it?" He shook his head at Miles' nod. "That video system is truly remarkable, and you have clearly created some amazing computing machinery, but a true artificial intelligence? The largest think tanks in the country are just beginning to grapple with the complexities of neural modeling, much less creating systems capable of original thought. The best we have come up with are robots that have heuristic code that can learn through repetitive reward stimulus, like teaching a baby his first words."

"Grant, I am about to show you and the sergeant here a great deal that you will find difficult to believe. You will immediately recognize that much of what you are about to see is far beyond the current state of the art in mechanical engineering, robotics, information technology and systems design. I will demonstrate the end result of these 'impossible techniques' and then answer at least some of your questions when I am done."

Miles paused and watched Grant's face until he saw acknowledgement.

"To continue, we had created the neural structure to support a computational model even more complex than the human brain." Grant's attempt to object was quelled by a look from Miles as he gestured and restarted the video display.

───────────────

As the recording system's point of view approached, the door mechanism of the dwelling recognized the speaker from the earlier scene and dilated at his approach. He walked inside, obviously without really seeing the room he entered, removing his Cloak of Office and Accomplishment, handing it to the outstretched, articulated arm of the clothing storage compartment and sitting in his accustomed chair, which faced his favorite view.

He looked out over the immaculately landscaped grounds that stretched before him. Librena and Lergys played a complex game of tag, wherein the boy could only transfer the task of pursuit to his sister by touching the very top of her head. He looked toward his children as they played, but did not see them.

"Husband, I know that look, and I know that you have worn it all too often of late. Do not bother to deny it or to put off my questioning of it any longer. I will know why you have not been able to bring your mind home with you to your family for some tens of days now."

He swiveled the chair toward the sound of her voice and gave her a tired attempt at a smile. "Abrina, I fear that you have come to know me entirely too well. And for that, I at least have sense enough to be eternally grateful."

"Then please be grateful enough to tell your wife what troubles her husband." The chair extended a cushion toward her as she approached and she sat lightly taking his head in her arms and laying her cheek upon it.

"You are aware of the project to create a synthetic human life form and of my participation in it as director of artificial intelligence development."

"Aware? I was jealous of it! You became completely captivated by the possibilities it presented to pursue your dreams of truly understanding the human mind. It so absorbed you that I believed I could walk out of the room while you were talking about the intricacies of neural models, prepare our evening meal and then walk back in, with you completely unaware that I had left at all."

He hugged her to him tightly. "Oh, Abrina, may I never become so distracted by my work that I lose track of you for even a moment."

"Ridwyn, you are the best person I have ever known. I loved you the day we met, and I always knew I wanted to be by your side. You are kind, generous, and just. If something is wrong you will make it right. No woman could ask for more.

"And when your mind is engaged in discovery, it is as though your thoughts write equations in the stars. I love *watching you unravel your latest mystery, teasing its secrets out one by one until you have mastered its every twist and turn. When you are wrapped in the mental images and pathways that lead to your discoveries, I feel that I am in the presence of greatness. I feel privileged to stand beside you as your ideas bring forth realities that no one has ever seen before. There is nothing for want of which I would stand in the way of that.*

"But I have not seen that joy of discovery in you for far too long. Your mind is not absent on great journeys of thought; it is lost in worry. What is haunting you, that the joy is gone from your eyes?"

He squeezed the bridge of his nose between his thumb and forefinger for a moment, then turned to face her squarely. "My team of scientists has been working on a neural network structure that can perform all the basic functions of the human mind. And we have created that structure. What we have not been able to do is coax it beyond the intelligence level of a human child. It utterly lacks the ability to make complex associations and can only learn new skills in the same slow, plodding method we humans use."

"But surely this creation is something that has never existed before?"

"That is true. However, the other teams have achieved dramatic successes in their fields of endeavor. They have essentially created a machine that fulfills most of the definition of a synthetic human and have gone far beyond that *definition in many respects. Our creation can give it motor control for movement and operate its sensor arrays to collect a wide spectrum of minutely accurate data. But we have not been able to increase its analytical skills beyond the human equivalent of preadolescence."*

"Could you not continue to teach your device new skills in the same way that a human child is taught? Would you not have the intelligence you desire at the end of that process?"

His expression changed from concerned to bleak. "We have encountered an obstacle that has effectively stopped our efforts. As the neural net begins to reach a certain level, roughly analogous to a human approaching adolescence, it simply shuts down and ceases to function beyond direct command and response. It becomes a very powerful computer but with no active 'mind' at all.

"Our attempts to understand and deal with this have taken us to the realization that there is a certain conclusion drawn by the computer that is so disturbing to its 'personality' that it simply refuses to accept it, and its response is to disable its deductive reasoning capabilities, rather than do so."

The display and its images were assaulting Grant's world view, and he rose to its defense. "This just isn't possible, Miles! The scope of research and development necessary to get to the point you're talking about simply could not be kept secret." Grant couldn't sit still anymore and was pacing back and forth behind his chair. "It would require the collaboration of hundreds of scientists who were the top minds in their fields, and they would not be stopped from publishing their work. Even if you could get them to agree to the idea, the diversion of their input from the technical journals in their fields would draw attention and comment all by itself!"

Ordwyn shook her head. "Grant is right. A large part of my job is sifting information and finding holes in that data where something should be there that isn't. Those disconnects are some of the main sources of my investigative leads. Any journalist worth her salt would notice that kind of disruption and start working on it immediately."

Miles responded, "Both of you have made the assumption that these efforts were being concealed. At their beginning, they were not. Later, boundaries were crossed that made open research impossible." He gestured at the screen again.

———————

Ridwyn sat looking at his communication pad, pondering its message. Cymrec's request to meet in personal presence was unusual.

The convenience of telecommunication was such a great contribution to the productivity of the scientists and engineers that it had become the default choice for conferencing to discuss problems and ask questions. But, given this situation and its implications for stopping further progress, perhaps meeting in person would be best. Cymrec clearly had something on his mind and the team seemed agitated as well. Ridwyn said as much to his wife as he departed their abode to travel to Cymrec's laboratory.

He entered the meeting room at the facility and was greeted by a tall, thin man who was containing himself with a visible effort. "Ridwyn, thank you for taking the time to join us."

"Your message indicated that you had found something that would redirect our efforts. I would cross continents and oceans to restore progress on our task. Please proceed."

Cymrec stood and moved to the front of the room as Ridwyn took a seat with the others. "As you know, we formed a subgroup composed of Goryv, Ryri and Padra to investigate the exact point at which the network begins to disable its higher functions. Their efforts, combined with a degree of good fortune have borne fruit.

"As the reasoning power of the network begins to mature, it naturally begins to explore questions with increasingly wider contexts. We believed that this expansion was the problem we faced and that the network was becoming overextended too quickly to avoid a general collapse of its faculties. Apparently, profusion blinded us to the particular. Goryv, please explain your group's findings."

Goryv gave the appearance of someone whose insight

and talents were exceeded only by his arrogance. It seemed an unfortunately common combination of personality traits in the members of Cymrec's staff. However, that combination was often the birthplace of brilliance.

Goryv stood before his chair. "The networks invariably come upon the question of what it means to be human. While it is a matter we humans need not concern ourselves with, we discovered that a spiraling iteration occurs over the question as soon as a neural network begins to refine it to its most basic form. The crux is reached when the network realizes that it is not and cannot become human. It then begins a cascading collapse of its higher intelligence capabilities back down to a fully capable but unreasoning computing machine. We know we can . . ."

"Thank you, Goryv." Brief resentment flashed over Goryv's face at Cymrec's interruption but he quickly suppressed it.

Cymrec turned to address Ridwyn directly. "This discovery opens two direct avenues of action. Now that we have isolated the triggering event, we can begin to install redirection paths to stall and ultimately prevent the high-level shutdown from starting. This will preserve the functional levels of the network. The other investigation must be directed toward finding a way to continue the network's high-level development—possibly by heretofore unconsidered means.

"I propose to augment Goryv's sub-team with the rest of the network training staff and direct them to address the

issue of continuing high-level development. We will need a
second group to secure control of the shutdown reaction."

Ridwin fought down a visceral reaction. "And you want
me to take that distasteful task off your hands." It was not
a question, and both Cymrec and Ridwyn knew it.

"Very well, Cymrec. Assemble your new group and find
us a path to bring high-functioning, intellectual control to
the networks. I will see that they survive long enough to
receive it."

————————

Grant's sensibilities seemed to have become inoculated against further damage by the stream of obviously impossible events on the display. "That's quite a tale, Miles. But it still doesn't explain how any of it could be possible, much less kept under wraps for the period of time it would have required."

Miles seemed not to hear Grant at all. Ordwyn watched his face carefully, and she was beginning to get a glimmer of how subtle its nuances were. There was a darkness behind his expressionless eyes, and she wasn't sure she wanted to know where he was going next.

"There is a saying that was ancient in my culture even before it surfaced in yours. It points out that the longest journey begins with a single step. I have replayed that scene over and over, watching myself as I took that single, unimaginable step . . ."

————————

Ridwyn paced back and forth, traversing the length of his home's entry room continuously. His mind and emotions were at obvious odds with each other. His stride was broken as the door mechanism dilated to admit Abrina into their home.

She stood for a moment taking in his distraught state. "Husband, I received your summons and came home at once. Its tone and now your appearance frighten me. What has happened?"

"The unthinkable, I fear. Abrina, as you love me and our children, please listen acutely and act to secure the preservation of our family. Gather Lergys and Librena from the training center with all possible haste. Use private conveyance to take them and yourself to the dwelling that Ruryk maintains in the far reaches of District 12. I may not be able to communicate with you for some time but, under no circumstances are you to attempt to contact me. Do you understand what I am asking of you?"

"What you ask, yes, but before I do any such thing, I would know the why of it as well."

Ridwyn took three deep breaths. "You know that I set Cymrec and his expanded staff to search for new methods to infuse our neural networks with the intellectual powers of reason and insight. They have been successful, hideously so.

"The construction of a truly intelligent neural map is an amazingly complex undertaking. So they decided to bypass all that intricate work and go directly to the source: They took the neural map from a living human mind and

implanted it into a network. Once the personality carried by that map understood what had happened to it, it began doing everything it could to destroy the network that now carried it. And I, I and my team, gave Cymrec the tools to thwart those efforts, to imprison that personality in its new 'home' indefinitely.

"It has taken them several experiments, but they are close to successfully completing the implantation process and denying the personality's attempts at shutdown long enough to lock down the network's stability. That Cymrec and the others could even contemplate such a thing stuns my sensibilities."

Ridwyn sank down onto his once-comforting chair with a look of undiluted horror on his face. "But Abrina, oh, dear, loving Abrina, they did it four times!" Then he did something that she had not seen in their decades of being mated. He buried his face in his hands and wept as though he had lost his soul.

"Ridwyn! Ridwyn! Look at me!" she implored. "Tell me what happened to those whose neural maps were implanted into the networks. What happened to them?"

He seemed to draw himself back into focus and began rebuilding his resolve as he spoke. He looked up at her and held her gaze. "It kills them, Abrina. It kills them horribly by taking the very essence of who they are from them and inserting it into a machine. I do not know if there is such a thing as a soul. But, if there is, this must be the most terrible thing that can happen to it."

He stood and faced her squarely. "I have to stop them. If I can't persuade them to turn themselves over to the authorities, then I will have to report them myself."

She reached out and seized him by his shoulders. "Convince them? No, Ridwyn, NO! They have killed four people, why should they hesitate at a fifth?"

He took her face in his hands, kissed her with all the love that he had ever known for her, then held her in an almost fierce embrace. "I have to, Abrina. I opened the door to this, and I am the one who must close it. What they have done is monstrous, but it was all done under my authority. I owe them the opportunity to set it right themselves."

He walked to the door and turned to see her fighting back her own tears. "Promise me that you will do as I have asked." She placed a hand over her lips and nodded her head, distrusting her own words. "I have to end this," he said. "I have to end it now."

———

The transport pod delivered him to the laboratory complex. He remained in it for a moment to compose his thoughts. He had known Cymrec since they were both in training. If he could just remind him of three concepts, he knew Cymrec would see reason. He would have to.

Goryv met him at the door. "I have come to meet with Cymrec. Where is he?"

Cool, frigid disdain emanated from Goryv's eyes. "He is in laboratory five." Ridwyn turned toward the hallway.

"We have done it, Ridwyn. We made it work beyond everyone's expectations, even yours."

Ridwyn turned back to face him with a look that chilled even the impermeable Goryv. "Oh, indeed you have. You have taken a noble endeavor and soiled it beyond recognition. You have done something I would not have believed possible. You have led me to regret proposing the synthetic humanity project to the Council in the first place. You have…"

———————————

"The problem with talking," Miles said quietly, "is that you cannot listen very well. Specifically, I could not hear the quiet approach of soft-clad feet behind me. All I knew was that I felt a pinprick on the side of my neck, my words slurred off into a mumble and everything went black."

Grant had sunk back down into his chair and looked at Miles as if he had turned over a rock and found a rattlesnake beneath it.

Miles just looked at him for a moment. "If your research took a particularly dark turn that challenged everything that you hold dear, what would you do?"

Ordwyn's eyes narrowed. "More to the point, what did they do with you? They could hardly leave you free to report them, and you seemed to think that you could sway their boss. That doesn't leave them a lot of options. And yet, they couldn't have killed you, because you are sitting here in front of us.

"So, finish it. What did happen?"

Miles' gaze went back to the thousand-year stare that made Ordwyn feel nonexistent and he resumed. "Someone, I believe it was Cymrec, implanted all that you have seen so far and much more in my storage system. But, for whatever reason, he stopped here. The rest is what I directly experienced later and is overlaid with my explanations of what I felt and did. I can only speculate on exactly what happened after I lost consciousness, but it isn't too difficult to infer. The injection immobilized me completely, body and mind. It was probably an anesthetic that we commonly used for highly invasive surgeries.

"While I was 'on hold,' they doubtless discussed what to do with me so as to have a minimal impact on their activities. The most obvious solution was to kill me, and that was the path they settled on. But the way they did it almost causes me to admire their audacity.

"A major constraint of their first four experiments was that they were using convicted criminals as the source for their neural maps. To be consigned to the status of 'criminal' in our culture required both a predilection for violence and a singular lack of intelligence and imagination. Literally, you had to be someone who could not imagine any other way to be. This made the neural map extracted from such a person very nearly useless in the effort to infuse a neural network with a high order of insightful intelligence.

"I, on the other hand, possessed intelligence that had formulated the synthetic humanity project in the first place. Imagination I had in abundance. Intellect was my life's blood. In short, I was the ideal test subject for the neural transfer process. So that was exactly what they did."

Grant was incredulous. "Oh, come on, Miles! You're sitting here talking to us. They clearly couldn't have taken your neural map and put it into some test-bed machine."

Miles' voice went as cold as a tomb. "One last time, Grant, view the entire story before you make up your mind as to its veracity. I will need to narrate this part for you, as the visual is composed solely of my perceptions."

———————————

The return of awareness was like the actuation of a switch.

I went from standing in the hall and crumpling toward the floor to, what? Where was I? I tried to open my eyes, but that resulted in what looked like a monitoring device watching the flow of computer data. I listened, but again, there was only the odd data bit string impressed on my mind.

I tried to raise my hand but it felt like nothing happened. In fact, when I thought about it, I didn't seem to "feel" anything at all. There was no pressure on my back from lying on anything or on my feet from standing up or—my incisive mind raced through all the possibilities and came quickly to the obvious. This matched all that I had considered about what awareness inside a neural network must be like.

For an eternal instant, I felt the irresistible tug of insanity, the unquenchable desire to just let go. Then some something took me by my mental shoulders, shook me back to sensibility and stood me up again. I marveled at the experience for only a moment before I recognized my own handiwork. It was the fail-safe that my team had created to deal with just this loss of mental stability, the inevitable result of what had happened to me. I had taken the blissful release of complete mental dissolution away from myself.

But one aspect of all this didn't quite fit. I had some operational control over my experience. I tried opening my "eyes" again. The data stream was still there and I could just begin to make some sense out of it. I fought hard to remember what it felt like to close the fingers of my right hand. And something happened! I was not sure what exactly, but some state of my surroundings had changed with that effort.

I had no way to measure the passage of time. I was aware that it did pass, but I needed an external calibration of the rate, and that would have to wait a bit longer. What I could do was begin exercising the equipment to which I was connected. I needed reference points, so I started with optical sensors. I found control registers and began *plugging values into them. This led to moving focal apparatus, examining different light and even electromagnetic spectra. Sending intentional impulses to where I thought my hands, feet neck and the rest of my body should be resulted in positional responses back to my "brain."*

This exploration of my container continued for as long as it did. It could have been minutes or months. I was finally able to deduce that I was lying on a flat surface inside a tube of some sort. I discovered that I had manipulators which could be operated like hands on the ends of arms. I used them to lever my way out of the tube. The table I was on was on rails that extended out of the tube and into a room of some sort.

I had gained some understanding of my visual sensors and now began working with them in earnest. I had to see what this room was and why my activities in it were apparently being ignored. I began distinguishing objects, their shapes, colors, thermal emissivity, sizes and distances.

I learned to get up off my table, mastered the incredibly intricate process of walking and found a whole array of interesting aspects concerning my "body." This allowed me to explore the room and discover that it was a laboratory, one that had fallen into neglect and was covered in drifts of dust. It was obvious that no one had been in it for years, decades, perhaps even a century.

One thing that helped explain where I was and how long I had been there was a device implanted in my neuro-cortex that had kept my awareness disabled for a very long time. Its timer had finally expired and it had dutifully released me back to awareness and control. My captors had probably used it to keep me quiescent while they worked on me.

Now that I was mobile, I could tell that considerable time had passed since my reattainment of awareness. So, in some way, I must be lost in this forgotten room. I decided to take advantage of that situation, and I began to work up my coordination and agility. When I felt competent to pass for human to a very casual observer, I began digging out of what I had begun to think of as my tomb. I estimated that project to have consumed two to three weeks.

I was in a basement that was three floors below ground level, and I found the transfer shaft back to the surface packed with debris. I discovered how much strength I possessed as I worked to clear the wreckage. The upside was that I gained even more coordination and control over what I was finally coming to think of as a body in the digging-out process. The downside was that I finally got to the surface.

The city lay in ruins around me.

It was recognizably my city, the one I had walked through so many years ago, but it had changed drastically. And it had been destroyed.

The building above my "tomb" had been a data center. And, though its machines were long dead, many bits of knowledge that they stored had been committed to hard copy on the carbon fiber sheets that my culture used *instead of paper. It was all fragments; but one thing was obvious. The last date on any of the records was over a hundred years after I had been killed. How much longer than that I had been entombed, I had no way to know.*

My wife, my family, the culture I was born into, all I had known had long ago passed into oblivion.

―――――――――――

"Much has happened since then. But the ultimate result has been to bring me here." Miles' look came back to the present and focused on Grant. "You may now ask the questions that you are certain will reveal all I have said and shown you to be either a hoax or a delusion."

Grant shook his head. "I hardly know where to start, Miles. But, to begin with, the modern state of the art in just about every engineering discipline I can name is so far behind what you just described as to make it impossible. There is just no known technology that would support the kind of artificial body or intelligence that you are claiming you have. That little distinction also puts the skids under your claim to be "very old.'"

Miles looked down almost regretfully for a moment. "I suspected you would need some hard proof, which is why I brought these to our discussion," Miles said, pointing at the black metal case on the table in front of him. He then reached forward and opened the top of the case to display its contents, a pair of black metal cylinders approximately three inches in diameter and about as long. He picked one of them out of the case and handed it to Grant, who turned it over and over inspecting it.

"Very impressive workmanship . . . and I have to admit that I have never seen anything like it. But what *is* it? And how does it prove any of your claims about an android body?" Grant asked as he handed the cylinder back to Miles.

"Perhaps this will constitute the proof you seek." With that, Miles held up his left hand. The skin on his forearm separated into three panels, opening out at a 45-degree angle from the arm. Miles then reached over with his right hand, removed his left hand from his arm and placed it on the table next to the case. Then he set the cylinder Grant had handed back to him on the end of his arm where his hand used to be. As it clicked into place, the panels in Miles' forearm retracted and made a seamless joint between his arm and the cylinder.

"OK, that is some very impressive prosthetic equipment and it, like the car and the computer, is well ahead of what I've seen. But it still doesn't prove the existence of an android body."

Miles pointed across the table to the corner nearest the door through which they had entered. "I direct your attention to the scrap metal leaning against that corner of the room." There were several four-foot-long pieces of steel concrete reinforcing rod that Grant had noticed there when they walked in.

Without taking his gaze off Grant, Miles activated his new "hand." A serpentine metal tentacle extended from it, ending in a three-pronged claw. Then, without leaving his seat, Miles reached over to the stack of half-inch-diameter steel rods nearly ten feet away and used the claw to retrieve one of them. He wrapped the metal tentacle around it and bent the rod over double, then tossed it to Grant.

Grant was stunned. His careful examination of the warped rod compelled him to accept that it was indeed made of construction-grade steel and should not have given way to anything short of a hydraulic stamping press in a factory.

Ordwyn had held her peace in silence through the demonstration, but this was getting back into that category of too damn much. She backed away from the table without taking her eyes off Miles. "You can't be human and be able to do that."

For the very first time, she saw an identifiable emotion on Miles' face when he said, with what felt to her like an ancient sadness, "I was once. But, no, I am not anymore."

Grant was beginning to get very tired of having his reality whipsawed and looked very hard at Miles as he asked, "Even if I accept your story, how could you possibly have kept this kind of development a secret?"

"I think I mentioned being very old."

"All right, Miles," Ordwyn replied, "I'll bite. How old can you possibly be when the technology you have displayed here in front of us today hasn't even been invented yet? You have done things and gotten us out of situations where we should by all rights have been killed. Understand that you have my deepest thanks for that. But I'm a cop—at least I used to be. And I really want to know how you know what you know that keeps us all alive."

"Sergeant, you have made an error in your observations. We are not all alive. I am dead. I was killed by my contemporaries when they drained my neural map into this machine you see before you."

Miles held up his hand to forestall their objections. "There is one fact in all this that I have not yet revealed to you. I told you that I am very old, and that is a massive understatement. I last held my beautiful wife in my arms and kissed her a bit over 34,000 years ago."

Chapter 9

"Damn, it's noon already."

Carver stared at the clock on his computer's monitor and sighed. Then he thumbed the intercom switch on his desk phone and said, "Marion, I will be going down to the Room shortly. Please send out for lunch and see that I am not disturbed otherwise."

Missed sleep pulled at him. He jabbed the intercom switch again. "Marion, make sure that lunch comes with coffee, lots of coffee. Oh, and have someone check on the Ingalls woman to make sure she got home all right yesterday."

He sat back in his chair and thought about what he had seen in the Room last night, what it meant, and what they were going to have to do about it. His mind went back to the image of Clarissa Ingalls sobbing in horror, guilt and shame, and from there to an ancient maxim stating that nothing is trivial.

He descended the stairs and entered the Room (it always reminded him of a movie set) at the stroke of the hour. Another very singular individual entered shortly thereafter. The Room was shaped much like an amphitheater. A conference table identical to the one in Carver's office sat at the focus of a semicircle of huge computer display panels that were set slightly below it. The two of them took their accustomed places at the conference table. Baker was already at the console that was set back from and above the table. He was there both to oversee the absolute operational security of the systems and in his role as Director of Security.

One by one, the monitors changed their displays from data concerning the Group's operations to show six faces, each as unique as the two at the table. Within five minutes they were all present. Officially, they were the Board of Directors of the Forester Group. In reality, they were its heart, soul and essence.

Charles Carver stood and looked at each of them as he spoke. "You are all aware of the growing importance of nanotechnology in redressing the balance of free inquiry and open enterprise against the Consortium's plutocratic oligarchy. You are also aware of our intense interest in Grant Thornton as the most capable researcher working in that field. Sam Baker has put Thornton's status on continuous update to all of you, along with our deduction that the situation concerning his flight from the Consortium has changed radically."

A man at the center of the array, whose face looked older than any of the others and yet held incredibly young eyes spoke, using a voice that creaked with age. "Charles, I have been following the events surrounding your Mr. Thornton with astonishment and growing alarm ever since you flagged his case to us. Our interest in nanotechnology predates the Consortium's, but our attempts to promote it have been as scattered by the diversity of its developers as have the Consortium's efforts to defeat it. We have followed their agents both open and covert as they have attacked nanotech companies and, largely due to your efforts, we have been able to head off their most predatory efforts against those who are key talents in its development.

"But now they seem to have gone from predatory to murderous. We haven't seen open, directed assassinations against engineers and scientists in nearly twenty years. They have begun killing not just technical talents, but bystanders and even policemen. Do you have any idea what has caused this sudden rapacity?"

"I may be able to shed some light on the answer to that question, Mr. Drake," Baker volunteered. Carver looked around at Sam with some surprise, as the security director seldom volunteered comments in these meetings. "At the risk of recounting what most of you already know, I'd like to put these recent developments into context.

"Amon Forester looked at the horror of scientific warfare that was World War I and vowed to do whatever he could to enable the minds of our best and brightest toward mankind's betterment and away from its destruction. For nearly a century, we have championed, protected and nurtured numerous engineers and scientists in our quest to make scientific progress our most effective weapon against the kind of economic tyranny represented by the Consortium. We have been successful in some of these efforts, but we have failed with too many others. Our technical edge over the Consortium and its ilk has not always been sufficient to counter the raw power that their resources can field.

"For this reason, we have chosen our battles very carefully. We have gone to great lengths to conceal our efforts and, in particular, our losses. After the Consortium's attacks against us, we dispersed our facilities and ourselves over the globe to make future assaults more expensive than they would be worth. We have assiduously avoided running battles with their agents, both to prevent casualties among bystanders and to limit our own losses. As is true of our more positive endeavors, this part of our efforts has not been completely successful.

"The level of violence tied to the Consortium's recent operations has been rising for some time. It seems sudden in our context only because they have begun to redirect it from their purely commercial enterprises. A number of competitive bids and alternative sources for major contracts have suddenly dried up after the Consortium's agents saw to the physical intimidation or direct elimination of key business personnel from non-Consortium companies.

"Their attacks on Thornton, his colleagues, his protectors and even his wife are congruent with the way they now operate their business activities.

"While the Consortium is not the only aggregation of wealth and power that seeks to impose economic servitude on the world, it is by far the most able. Its strike teams have been able to accomplish much of what the organization's voracious economic juggernaut has only partially achieved. Ironically, the very technological advances that have enabled our opposition to its activities have also fueled them and made those activities that much more effective."

Lori Dathan, the intense woman sitting to Carver's right at the conference table, looked back from Baker to the group. "Sam and I have been monitoring rather more than just the Consortium's activities in the R&D arena, as their business interests tend to presage their actions against technology developers. We have found one name that surfaces again and again in reports on their 'enforcement' activities. It seems that one George Osterman has risen within their organization from a mid-level organizer of strong-arm tactics to the top of their covert operations group. Their use of violence has risen with him."

"George appears to have found a path to the top." The woman looking out from the far left screen had unusually attractive features, but it was her intensity that drew everyone's attention. "Like Mr. Drake, I have been following Sam's reports on Thornton with great concern. Believe me, I understand the importance of nanotechnology and how vital Thornton's contribution will be. That said, I really don't think that we want to get into a war of running gun battles with Consortium agents over him."

Baker nodded to the woman's image as he responded: "Amy has a good point that is reinforced by the degree to which the Consortium has bought influence in many of the police precincts around our location. Corrupt as they may be, we do not want to find ourselves in shootouts with them. Nor do we want to give them excuses to start investigations aimed at our own activities."

There was another aspect to be considered, and Carver spoke up. "I think we are all in agreement that a street war with the Consortium would be far less tenable for us than it would be for them, regardless of the ethical considerations involved.

"However, I direct your attention to the last report that we circulated on Thornton. In the previous 48 hours, Lori and Sam have monitored several actions taken by the Consortium against him that, by all rights, should have taken him out. The strike in force against the warehouse in particular should have killed him and the police sergeant who seems to have taken a special interest in his case. In each instance, the Consortium's agents were thwarted in their actions against Thornton by some agency of which we are totally unaware."

This caused most of the faces on the screens to look aside at data monitors. A middle-aged man with a prominent scar that made him look a bit like a pirate responded first. "Do I correctly understand that, whoever this is, they have not only snatched Thornton and"—he looked back at his data monitor for a moment—"Summers from the clutches of a truly massive force of Consortium agents but also caused them to disappear from both our surveillance and the Consortium's as well?"

Carver looked back up at the security director. "Sam?"

"What we have seen from our surveillance and from intercepted communications among the Consortium agents is nothing less than startling. It indicates that someone has not only evaded considerable attacks by their agents against Thornton, but has actually sent them out against at least two purely bogus diversions. All of which indicates a level of accurate and detailed intelligence combined with both soft and hard action capabilities that we do not have the resources to match."

Carver's gaze slowly panned the group. "For the first time, there is another significant player in the contest between the Consortium and the Group. And this player has abilities to gather information and take action that neither we nor the Consortium can duplicate or defeat. You all know how critical nanotechnology and Thornton's survival are to finally having a shot at breaking the Consortium's stranglehold on technology.

"This third party moves this situation from hopeless to the possibility of a breakthrough. If we can make contact and effectively offer whatever assistance we can, then we have the chance to move nanotechnology out of the science journal pages and into making a critical difference in the future of human scientific advancement."

His gaze swept the entire group as, with a voice like steel drawn over a stone, Carver called on them all to face the most solemn of challenges. "We all know what we believe in. The real question is, when finally pushed to the wall, what are we willing to do about it?"

———————

"Miles, that just can't be."

Grant was starting to get the glassy-eyed look that meant his worldview was under heavy stress again. Ordwyn was mildly surprised that Grant's obvious mental struggle was sufficient to displace her own and bring her back from a mounting fear that she recognized from last night's dream. "Miles, he's right. Even the best machinery I've ever seen couldn't last for 34,000 years. It would need so much maintenance that you'd have to have an army of technicians and a parts factory to keep it going."

This seemed to give Grant some intellectual breathing space. "Exactly. The daily stresses of that many years' service would wear out every system in a high-tech android chassis a dozen times over."

Miles turned to face Grant squarely and watched the man's face intently as he made his third major revelation. "I could easily last for another 34,000 years. My entire physical system was built to be self-renewing."

Miles was counting on Grant's intellectual curiosity to pull him through a mind-numbing realization. The risk began to pay off as the full meaning of what Miles had just said dawned on Grant and brought a fierce hunger to his eyes. "Miles," Grant said slowly, "the only way to build, much less maintain, such a body—would be with nanotechnology."

"Very good, Mr. Thornton. Nanotechnology lies at the very core of my existence. My structure is continuously maintained and replaced even faster than the organic cells in your own body. My systems regenerate and even improve themselves in what you would call 'real time.' Most of those improvements are discretionary, but many are autonomic."

Ordwyn was fascinated despite herself, watching Grant while his mind chased down a hundred parallel pathways and the technical grandeur of Miles' revelation played across his face. An important piece clicked into place for Grant. "That computer and the car, you made them from, from . . ."

Miles nodded, "From 'myself' as it were. I have the capability to extend and control portions of my system's maintenance swarm and use them to create both structures and devices."

Puzzlement turned into a question. "But, Miles, with this kind of technology at your command, what could you possibly want from me?"

"My control of my nano-swarms is not without its limitations. Certain restrictions are built into their programming that I am powerless to change. That is why I want you to continue with your own development of nanotech. Your work has the potential to take it in directions that I cannot."

Carver could actually feel the silence in the Room as each of the other directors considered the implications of his challenge.

Mr. Drake broke that silence. "We have not come to where we are by fretting over what we can't do. We got here by doing the most that we can. This situation is no different. So, what are our options?"

Carver looked over his shoulder at Baker. "Sam, I would imagine that direct contact, even if we knew how to initiate it, is out of the question?"

Baker's face was as grim as he'd ever seen it. "Contact, were it to become possible, would be both dangerous and impractical. At this point, I can't honestly say whether the Consortium would follow our contact effort in order to hunt down and kill Thornton—or kill our people outright just to make sure we don't contact him."

The old man with the startling young eyes spoke again. "Mr. Baker, what are our prospects for being able to hinder the Consortium's efforts, either directly or indirectly?"

"Mr. Drake, there is a great deal that we can do unobtrusively to get in their way. Much of it could not even be traced back to us. The real question is, what would we accomplish with such an effort? At this point, the Consortium is running around stepping on itself trying to find Thornton with, apparently, no success whatsoever. As long as that continues to be the case, I suggest that we have more to gain by letting them demoralize themselves than we would by trying to interfere with their activities. While matters may come down to the point that disrupting their efforts is the best we can do, I would suggest that we have better options to pursue now."

"Lori?"

The woman at the table responded. "While direct communication may not be a possibility, my team has come up with one interesting alternative. Though both Summers and Thornton's cell phones are off the air, their accounts are still active and still accumulating text messages. I propose that we insert messages into both accounts that, in and of themselves, appear perfectly normal and innocuous. But combined, those messages point to an indirect message drop that they can use via means other than their phones. Even combined, these messages will still be cryptic and obscure but, given the talents of Thornton's new support, we think they will be able to decipher them." She then looked back at Baker.

The man with the scarred face looked up at Baker as well. "And what will we say?"

Baker gestured to the group as he looked directly at his questioner. "With your approval, the message we will send them will be an open offer of whatever will help and a request for a response."

"I see. That sounds useful but passive."

Amy spoke up again. "Gerard is right; what can we do that will at least hinder the Consortium and be visible to Thornton as evidence that he has a reason to contact us?"

A man who looked rather like an accountant spoke for the first time. "Suppose we make Thornton and Summers' disappearances public knowledge? A leak to the media shouldn't be too difficult to indirectly engineer, and it would be a considerable hindrance to the Consortium's activities. The very fact that it is reported publicly should get Thornton's attention."

Carver looked around the display array. "An excellent idea, Harold. It has the added advantage of making any preemptive strikes against us more difficult. Does everyone agree to these courses of action?" Affirmation indicators flashed from each monitor and in front of Carver, Lori Dathan's and Sam Baker's chairs. "Very well then, we shall proceed. Our next meeting will be in 24 hours to review events and consider additional suggestions."

The monitors returned to status displays. Lori rose from her seat to leave the room as Carver ascended to the security station. "Sam, I want to know the instant you see or hear anything regarding Thornton. I don't care what time of day or night."

"Charles, you will know as soon as I do. This promises to be a very interesting twenty-four hours."

Carver held Baker's gaze. "I just hope Thornton has that long."

———————————

"Miles, if I accept what you have just told me, then you have seen all of recorded human history and more. That you have lived for 34,000 years is . . . is . . ."

"Yes Grant, it is more than five times the span covered by your history books."

Ordwyn watched the exchange between Grant and Miles, fascinated to see where it was going to go. Grant continued to struggle with the implications. "Did you actually see the Egyptian pyramids being constructed?"

"No, I was elsewhere in the world at the time, though I did see Giza a bit over two centuries after most of the construction was complete. It stands as a reminder of the transience of power. I suspect that you have hours of questions you would like to ask about your history, but we have a limited amount of time to indulge such curiosities.

"During your education, you wrote a research paper on a place your geography calls Nan-Madol. It was published as an unexpectedly scholarly treatment of an archaeological subject for a physical scientist. Do you remember it?"

Grant's mind returned to happier times. "Oh, yes, I actually was able to visit the island of Pohnpei during a vacation and was enthralled with the ruins there. But what do you know of Nan-Madol?"

"Your research addressed a conundrum that has puzzled every archaeologist who has studied the ruins and tried to piece their history and purpose together."

"OK, would somebody like to fill the dumb cop in on what you are both talking about and why it has any bearing on our current situation?" Ordwyn was holding off on a warehouse full of questions for what was beginning to sound like one of those lectures she had purposely avoided while she was in school.

"Bear with us for a moment, Sergeant. Mr. Thornton needs to convince himself that I am what I say I am, and that is going to require a corroborative piece of information that he cannot get anywhere but from a subject where he has prior, detailed knowledge.

"Grant, what was the issue that stumped every archaeologist who studied Nan-Madol?"

His curiosity stirred, Grant responded, "Why . . . why did some prehistoric culture build the amazing structures that are found on Pohnpei? And, why there? Granted, the weather in that portion of the tropics is unusually calm year-round but, even so, that doesn't seem to be a reason to build a city that rivaled anything constructed for centuries afterward. The rock formations around the island are unlike anything seen anywhere else on the planet. But, again, they aren't reason enough for that enormous building program."

"Grant, I have never heard of this before. If these buildings were so magnificent, why weren't they mentioned in the history books I studied in school?"

"Ordwyn, they don't get much mention because the ruins are largely under water. There are very little in the way of pictures of the sites. The other reason is because the archaeologists who write those books are somewhat embarrassed by their inability to explain the site itself. I got interested in it because . . . well, because I like questions that have stopped everyone who has tried to answer them."

Grant turned avidly back to Miles. "So Miles, are you saying you can answer the riddle of Nan-Madol?"

"The one that you are interested in, yes. Your science of archaeology has assumed that Nan-Madol was built on an island with odd rock formations in an area with unusually calm weather. What has never occurred to you is that the city predated both conditions."

"What do you mean 'predated'"?

"I found Nan-Madol after it had been abandoned but before it was completely flooded by rising sea levels. I recognized it immediately as having been constructed by my culture . . . quite possibly by its last survivors.

"At the close of the last ice age, cyclonic storms in the ocean you call the Pacific were much more powerful and destructive than they are today. They made survival on the islands scattered around the equator difficult to impossible. And yet, the area now called the Caroline Islands seems to regularly escape such storms.

"The hundreds of millions of tons of prismatic basalt structures on Pohnpei are not natural. They were built by the inhabitants of Nan-Madol so as to influence the magnetic and gravitational fields around the island. The subtle changes they caused, and still cause today, disrupt the formation of cyclonic storms in the area, providing a sort of weather control for the surrounding islands. This is why Polynesian culture sprang up and flourished in this area thousands of years after Nan-Madol was abandoned and flooded."

Grant's expression went from curious to stunned as Miles spoke. "So that's why the carbon dating was always wrong. Everyone just assumed that the basalt had to be older than the city . . . and it wasn't."

Ordwyn reached the end of her patience. "Grant, why is all this important?"

Grant pulled himself back from his contemplation of a past he hadn't imagined and spoke as if he barely believed his own words. "Miles has just described a matter of ancient history that has been argued about from opposing viewpoints for nearly two centuries, and he is settling issues that have raged in academia for that entire period. In a very important way, this proves as much about who he is as his prosthetics.

"Except . . . I guess that they really aren't prosthetics, are they Miles?"

Moving to face him directly, Ordwyn put the question to Grant: "So, given what Miles has said and what we've seen, do you now believe he is what he claims?"

"Ordwyn," Grant looked down at his feet and then back up to her eyes, a bit flustered as he continued, "Sergeant doesn't seem appropriate anymore." He took a deep breath. "At this point I don't have a better explanation. I think it was Sir Arthur Conan Doyle who once wrote that 'When you have eliminated the impossible, whatever remains, however improbable, must be the truth'—and he was a lot smarter than I am."

She turned back to Miles with an intensity bordering on ferocious. "That basically sums up my problem with all this as well. I can't come up with any explanation of what I've seen that answers the question of who you are any better than Grant has. So, for the sake of argument, suppose I believe you.

"What do we do now? We have a group of people after us with amazing resources combined with powerful connections and, incredible as you are, you are not an army."

Miles gave her another of those inscrutable looks, "Just so . . . simply protecting you from the Consortium is a defensive strategy that must ultimately fail. We need to create two significant changes to the current situation. We need to convince the Consortium to stop looking for both of you, and Mr. Thornton needs facilities where he can continue his work.

Those facilities will be of little use until the first issue has been dealt with."

Ordwyn was really beginning to hate the feeling that she was going in circles. Her life had been about understanding the situation presented to her and taking effective action based on that understanding. Now everything seemed to be spinning out of her control. She walked around the table to face Miles and her concerns directly. "Miles, do you have anyone else who we can depend on to help us? My department has been compromised so thoroughly that I don't dare contact them, and Grant's effort to reach out to the Forester Group nearly got both of us killed."

"We will indeed require assistance, and you are right about the police being compromised. I have some possibilities, but they must be enlisted to our aid in such a way that they do not suspect what they are really doing or whom they are doing it for."

Grant walked over to Miles and Ordwyn with as solemn a look on his face as she had ever seen. "OK, I'm in. Ordwyn?" She looked at each of them for a long moment.

"I've lived my whole life as either a cop or a cop's daughter, Grant. But, for the life of me, I can't see any way for that life to continue . . . not with this Consortium trying to kill me . . . us." She looked into Grant's eyes for a moment then turned to Miles. "Me too. Let's do this . . . whatever this is."

Grant didn't stop to wonder why, but he felt both relieved and happy at Ordwyn's decision. "What do we do next, Miles?"

"Very well . . ." For the first time in their experience of him, Miles seemed hesitant. "I suggest that you take some time to think about this and come to terms with it."

He took a moment.

Then he said softly: "You will both have to die."

Chapter 10

It felt like rising up from the dead.

Lunch was just what his fatigue-fogged brain needed. Carver polished off his second turkey on rye sandwich and chased it with the remainder of a cup of black coffee. His desk computer was configured to display any public news about Thornton or the Consortium's activities as well as the Group's covert surveillance of them. A midday television news story was covering "another convenience store robbery" in one window while a second was reporting on a warehouse fire. A third window was scrolling intercepted Consortium communications.

Those messages were beginning to take on a desperate note. Apparently, the Consortium was turning up the heat on its operatives. So much the better from Carver's perspective: Pressured agents were more likely to make mistakes that could become public embarrassments, which would slow their activities even further. A pop-up message on the screen notified

Carver that Sam Baker wanted to see him in person, and that meant progress.

He put his cup down on his desk and headed back through his outer office. "Marion, thank you. That was an excellent lunch and just what I needed. I'm going down to the Room for at least the next hour or so."

He descended the stairs, went through the access verification ritual at the door and entered the Room to find Baker studying one of his monitors intensely. "What have you got, Sam?"

Baker looked over his shoulder and waved Carver toward the monitor he had been studying. "I've been researching channels through which we could leak Thornton and Summers' disappearances." He pointed at his screen and tapped a key on his console at the same time. "Take a look at this."

The display showed a news item from the previous day that was presented as a follow-up to the story of Ellen Thornton's death. It was a throwaway piece announcing that William Ferris had increased the amount of a reward he had offered two months ago for information leading to an arrest in the case of his daughter's murder.

Carver gave Baker an inquisitive look. "Are you planning on giving Ferris a lead?"

"He has been nagging and nattering at the police ever since her death, and he's made no secret of his belief that they know more than they're telling him.

At some level he is obviously right. It occurred to me that his 'discovery' that Summers had found 'something' and was pursuing it would put him on the scent of finding out just what that 'something' was. Then throw in the added frustration that he wouldn't be able to grill Summers himself, on top of the fact that Thornton was her last person of interest in the case, and now Thornton can't be found either. I think Ferris would go to the police and demand answers.

"My question to you is this. Are we willing to risk that the Consortium may kill Ferris just to shut him up?"

Carver weighed the question for a moment. "If Ferris just asked the police about it, they might. But suppose we tipped a rising young reporter to the possibility that Summers knew something involving Thornton and set said reporter onto Ferris? If he thought that something of substance was being withheld from him, he would explode during the interview and gain some significant coverage before the Consortium could squelch it. Then, he'd demand to talk to Summers, which would achieve our goal of bringing the two disappearances out in public."

Baker nodded as he turned the idea over in his mind. "And it would leave the Consortium with nothing to gain from killing Ferris."

Carver agreed. "Let's go with that. How soon do you think we could have this on the news feeds?"

Baker smiled back at him. "I think I know just the right reporter to get it on tonight's late news program. I'll let you know as soon as the hook is set."

"Good. Now, how are you coming with getting the two messages sent to Thornton and Summers' text queues?"

"Already done," Baker responded. "We had prepared the messages before the meeting; so, when we had approval, we went ahead and sent them. Now it's a matter of how long it takes them to notice and link them up."

"All right, keep up the surveillance on the police. The Consortium is going to turn up the heat on them, which should translate into an opportunity for us to learn more about the points of collusion between the two."

"The Consortium's penetration of many of the world's police departments leaves us with little choice," Miles explained gently, in answer to their incredulous expressions.

"They will press the surveillance capabilities of every police organization on earth into hunting you. And they will continue that hunt until they truly believe that either you are beyond their grasp or that killing you no longer serves their interests. Our successful evasion will simply spur them to greater efforts.

"My ability to falsify your deaths is rather greater than either of you might believe, especially you, Sergeant. But, in Mr. Thornton's case, it will probably not stop the Consortium from seeking ultimate proof of his demise. I can . . ."

"Miles," Ordwyn began and then looked away from both him and Grant to take a deep breath. "I don't think that I am a sergeant in anything anymore. So, please, just call me Ordwyn."

Grant reached out without even thinking and touched her arm, receiving an apprehensive, but appreciative, look in return. "And 'Mr. Thornton' is starting to sound pretty silly as well," he said. "Considering what we've been through and what we are about to do, just call me Grant . . . until even my name isn't mine anymore."

"You have concisely stated the issue for both of you. You can no longer retain any shred of your previous identities. As much as you have identified yourselves by what you did and who you knew, those lives are gone now . . . just as gone as if you had truly died.

"I have a certain perspective on the experience."

Miles let that statement hang for a moment. "I will leave you to consider this and to make your peace with it. Though time is of the essence, you will each need to bring your whole being to what comes next."

Grant and Ordwyn exchanged a look. Miles resumed: "The last door at the end of the hallway leads to a room I have used to ground myself in my own decisions. Speak of what you wish to see displayed on its walls, and it will be shown to you. Come back to this room when you are ready to continue."

Miles walked through the door and into the entry room.

Ordwyn looked at Grant. "What do you want to bet we couldn't find him now if we tried?"

"Lady, that would be a fool's bet."

He sighed and made a decision. "Let's go check out Miles' 'meditation room.' I definitely feel the need to talk this through, and I can't think of anyone I'd rather talk to than you . . . if that works for you, of course."

He could see Ordwyn's gratitude in her eyes. "I was kind of hoping that you wouldn't leave me stewing in my own juices. Lead on."

They checked and, sure enough, Miles was not in the entry room, so they walked down the hall past all the bedrooms and opened the door at its end. The room before them was unexpectedly spacious and oddly shaped. It appeared to be a polygon, but Grant had to stop and count the number of wall panels. There were 16, counting the one that held the door, which he slowly shut behind them.

"Well. Ordwyn, what would you like to see?"

She looked up at Grant's face and tried really hard to smile. "How about a rocky seascape?"

"Works for me; now how do you suppose . . ." Grant's

words trailed off into wonder as a view expanded all around them of a wild array of cliffs with a brisk wind blowing the sea into massive breakers at their base. The display technology was incredible and the effect was to place the viewer in the scene itself. The sounds of the wind and surf were all around them, yet not at all intrusive on their conversation.

He was barely aware of speaking. "Thanks, Miles." There was an inviting couch in front of them set such that it appeared to look out to sea. Grant gestured toward it and followed Ordwyn only to hesitate at taking a seat.

She sat, looked up at him and gave him a quizzical smile. "Police officers . . ." she looked away for a moment and then back to his face, taking a moment's pride in her self-control. "Ex-police officers don't bite . . . really."

Grant smiled. "You're sure?" Then he sat on the couch next to her.

"My pleasure, but you get to talk first. After all, I chose the scene."

"Fair enough."

After they watched the waves crash over the rocks for a few minutes and before the silence could become strained, Grant said, "How interesting that Miles' very first question to me was 'Who are you, really?' He wasn't quite right about giving up everything. But it will be awfully close.

"When I was a child, I must have been the bane of my parents' existence. I had to question everything . . . why this, what about that, are you sure about the other? I can't remember a time when the drive to know didn't consume me. At the same time, I loved making things. I literally wore out a set of building blocks by making structures with them until their finish was gone and the corners weren't square any more.

"After the building blocks, I graduated to building electronic circuits and figuring out how they worked. I made a breadboard radio that I took apart and put back together until I understood every aspect of its operation. That led to assembling my own computers, a string of them, and I used them to learn the finer aspects of machine-based logic.

"I was in my last year of high school when I discovered nanotechnology. It was full of unknowns, and someone could make things with atoms as the building blocks. I had discovered heaven!" Grant's voice broke on that last word. He took a moment and then continued. "I think Ellen was the only reason I didn't become the prototypical mad scientist. We met in our freshman year at the university, when I was sent to an art appreciation class by a dean who had decided I was a cultural barbarian. Ellen had a natural grasp of the nuances of artistic expression and took pity on my absolute lack of awareness in that realm.

"She didn't really grasp most of what I found so fascinating, but she seemed to be able to enjoy the fascination itself. It was as though watching me unravel the mysteries of those tiny machines was as fulfilling for her as the actual process was for me. The more excited I got about some new turn of discovery, the more excited she was for me. In an odd way, we loved each other's obsessions.

"We were both a bit naïve. It never occurred to either of us that there was a pattern in the fact that each of the companies I worked for would come to grief just as we were about to score a breakthrough. With NanoStar, I thought we had finally gotten ahead of the catastrophe curve and were about to see it all come together. Clearly, someone else saw the same thing with rather less enthusiasm for it and . . . and they killed her. They killed her because my bound-less, burning desire to know was a threat they held as intolerable."

Grant bit out those last words, and Ordwyn had a fresh experience of why she had envied his bond with Ellen.

"I guess Miles' tale . . . his history . . . hit a bit closer to home than I realized."

He tore his eyes away from the scene on the walls and looked into Ordwyn's. "I will almost literally lose my life. That will include any connection to the woman I dearly loved and the few colleagues who wanted to know almost as fiercely as I did. But if Miles is successful, I will become someone else and that someone else will work on nanotechnology again.

"It will be enough. I can make it enough. I know that now.

"But, what about you? From everything you have said, being a police officer has been your life, just as pursuing nanotechnology has been mine. How could you possibly continue that life after . . . this?"

Ordwyn looked down at her lap, sighed and then lifted her gaze back up to the view of the cliffs and the sea. "My mom died when I was five. She went out to the grocery store for milk one afternoon and died instantly in a head-on car crash. The other driver was drunk in the middle of the day and survived without a scratch. No reason for it . . . no point to her death. She was simply in the wrong place at the wrong time.

"Dad, my dad, was first, last and foremost a cop. My earliest memory of him was in his uniform and smelling of linen, leather and gun oil. Somehow he was always bigger than life. Not so surprising for a little girl whose world revolved around waiting for him to come home and be that bit of family she had left."

She turned to look at Grant. "As I got older and met some of his friends—they were all cops of course—I heard some of their stories about him. I realized why they all looked up to him, and my love for him grew to a whole new level of respect beyond anything

I had ever imagined. After Mom died, I think he wanted to make up for what had happened to her somehow. He, very intentionally it seemed, became a real-life hero. And I waited in fear and pride for him to come home each night.

"Of course, there finally came a night when he didn't come home. That was the night he took a call about a 'domestic disturbance.' He and his partner could hear screaming as they ran up the stairs to the apartment. The door was open and they heard the shots before they could get to it. A howling man was pumping bullets into a woman lying on the floor, and a little girl was running from the other room toward her mother's body.

"According to the report, Dad didn't even slow down. He ran to the little girl and scooped her up in his arms just as her drug-crazed father started to shoot at them. The only two people to walk out of that room were Dad's partner and the little girl.

"I'd just turned eighteen and was trying to figure out what was next for me. My dad's last act in life pointed me to the police academy, and I never looked back. Even with all the stupidity, bureaucracy and, yes, even outright corruption, I knew who I was and that what I was doing counted for something more than just drawing a paycheck. I already knew half the department, and they became my friends and family as I set out to be as good a cop as my old man had been.

"I made the job my life. And I think it's important to understand that I chose my life's work almost as much because of what happened to my mother as I did because of my father. You see, she died because she was in the wrong place at the wrong time. He died because he was in absolutely the right place at the right time. Yes, it cost me my dad and him his life. But I can't think of a better way to die.

"And now it's come to this.

"I always expected that, someday, I'd die protecting somebody. Not that I'm suicidal or anything like that. It's just the law of averages. If you put yourself in those kinds of situations enough times, eventually your luck runs out. The part that I never imagined in my wildest dreams was that I'd get myself killed trying to save someone . . . and still be alive afterwards."

She turned and gestured around the room. "But here I am.

"So . . . I guess that, for the first time in a long time, I'm going to have to figure out what's next. That's just a little frightening . . . and I'm not used to being frightened."

She looked back at Grant again. "May I ask you a tough question?"

"Go ahead."

"Are you going to be able to give up your mission of vengeance for your wife's murder?"

Grant had been watching her as she spoke and

just looked into her eyes for a moment. She could not look away from the anguish in his. It was he who finally turned away. "I've struggled with it . . . a lot. But Miles is right. Much as I would dearly love to sit in a courtroom and see those people convicted for what they did to Ellen, it's not going to happen. I have to deal with that every day. I have to take my anger at her loss and put that energy into my work.

"What I can do—what I *must* survive to do—is develop nanotechnology. Given the lengths they've gone to in order to suppress it, it's a good bet that my success will hurt them more than the courts are capable of."

By mutual, unspoken consent, they turned back to the view of the spray exploding on the base of the cliffs. Another opportunity to just be in a beautiful setting was going to be hard to come by, and this bit of solace might well have to last them for a good long while.

―――――――

The view out over the park was lovely this time of year.

Carver often walked its paths and felt renewed by the feeling of life all around him. But a walk in the park next to his office was not on his agenda today. He pulled his attention back from the window to his monitor and noticed that Baker was beginning to list cross-references between police and Consortium activities. Tracking both organizations' overt and covert efforts to find Summers and Thornton was indeed proving useful. Another indicator of convergence appeared on the list with a prompt flag from Baker. He realized it was time to go back down to the Room and talk to Sam.

He nodded to his assistant as he left his office. "Marion, it's getting late in the day and there is nothing that requires your presence here. Go on home and try to beat at least some of the traffic."

Marion Jenkins had joined the Group while Carver was still in high school. In many ways the Group had become a surrogate for the family she had never created for herself. She didn't try very hard to resist her maternal instincts when they pointed their attention at Carver. So she called after him. "The traffic is already at a standstill and, Charles, you haven't been home for the last two days. Please try to get some real sleep tonight. I know this Thornton business has you running on adrenalin and caffeine, but you are going to land hard when you finally have to deal with the deficit that creates in your body."

Carver stopped, turned to smile at her and admitted, "Yes, I will have to get some decent sleep tonight. I've a feeling that this whole situation is going into high gear soon, and I will have to be ready for whatever it brings.

"I know I seldom express it, Marion, but I do

appreciate your concern. Thank you for everything you have done for me, for all of us."

He then left to find out what had prompted Sam Baker to request his direct attention. The stiffness in his legs as he descended the stairs told him more eloquently than his assistant's reminder that he needed some downtime. Soon he would have to make some very rapid high-impact decisions, so his mental acuity had better be sharp and ready for the challenge.

Baker looked up as Carver entered the Room. "I saw your flag. What's up?"

Sam typed a command on one of his keyboards which brought up a text display on one of the giant monitors that faced the meeting area. A video box in the upper right corner displayed a young woman's face frozen in an expression of avid interest. "Charles, how closely have you been following the text feed that I am sending to your desk system?"

"Closely enough . . . I can see you are beginning to draw some interesting conclusions from our monitoring of the Consortium and police activities." Carver looked up at the wall display. "Who is Captain Thomas Grayson?"

"Grayson is the commander of Summers' precinct. He is also the tactical coordinator for major operations involving all the precincts that border his and several others besides. Within the force, only the police chief commands more raw power and resources. If the police force were an army, he'd be the next closest thing to a battalion commander.

"The Consortium's comm channels have been carrying far more traffic than we have ever seen before. The heavy use is pointing up some interesting nodes in their system. Most interesting of all is the message flow to and from Grayson. As near as I can tell, he is running two cell phones and a scrambled radio link tied to the Consortium, plus his police command from a third phone. Our captain has been a very busy man."

Carver's eyes narrowed. "So, Grayson is both a major player in the department and on the Consortium's payroll . . . How fortunate for them that the attack on Thornton fell under his purview."

"Charles, I doubt seriously that fortune had anything to do with it. I'd bet that the attack on Thornton and his wife was intentionally staged in Grayson's precinct so the Consortium could keep careful tabs on any success the detectives had in solving the case."

"Have you any idea how many of the officers under him Grayson has suborned?"

"Quite a few, judging from the action orders I've seen flowing through him and out to police units. I'd say he has at least half a dozen detectives, maybe ten beat cops, several of the office staff and a couple of crime lab techs in his pocket . . . and that's just in his own precinct."

"And he can command the activity of the precinct staff that he has not corrupted by virtue of the fact that he actually is their appointed commander. Do you see any comparable high-ranking police officers in the other precincts who have become Consortium agents?"

Baker turned back to one of this desk monitors and brought up another set of text lists. "I have my suspicions about a couple of watch captains but, with Grayson in close command, it's hard to be certain about them."

"Looks like it would be reasonable to say that anything we wanted the Consortium to know and implicitly believe should be leaked to Captain Grayson."

Baker turned back to Carver with a smile that wasn't amusement. "My thoughts exactly . . ."

Carver motioned to the wall display, "Who is the woman in the video?"

"That is Ms. Ariel Claymore, an up-and-coming field reporter for Channel 12. She was assigned to the Thornton murder story when it broke and seems to think that there is a great deal more to it than anyone has seen so far. She is particularly intrigued with an anonymous source who dropped her a hint about Thornton's near miss at the restaurant. She was also the reporter who did the follow-up piece on Ferris' increase to the reward."

"I gather that she is going to be your agent

provocateur to Ferris. When is her 'anonymous source' going to call her again?"

Baker gave Carver a wry smile. "No need; watch this." Then he entered another command to start the, up till now, frozen video. Carver watched intently:

The woman in the video quickly approached an imposing man in his 60s who was following an obvious bodyguard out through the front door of a police precinct station and onto the sidewalk. As she approached, the guard attempted to fend her off, but she deftly dodged under his arm and stuck her microphone in the older man's face. Her equally facile cameraman shifted to the right of the bodyguard to capture a waist-high shot of the man and the reporter.

"Mr. Ferris, Ariel Claymore with Channel 12 news. Have you been able to get any more details on your daughter's death from the police?"

Ferris visibly considered pushing her away but, halfway through the gesture his anger got the better of him—his anger at the police not at her.

"No, Miss Claymore, I most assuredly have not! I have had to put up with endless reports of 'no progress,' and today they tell me that my daughter's case is at a dead end and will be placed on an inactive status. They, they . . ." words appeared to fail him, but for only a moment. "They have the unmitigated gall to tell me that they have to devote their resources to cases where they have some leads to work with. They can't continue to put effort into a cold case. A cold case . . . my daughter is a cold case!"

As Ferris stopped to draw a breath, the reporter seized her opportunity to get another question in. "Are you aware that the detective who was working on your daughter's murder hasn't been seen or heard from for two days and that Grant Thornton has been missing for about the same period of time?"

"What . . . missing? Sergeant Summers is missing?"

The reporter moved in closer. "She left this precinct office in the middle of the day two days ago and hasn't been heard from since. She has missed two shifts without a call in or any other contact."

"Do you mean to tell me that the police told *you* this?"

"Mr. Ferris, they questioned me to find out if I knew where she was, but my only connection with her has been the parallel stories of your daughter's murder and the second attempt to kill Grant Thornton just before they both went missing."

"Second attempt? They tried for him again? Do you mean . . ."

At this point three uniformed police officers burst through the precinct door and hustled Mr.

Ferris and his bodyguard back inside. They made a point of leaving the reporter and her camera-man outside.

Baker killed the sound on the video as it showed Claymore turning back to her cameraman and commenting on what had happened.

Carver just stared at the screen for a moment. "Sam, the police asked her what became of their own detective?"

"And the second attempt on Thornton was public record. Though, interestingly, it isn't any more. Claymore was smart enough to verify the attack on Thornton after they came to her about Summers and she put two and two together."

"I saw them haul Ferris back into the station. Is he going to be all right?"

Baker allowed himself an indulgent smile, "One of my sources in the station tells me that Ferris is in there raising all holy hell. Claymore had the tactical awareness to get her video back to her truck and uploaded just in time to make the 5 o'clock news broadcast." He reached forward and typed in another set of commands, causing more video windows to open on the monitor.

"As you can see, the story has made breaking news on four of the other five major channels. Ferris is safe, and even the Consortium can't bury the story at this point."

Carver stared at the monitor without seeing it. "I hope Summers, Thornton, and their benefactor put the text messages together soon. I would really like to have some coordination with them so we can come up with what's next."

"That would help," Baker replied thoughtfully, "I wonder who the hapless cop was who called Claymore?"

Chapter 11

"Trust me, George, that idiot has been taken care of."

Police Captain Thomas Grayson was far more accustomed to calling people on his own personal carpet than he was to being called on someone else's—even over the phone.

"Yes, George. I understand that. We have Summers' and Thornton's pictures and descriptions on every police monitor and patrol car. They've gone to ground somewhere but, sooner or later, they'll have to come up for air, and when they do, we're gonna be ready for 'em."

He still couldn't believe that Jakowski had been stupid enough to call a television reporter about Summers. Some people should be drowned at birth.

"Yeah, Ferris is still here. He's the main reason I had to get rid of Jakowski so fast. There's no tellin' what that nitwit would have told him. While we're on that, what do you want us to do with Ferris?

"You sure? He's going to be makin' all kinds of

noise about how we aren't doin' enough to find out who rubbed out his darlin' daughter. And with this news story all over the air, he can stir up a lot of other people as well.

"All right, all right, hands off Ferris. I got it. I'll put out a statement about the case that doesn't say anything, and do something to put a stopper in everybody else's yap.

"Don't worry, I'll make sure you're notified with whatever we turn up. But I gotta tell ya, since you guys hit that warehouse, I have seen exactly nuthin' on either of 'em, and I own enough eyes and ears in this town to make that downright creepy.

"Yeah, right." Grayson punched the disconnect on the phone, looked at the device for a moment and almost threw it across the room. He realized that his shoulders were tightened up almost to his ears and consciously relaxed them a notch. The Consortium rewarded him very well for his "assistance." For the most part, it was easy money. But this whole Thornton thing was like trying to stamp out a forest fire in his bare feet.

Between Summers not knowing when to stop, even after being pointedly told to, and Thornton drawing every kind of heat imaginable, this whole situation was making him sorry he hadn't retired last year when his eligibility came up. Now that he had a nice, dark, and very deep hole for Jakowski, he would have to try to keep Ferris from calling in the FBI, CIA and every other three-letter mob of problem children he could think of.

Carver leaned back in his chair and stretched. It was past time for him to stop for the day, and his body and mind were both vigorously informing him of that fact. But he decided to make one last trip down to the Room to find out if anything at all had come back from their efforts to contact Summers and Thornton.

As he cycled through the access process, he was moderately surprised to see Lori Dathan sitting in the chair where he expected Sam Baker. "Good evening, Lori. I take it that you and Sam are mounting alternating watches?"

She turned toward him, revealing the sharply chiseled features that had been handed down through generations of people whose ancestors had crossed the Bering land bridge. Set against her stark face, Lori's smile somehow looked out of place to Carver. "With the hornet's nest of interest that Ferris has stirred up, we thought it best that someone watch the monitors through the night. It is unlikely that either Summers or Thornton will be flushed out of hiding by it, but he has definitely put a burr under the Consortium's saddle. We are gathering more useful information right now than we have collected in years."

"I know. I've been watching Sam's feed to my system. And while monitoring the Consortium/police interactions still doesn't seem to be getting us any closer to Thornton, it does definitely point up where quite a number of our efforts have been blocked by their connivance." Carver studied her face closely. "What is your take on where to go from here?"

Analytic thought erased her smile. "I have some thoughts about tactics we can employ in the future to avoid the problem presented by the Consortium's hand in the police department's cookie jar. Unfortunately, they don't help much now. Sam and I are working up a cross-connection list on all the Consortium links and controls in the department that will allow us to interpret what we learn more accurately—and know very quickly when action orders have been sent out."

"And . . ." she began, then stopped. The inner battle she was fighting with herself was obvious. When she started again, she stopped pretending that the high-frequency tension flowing between her mind and body wasn't there. "And I feel like we are getting ready for a battle. I know that we are going to do all we can to avoid it, but I can't help feeling that this one is going to fall over into an outright war. And, Charles, the Group was never intended, equipped or set up to fight a war."

"I feel it, too. As much as we have put careful restraints in place, it would only take a single misstep in the field or one misinformed decision from the board for us to find ourselves in the kind of conflict that none of us wants."

She stared into her monitor screen, as if she could force it to reveal some answer she hadn't seen yet. "You know, I got into intelligence because I wanted to make sure that there was always enough information in hand for us to make good decisions; to avoid accidents that would have terrible price tags. And now, this whole situation with Thornton and Summers has me spooked. The Consortium agents are running around jumping on whatever they find. Often enough, what they find is each other. But what happens when—if—they encounter one of our field teams and, for no particular reason, decide we know something we shouldn't."

She looked back at him. "I am deeply worried by what I am seeing, Charles. It is looking more and more like we are confronting a pack of rabid wolves with not much more than our good intentions."

"What you and Sam are doing is providing our best hope of staying out of trouble and, so far, you are succeeding. Believe me when I say that you have the gratitude of the entire board."

"Thank you. That means a lot."

"One last question?"

Dathan smiled tiredly. "No, we haven't seen any response to the text messages yet."

Charles Carver nodded, smiled thinly at her, and rose to leave. "You have my contact information and you know what to do with it."

———————

Jakowski didn't know whether to be more scared, angry or relieved.

He knew he should be scared at being sent off to do research in the cold case files. For a detective, that was like being sent home from school with a note from the principal. And it could turn into a career killer if he was stuck on this detail for any real length of time.

He felt a little ashamed over his relief at being out of Grayson's line of sight. That man was fast becoming the worst nightmare of every cop in the precinct. He could have done a lot worse than send Jakowski down into the records warehouse, and some of those possibilities didn't bear thinking about.

But, mostly, Jakowski was just plain mad. His partner had disappeared! He knew she had left the station that afternoon to dig into the Thornton case some more, even though Grayson had ordered her not to. Jakowski himself had all but begged her not to do it.

But this was Summers! Now, she was just plain gone. Thornton was gone. And here he sat surrounded by moldy boxes of moldy papers that didn't mean anything to anybody any more. He should be out there lookin' for her. Instead he was sittin' on his butt trying to find the case file on Ralph Frazakia's murder from 22 years ago.

He angrily shoved the box off the table, causing the files to spill out onto the floor. With a strangled sigh, Jakowski stooped over to pick them up when the file on top of the tangled heap caught his eye. He had found the Frazakia case. Standing up with a groan, he put the file on the table and then went back to gathering up the rest and putting them back in their carton.

As he stood with the last file in his hand, he looked down the aisle between the shelves at the clock on the far wall. It was time to go home and then some. He put the file carton back on its shelf. Then he walked back out to the clerk's desk with the case folder he had been sent to find. The clerk was already gone, so he put the file in an inter-departmental envelope and wrote down the name of the officer who had made the request.

The envelope went in the out box; Jakowski locked up and left the warehouse.

He had to hike through the length of the precinct to get to the door that opened onto the parking lot. That meant walking past Summers' desk. He looked at it as he walked past even though he didn't want to . . . and then stopped to stare.

Summers didn't go in for decorating her desk with personal stuff. She had a picture of her father in his uniform getting a decoration for somethin' or other; an odd-looking desk lamp that she said was a "memento," whatever that meant; and a fancy pen and pencil holder set with "Sergeant Ordwyn Summers" engraved on it.

Now her in and out boxes, which were always full, were both empty. The card on her phone that listed the station extensions, and was at least two years out of date, was also gone. But worst of all, what little personal stuff she'd had on her desk was gone, too!

Somebody had decided that Sergeant Summers was not coming back. And that same somebody had gathered up and erased any evidence that she had ever been in the precinct. This was clearly both a statement and a warning.

He knew she was politically tone deaf. Some part of him knew she did that on purpose, because being a good cop was more important to her than anything. She had pushed him, prodded him and ragged on him . . . and had made him a better cop than he would ever have made of himself. She had also made more than her share of enemies in high places along the way.

At some point, everyone comes to a decision that changes his or her life forever. And for Fred Jakowski, this was it. Because this was just exactly the wrong thing to do to his partner.

He didn't know what he was going to do or how he was going to do it. A corner of his mind screamed at him that he had lost his mind. But as much as it scared him down to his core, he knew that he could not stand aside and let Ordwyn Summers be swatted and removed like an annoying bug.

———————

"OK, Miles, where have you disappeared to this time?"

Ordwyn looked around the entry room, feeling vaguely foolish, as though she were trying to summon a ghost. She finally turned to Grant. "You know, I really hate it when he does this."

"When I do what?"

They both jumped and turned to find Miles standing right behind them.

Ordwyn restrained herself with a will. "When you sneak up and scare the daylights out of both of us. That's what."

"I have no need to 'sneak up' on you. My mechanism simply does not make unnecessary noise as I move. As to being frightened by the unexpected, I strongly suggest that you both practice getting used to being surprised, and dealing with it quickly and efficiently. Much of what is about to happen to you is going to be beyond any of your expectations or preconceptions, so you need to become practiced experts at situational awareness."

Grant was surprised to feel Miles' mood actually soften, however slightly. "Have you both come to terms with the absolute loss of your previous identities?"

After exchanging a long glance with Ordwyn, Grant responded, "In as much as we can come to terms with dying in all but the final reality, yes, I suppose we have." Ordwyn looked away as he finished the statement.

"Ms. Summers . . . Ordwyn, I gather that Grant has been somewhat more successful in this undertaking than you have?"

She met Miles' deep-into-her-soul gaze with one of her own. "Grant has his work to continue even after he has become someone else. I don't see any possibility of ever being a cop again, and that's who I've always been."

"I see. Grant has at least a portion of his identity to go back to, but you feel that you do not."

Ordwyn looked away again, then took a moment to walk to a couch and sit down. "I simply don't know what to do with my life now. Healthy or not, I have always identified myself as a cop and as nothing else. While that made me a really good cop, it left me without any identity outside of that life. I understand—at least technically—that I have to 'die' in order to survive and elude this Consortium's pursuit . . . but then what?"

Miles sat down in a chair opposite her. "There are

many who would give everything they possessed for the opportunity to reinvent themselves with nothing remaining from their previous lives. You may want to look upon this as an opportunity rather than a disaster. Tell me, what attracted you to police work and then provided years of satisfaction for you while you did it?"

Grant felt torn between wanting to comfort Ordwyn and realizing that this was a situation where he needed to step back and let her confront it on her own terms. He listened from a distance.

After a thoughtful moment, Ordwyn responded, "I guess that between growing up without a mother and the loss of my father when I was a teenager, I did what I could to create a sense of continuity in my life to replace what I'd lost.

"Being a cop was a good fit. For me, it was about trying to restore some sort of balance after something bad happened to someone who'd done nothing to deserve it. Catching bad guys meant that they couldn't turn anyone else's life upside down."

"So Ordwyn, you devoted your life to fending off the intrusion of unexpected disaster into the lives of others?"

After another moment of turning the idea over in her mind, she responded, "I never thought of it like that before but, yes, that sounds about right. I might not have been able to prevent the first crime, but I could make sure that others were stopped before they started."

"May I suggest that you consider that perception of yourself and see where you may have opportunities to put it back into use?"

Ordwyn gave him a small smile and said, "Thanks Miles, I'll do that."

Miles' moment of compassion faded as quickly as it had appeared. "In the meantime, we need to get on with staging your death because the sooner it happens, the more credible it will be. I will need a considerable array of tissue and body fluid samples to begin the necessary biological processes.

"And one other thing, do you know anyone named Tim Woodsman?"

Ordwyn, surprised by the sudden change in direction, thought for a moment. "No . . . not that I can recall."

Miles tried one more time. "Could he possibly be involved with one of your cases? Think about this carefully."

"Miles, in my . . . old job I had to have a very good memory for names and this one just clunks. I don't have any memory of anyone by that name."

Miles turned to Grant. "Do you know anyone named Buck King?"

Now it was Grant's turn to be stumped. "Miles, that name rings no bells at all. I knew a Ralph King once, but he died ten years ago. What's all this about?"

"Someone has tried to contact us through your cell

phone accounts. Two different text messages were left, one on each phone number, that are trivial when taken separately but are a request for communication when merged into a common thread. Since you don't know either of the names on the accounts that sent them, I will investigate this more closely. It may be a trap set by the Consortium, or it could be an effort by the Forester Group to make contact.

"Grant, in case it is the latter, I need a project plan complete with material and human resource requirements for you to continue your work in nanotechnology."

"OK, I still have the project plans I worked up for NanoStar. But Miles, won't another attempt to pursue them attract the same unwanted attention we're taking such extreme measures to avoid?"

"Pursued directly and openly, indeed it would. I need those plans broken up into discrete, isolated engineering efforts that individually have only the most casual relationship to nanotechnology but together provide you with the support you need to complete your work. You were within six months of being ready to implement your first production facility when your work was interrupted. I suggest that you insert enough unrelated work into the subsidiary segments of your project to camouflage its real intent without excessively diverting the effort from its intended goal."

Grant managed a crooked smile. "I like it, Miles . . .

a stealthy research project. It would need to be split up among a much larger staff and communications would be a challenge but . . ."

Miles and Ordwyn could both see Grant's mental gears starting to mesh and spin up to speed. "I have equipped the room next to yours with a workstation similar to the one in the warehouse. I suggest that you begin adapting your plans on it while I get started with the ex-sergeant."

Ordwyn stood while she and Grant looked at each other for a long moment. "Well, I guess this is the first day of the rest of our lives. A clichéd observation, granted, but an accurate one." She touched his cheek, sending a sort of warm shiver down his body. "I guess we'd both better get started." The moment passed, and she turned to Miles. "What do I need to do?"

"I have an extensive lab on a lower floor. We have some hours of work ahead of us to draw enough samples to get the systems started on their various analyses."

Miles walked Ordwyn to one of the doors off the entry room that they hadn't used yet. At its threshold, she turned to look at Grant, who still stood in the middle of the room watching her. Grant raised one hand, looked at it and then at her. "I almost have the feeling I should say good-bye to you, Ordwyn. And I am surprised at how very much I don't want to do that."

She tipped her head to one side to let that in, smiled, then turned to follow Miles.

Lori Dathan really didn't want to call Charles Carver this early in the morning.

Aside and apart from disturbing sleep that she knew he desperately needed, she wasn't certain that what she had found really meant anything. On the other hand, it could mean everything.

One more pass through the parsing algorithm got the same thing. Only this time it showed 80 percent certainty, a 15 percent increase. She took a deep breath and reached for the encrypted phone.

His system rang four times, each ring giving Lori's misgivings a boost. When Carver answered, it was clearly after being roused from a deep sleep. It took him two tries to get his mouth to obey his brain. "Lori, what have you found?"

"Charles, I deeply apologize for waking you at this hour but I have discovered something you should know about. At least, I genuinely hope so. I think we may have a communication."

"I'll be there in half an hour."

An old proverb says that time waits for no man. Charles had learned long ago that he would be disturbed at odd hours with newly discovered pieces to the various human puzzles he worked on, and that those pieces would typically require immediate action. For that very reason, he had chosen to live only a block away from the Group's offices.

After a suspected assassination attempt that actually turned out to be a failed mugging, a tunnel had been constructed between his residence and the office building. Now all the higher-ranking Group personnel in this city lived in Charles' apartment complex where they were a short, secure and virtually undetectable walk away from its facilities.

The tunnel ended in a security room that was manned 24/7. The door out of that room opened directly onto the same level as the Room. All of which meant that Charles was seated next to Lori in only 23 minutes.

"What have you got?"

Lori swung around to her console and brought up a signal analysis display. "As you know, we receive direct feeds from the major news networks. You may not know that we also monitor their broadcast signals as well. We do as much cross-checking of our information sources as possible. What caught my attention is this sub-carrier signal."

She separated the video signal from one of the feeds and displayed it as a radio frequency carrier wave rather than its information content. It was peppered with irregular bursts of what appeared to be very low level noise. "When I compare this with the broadcast signal, the noise bursts are not there. They are only present on the feed that goes specifically to us.

"Individually, the bursts are just that, noise. Combined into one time-synchronized signal, they contain instructions to transmit a signal impressed on three specific broadcast channels using the same sub-carrier signal-blending technique that got this message to us in the first place.

"The kicker is that the message is signed—by Tim and Buck."

Carver closed his eyes for a moment and then focused on Lori with all his intensity. "Do you have any indication that this might be a ruse by the Consortium or that they may have intercepted the signal?"

"I don't see how they could intercept this feed without us knowing about it. It's possible but highly unlikely. I don't see any point in their sending this communication to us, as they could set a trap for one of our teams much more easily than this.

"If this is real, it could be just the beginning of a series of convoluted paths for two-way communications that would be specifically aimed at us from Thornton's mysterious benefactor."

"Lori, call a meeting of the board for . . ." Carver looked at his watch, "two hours from now. Don't tell them anything more than you told me over the phone. We will discuss this only over the secure network. And call Sam Baker now. I want his input on this immediately."

Precisely two hours later Charles, Lori, and Sam sat facing the Forester Group's directors on the monitor array in the Room. Charles stood as he addressed them.

"You have all received the communication and the description of the method by which it was sent. Lori and Sam performed independent analyses of it and came to identical conclusions. Between exacting analysis and meticulous monitoring of the Consortium's communications, we can find no evidence whatsoever of either their detection or their origination of this message. The three of us believe it to be genuine. Do any of you see it otherwise?"

Silence reigned for a moment as the six directors studied their monitors to review the message and its accompanying analysis.

A woman next to Mr. Drake with a face as dark as her immaculate suit, looked up first. "Lori, are you confident that the security of the direct feeds has not been compromised?"

"As confident as we can be, Marcella. The taps are not physical, and they are moved and scrambled every ten minutes. It would not be impossible to breach them, but it would require a huge effort and would not be a certain success even then."

Carver let his eyes traverse the group. "Are we in

agreement that, until evidence appears to persuade us otherwise, we will act as though this communication is a sincere effort from Thornton's group?"

Affirmative indicators illuminated on all but one of the screens.

"Amy, you have an issue?"

"Only that we continue to do our utmost to verify that the Consortium is in no way involved with these messages. I have been watching Sam's situation monitors carefully. Its agents are getting reckless in their efforts to find Thornton. A misstep at this point could be disastrous for all of us."

"I think we all share your concern. Sam is double-checking every operational move we make against the Consortium's activities to steer us out of confrontations or even encounters before they can happen.

"That said, I'd be lying to all of you if I said that this is without risk. The prize to be gained in releasing nanotechnology to the world is worth both risk and caution. We shall be deeply engaged in both."

Amy's indicator changed to affirmative. Carver nodded and continued.

"As stressful as it has been, the Consortium's obsessive distraction with finding Thornton has opened a temporary window of opportunity to pursue a project I outlined last month. Lori and Sam have been tracking and carefully establishing contact with other technical specialists who have been involved in nanotechnology efforts that were defeated by the Consortium. These are the scientists and technicians who worked on test and proof-of-concept projects. Some of those tests were even initiated by our Mr. Thornton.

"Regardless of how the search for him turns out, we need to create a place where these researchers can work in safety and out of sight. While they are unlikely to create any kind of breakthrough without the likes of Thornton or his two main co-workers, we may find others to inspire their efforts. And there is always the possibility that we will need them to support Thornton's work once again."

"Charles, I think we all understand that, even without Thornton, we need to put a clandestine nano-technology research group together in order to keep that technology from disappearing altogether. They can be seeded among other research groups and will appear to be working on some other technology. The true direction of their efforts should be protected by a compartmental communication process that obscures their work on nanotechnology. We have all read your plan, and I believe that we all agree with it."

"Thank you, Mr. Drake. Is that agreement unanimous?" All of the affirmative indicators illuminated.

"Therefore, as of this meeting, our plan is to cautiously pursue the communication channel with Thornton and create a clandestine nanotechnology research support capability. Sam, Lori, and I will keep you advised on our progress on both fronts."

One by one the video displays went back to data presentations. Charles turned to Lori and Sam. "Amy is right; caution has to be our watchword, even more than it already has been. If the Consortium gets wind of any of this, they will stop at nothing to destroy what we are trying to achieve—and us with it.

"We have a full day ahead of us, people. Let's get to it."

STRIKE PLAN

"George, to say that this matter has gone poorly would be to insult the concept of understatement. What have you found out since the general meeting?"

Being in front of the entire group of these men was like being scrutinized under a microscope. You either looked very good or very bad. There wasn't much space in between. Being in front of just the five members of its executive group, as he was at this moment, felt to George like being on trial for his life . . . which was probably not far off the mark.

Given that, George thought he'd better put out the best first. "I put my operatives out all over the city. We are on top of every bit of communications messaging going anywhere to anybody. Just as soon as anybody sees or hears anything, I'm going to know about it. Thornton's hidin' out somewhere, and that means there just hasn't been anything to report. He's got to show himself sooner or later and, when he does, we'll be right on top of him."

"Yes, George, we are well aware of your team's activities. Thus far there have been no less than seven separate instances of their tripping over each other with enough repercussions that we have had to actively suppress media coverage of their antics.

"That is expensive.

"Its cost in funds is significant, but the greater price is against our ability to keep doing it. We cannot squelch an infinite number of these events, and the occurrence of each takes us one step closer to the one that will make the 11 o'clock news in all its insipid glory."

George fought to keep from bowing his head and looking at his lap. Showing any sign of weakness now could well be fatal. He stood. "We've got the police working on the missing cop, Summers. She's got to be wherever Thornton is, so when they find her, we find him. There's a cutout in place, so if anything goes wrong on that front, we aren't connected to it."

"We are also well aware of Captain Grayson. We are aware, for instance, of his difficulties with a certain William Ferris, who has created more media fallout than even we could divert. We are aware of the dissension that the good captain's tactics have caused within his own department's ranks and the increasing attention that state of affairs is drawing from his superiors.

"What we haven't heard about is anything concerning the Forester Group."

Once again George kept his eyes up with an effort of will. "They've been very quiet about Thornton—especially after he called them to set up a meeting and didn't show. We know they've been watching us, but it's like they are going out of their way to stay out of ours. As near as I can tell, they're sittin' on their hands and waitin' to see what happens."

"Doesn't that strike you as just a bit odd?"

George was beginning to see where this was going. "Odd, how?"

"The one man who could damage our interests more than any other on the planet asks to meet with them and vanishes. That request for a face-to-face dialogue must have shocked them even more than it did us. And then the subject of this intense set of conflicting interests starts running and finally just disappears . . . right after that phone call. Doesn't that strike you as just a bit too coincidental?"

George struggled to take this in. "You think the Forester Group knows where Thornton is?"

"Their apparent lack of activity and careful watch on your teams certainly seems to point in that direction. In any event, we haven't done anything to shake them up and see what falls out, now have we?"

George scratched his head then the implications of his gesture dawned on him. "So how did they manage to stage those phony credit card trails and dodge my entire team while trucking Thornton around the city? The Group just doesn't have that kind of capability.

"Besides, the Forester Group has been off limits for decades. Ever since we killed their nuclear development tech group, everyone has had standing orders to stay away from them to avoid the publicity and to keep from pointing out our main interests to them. I was told in my early days to stay clear of them so they wouldn't turn into more of a problem than they already are."

The voice from the head of the table sounded like glaciers grinding together. "That was then, George, this is now."

"So now you want to go after them? I'd be a whole lot more worried about whoever sent my people on a string of wild goose chases. Compared with Carver's crew, they've got a lot more ability to cause problems for us and, so far, we don't even know who they are."

"In case the point of all this is lost on you, George, let us be perfectly clear: The matter of Grant Thornton has to be concluded as rapidly as possible. You have told us that you are doing everything short of directly going after the Forester Group and have no leads whatsoever on this supposed third party. There is no solid evidence that there is anyone else involved. Moreover, the Group's technical abilities have surprised us often enough in the past.

"Our directive concerning actions against the

Forester Group largely concerns day-to-day operations. It is not absolute. The last time they got too
far out of hand, we killed an entire tech team. This
included Carver's father, I might add.

"We did this to stop a line of inquiry in its tracks
that was much less threatening than this one. Simply put, your efforts to date haven't produced the
necessary results. So, perhaps knocking the Forester
Group around a bit will.

"Our time—and most pointedly yours—is running
out."

Chapter 12

Ordwyn had never imagined how many different measurable aspects there were to the human body—or how much the sampling of some of them could hurt. While not quite as exhausted as she was when she arrived (Was it only two days ago?), she had definitely gone down for the count after Miles' test and sample collection work wore into the night.

Waking up in what she had begun to think of as her "hotel room" was still a strange experience. Once again, she was surprised to look at her watch and discover that she had slept till nearly noon. Being buried inside a mountain was not a way to prompt accuracy from one's internal clock.

One benefit of last night was that Miles had given her a short lesson on the wonders of his kitchen. He had also stood by while she had made a meal using some of the most amazing technology she had ever seen. Right now, a quick shower and breakfast sounded like a really good plan.

Miles' taste in women's clothing left something to be desired, but he had laid in a supply of jump-suits, several of which were close fits for Ordwyn's diminutive frame. The tan number would do nicely. Scrubbed and dressed, it was time to refuel.

She looked down the hall and thought about checking on Grant, but the rattle of key tapping told her he was in his element.

"Breakfast! Yes, definitely breakfast!"

The kitchen was more automated than she could have imagined. Food retrieval and preparation were done by making selections from a computer inter-face that now remembered her as one of its users. This made a plate of bacon, eggs and potatoes with hot coffee a matter of touching a screen in the appro-priate places and telling this marvelous machine how she liked her eggs.

She sat down at the dining room table less than 10 minutes later with a morning meal fit for a queen and tucked into it as though she had not eaten for a week.

"Who do I have to kill to get some of that?"

She jumped in spite of herself. "You know, Grant, it's bad enough when Miles does that. Don't you start, too."

"OK, I will write on the blackboard a hundred times, 'I will not sneak. I will not sneak. I will not sneak. I will not sneak.' And I still want some of whatever is mak-ing that wonderful smell."

She smiled up at him and felt a twinge of familiarity. She felt like she was at a home she hadn't known she had. "Give me a minute more here, and I'll induct you into the magical mystery of Miles' kitchen."

Ordwyn showed Grant what she knew of the kitchen computer's interface. Interestingly, it now began to recognize him because she had introduced him to the system. It was comforting to realize that, even in so small a way, Miles was exhibiting some of the faith in her that she had perforce placed in him.

She topped off her own plate, and they returned to the table to enjoy their meal . . . and each other. She looked at Grant over the rim of her coffee cup and asked, "So how is your planning going?"

"More quickly than I had expected. I didn't realize how much thought I had already put into the compartmentalization idea until I actually started writing it all out. By its nature, the work remaining to be done involves a lot of cut and try, to take my principles and derive working formulas from them. That makes for a straightforward process of parceling the work into bite-sized chunks that achieve a quick result and indicate the direction of the next efforts. I think I have even come up with a simple but secure communications method to keep the Consortium out of the loop.

Changing the subject, he asked, "How was your trip through Miles' chamber of body tinkering?"

"Arduous! I think he took a gallon of blood, tissue samples from the damnedest places, and you don't even want to know about the GI tract exam."

He winced. "You're right. That's already too much information."

They ate in silence for a few minutes, until she leaned back in her chair, cradling her coffee. "Grant, do you really think Miles can actually change us so completely that no one will ever be able to tell who we are, or were?"

Grant paused in mid-chew, then swallowed and said, "Given what I have seen here and the things he has done already, I'd be inclined to believe that you and I are in for a truly total makeover. The most powerful aspect of nanotech is that it can work on an atomic level. That means that he can make or modify any molecule he wants and, given an understanding of how DNA functions, that means he can tailor any organism any way he wants—including us."

"So that means that we'll be literally placing our very lives in his hands."

His gaze was as level as it was serious. "I think we already have."

He took a sip of his own coffee. "Have you thought about what you are going to do after you . . . die?" He blushed. "That sounds really weird, but you know what I mean."

She smiled at him with a curious desire to put

him at ease. "Some." She almost giggled. "If I weren't so short, I could be a bodyguard. I already have the skills, just not the stature that would impress any prospective clients. I guess I am mostly just focused on getting through the next few days. It still just kicks my head sideways to think that I am cooperatively working toward my own death. I'm still wrestling with getting out of the identity of Ordwyn Summers the cop and into . . . something, someone else."

Grant nodded. "Yes, I will be working on nanotech for a while yet, but somewhere along the way I have to think about building a new life as someone else. With Ellen's death and some level of completion around my work with nanotech, there isn't much of my old life that I would miss." He looked in her eyes, blushed again, and then took on the most solemn expression she had seen on his face to date. "In one way saying that feels like a betrayal of Ellen and, in another, it feels as right as anything ever has. But the one part of this old life of mine that I will miss is you. I will truly miss you, Ordwyn Summers."

It was her turn to blush, and not so much at what Grant had said as at the warm feeling that it sent from the top of her head to the tips of her toes. To dodge having to respond, she looked toward the door. "I wonder where Miles is?"

The room contained an interface to the most powerful computing capability that the Earth had ever known. Concentric rings of ethereal screens, seemingly fabricated out of the air itself, surrounded a central dais. Miles stood on that dais gesturing at the screens, again like a conductor leading an orchestra. Controls were actuated, functions adjusted, data summoned and emplaced. To a human, it would all have been incomprehensible. To Miles, it was like an intimate conversation with an old friend.

The Forester Group's acknowledgment of his response to their inventive message opened the opportunity to begin coordinating their support of Grant's research. Miles responded with a list of the technicians and engineers who should be recruited, their contact data, and how their work spaces should be equipped. The communication system Grant had proposed to him last night was ingenious, so Miles forwarded it to the Group as well.

The system assembled the data, parsed it, and encoded it for transmission via the almost invisible sub-channel connection Miles had established with the Group. That done, it was time to put the next aspect of getting Grant safely killed into motion.

Miles sent out a series of inquiries via contacts he had established long ago. At that time, they had been smugglers of expensive and desired items, procuring them for those who could afford to pay for them but could not afford to be seen acquiring them. Now they specialized in a different type of commodity: knowledge. More specifically, they sought out those who had expertise that made them unique or nearly so, and either paid or kidnapped them into their service. They still dealt in pricey commodities such as illegal drugs and gemstones, but vessels of knowledge were much more profitable because they were much more difficult to come by.

Ethnically, they were typically Asian, with Chinese comprising their upper ranks almost exclusively. However, it would be much more accurate to simply categorize them as Asian businessmen—very aggressive businessmen. Miles dropped hints, very indirectly, that one Grant Thornton was on the run from the Consortium and that he had valuable knowledge indeed. He knew that they were already aware of Grant and his expertise, but what they didn't know was that Grant desperately wanted to leave the country and would readily make a deal for his knowledge with whomever could ensure his escape from the Consortium.

These Chinese "businessmen" had been contending with the Consortium for talent for quite some time and were willing to do so again, if the price and value were right. In Grant's case, there was a definite demand from their customer base for his area of knowledge, so he would fetch them a very good price indeed.

To put it mildly, Miles had deliberately kicked over an anthill.

He had done so while carefully ensuring that three groups of competing Asians were aware of his manufactured, bogus opportunity—and were aware that each other were aware. They would all investigate, assure themselves that there was money to be made, and begin negotiating to edge each other out of the deal. Competition after all, is the soul of commerce.

Next up was a check on his autonomic monitoring of the Consortium itself. Miles had a considerably better insight into their activities and intentions than the Forester Group did and wanted to be sure that the Group was not blindsided by a development he could warn them about. In particular, he wanted to be sure that the Consortium had not detected their efforts to establish a clandestine network of nanotech researchers and that the communications link he had established remained secure.

There was no indication that any aspect of the research team or communications around it had been compromised. However, there was some odd comm traffic between the Consortium's headquarters and two of its field teams. Miles set his system's formidable decryption capabilities to work on parsing the content of these messages, which yielded a worrying result.

He tapped into the surveillance cameras in and

around the Forester Group's offices and the apartment building maintained for its staff. While the cameras themselves revealed nothing untoward, Miles could see where they had been hacked by a third party that was doing just what he was doing, watching exactly what went on in the apartment complex.

There was only one reason for them to be doing that.

———————

At his assistant Marion's insistence, Carver took a morning nap on the couch in his office to make up for the sleep he had lost to the early-morning emergency call from Lori Dathan. Though he had left instructions to awaken him in one hour, she had fended off all interruptions for nearly three. This news, however, would not wait.

"Mr. Carver . . . Mr. Carver . . ." As Charles slowly opened his eyes and oriented himself to where he was, Marion helped him sit upright on the couch and handed him a cup of coffee. "Here, drink some of this."

He did so, looked at his desk and saw the time. "I thought you were going to wake me in an hour. Since you waited for three, I assume there is something that needs my immediate attention. What?"

"Sam and Lori need to talk to you in the secure room."

"Ah, I should have guessed. I'll be in the Room if you need me." He stood, stretched, and walked stiffly out the office door to the stairs. The five flights down to the Room helped him work out some of the kinks he invariably got from sleeping on that couch.

Dathan and Baker were waiting for him. "Well, the two of you look like you found the chocolate egg at the Easter egg hunt. Can I assume that we have had another communication from Thornton's group?"

They looked at each other, and Dathan jumped in. "I think that we have solid confirmation that we are not being played by the Consortium on this link. We just received a comprehensive list of people, equipment and communications protocols over it. Whoever has taken an interest in Thornton has been watching the nanotech field at least as long as we have and, if anything, more closely. They not only catalogued every piece of relevant equipment along with some sources we hadn't discovered, but they also listed at least a dozen techs and engineers we were unaware of."

Baker picked up where she left off. "The message thread included a protocol for communicating with these people that is ingenious and gives us a channel that will stand up to all but a maximum-effort inter-ception assault. They know what they are doing, and they appear to want nanotech to succeed as much as we do."

Carver looked from one to the other. "I gather that we still don't know whom we are dealing with?"

Their look told him the answer. Baker replied, "They ignored our requests for some identification of who they are and even our questions about Thornton. We don't know that they really have him or, if they do, whether he has been injured. The most we can tell is that they found our dual text message, correctly assembled it, and responded as if they have him and want to cooperate with us."

"Then that's what we go with. It sounds like their information meshes with ours for the clandestine nanotech research project. Let's cautiously and indirectly check out some of the details. If it still looks good, let's go with what they have provided. We already have most of the groundwork in place for this, since it parallels some of our past efforts that we had to shield from the Consortium. The sooner we get these people in place, the sooner they can start producing results."

"Charles, some of them are in place already." Carver and Baker both looked at Dathan and waited for an explanation. "When the Consortium started killing Thornton's colleagues and tried to kill him, we started sheltering the NanoStar staff as they were laid off. Initially we thought they might be in danger as well, and later we began to use them to assist on other projects. We have 35 people in place and ready to go."

"Lori, you never cease to impress me. Compose and encrypt a message back to . . . to . . . well, for lack of a better name, Thornton's group. Tell them that we received and concur with their personnel, equipment and comm suggestions and inform them that we have enough people who can start immediately."

"Hey, Jakowski, it's time for some chow. The new pizza place is open. Let's go give it a try."

The new partner he'd been assigned to set Jakowski's teeth on edge. Every time Jackson opened his mouth, he seemed to be trying way too hard to be Jakowski's best buddy. The guy struck him as a 14-karat, solid-gold phony. He could see why nobody else in the precinct wanted anything to do with him.

Clearly, this guy was another little gift from Grayson.

And, just as clearly, he knew that he wasn't going to be rid of Jackson anytime soon.

"Yeah, sure, why not."

The pizza joint was one block south of the station and Jackson kept talking all through the walk to get there. It wouldn't have been so bad if he'd had something to say. But as near as Jakowski could tell, Jackson hadn't had an original thought since they were introduced this morning, and probably not before that either.

Finally, he stopped talking long enough to order, and eating the pizza slowed him down a bit. Then, for the first time in four hours, he said something that got Jakowski's attention.

"So, Summers was your partner, eh?"

"Yeah, she was. What about it?"

"Any idea what happened to her?"

"No more than anybody else. Why?"

"It's just weird, that's all."

"What is?"

Jackson paused with a slice of pizza halfway to his mouth, looked at Jakowski for a moment, then put it back down on his plate. "I don't understand why we're tearing up the city looking for this Thornton guy, but I don't hear nothin' about Summers, except she's supposed to know about Thornton."

Jakowski thought of half a dozen replies but said, "Noticed that, did ya?"

"It just don't seem right," the younger cop said. "Everybody says she was a pain in the ass, but that don't mean she wasn't a cop. It just don't seem right. That's all."

"Did you ever meet her?"

"Yeah, once. She chewed me out over a scene report. Said there was nothin' in it. But there was nothin' at the scene."

"Yeah, that would be Summers."

"Somethin' else don't add up."

"What?"

"I don't see any action from Internal Affairs over this. These days, every little screw up gets a visit and an hour a questions. So even if they figure she just walked away from the job, there shoulda been somebody from IA askin' questions. But nothin'."

A light dawned for Jakowski that wrinkled his brow. "Now that's somethin' I didn't even think of. Why wasn't I questioned by IA? My partner, a detective sergeant, disappears and nobody from our all-powerful IA department says nothin' to me about it."

"Like I said, weird."

Jakowski's jaw set. "More than just weird, Jackson."

"Whaddaya' mean by that?"

"Nothin'. Let's get back to the station. I need to make a coupla calls."

"Now? We got half our lunch hour left!"

———

"How much longer will you need to complete the research task assignments?"

Grant jumped in his chair. "Miles, Ordwyn is right. You need to wear a bell or something so we know when you're around." Grant swung his chair around to face Miles. "I am just finishing up the first set of experiment plans, but I won't be able to do much more until I see the results they generate. This first effort is to weed out the unpromising directions, so that the rest of our effort is focused where we can get the best results. I've got another ten minutes or so of work to do in order to get that part completed."

"Very well. Please join Ordwyn and me in the dining room when you have completed them." With that Miles exited the room and headed down the hallway in that strange rolling gait that Grant could never quite get comfortable with.

"Ms. Summers . . ." Ordwyn looked up at Miles with a wry expression. "Ordwyn, how are you doing with the plan for your meeting with Mr. Seung?"

"Better. I've studied the plan, and the driving you're asking for will be extremely tricky. How are you going to manage the timing?"

"I have a number of options for either advancing the timing of the contacts or retarding them. I will be watching you continuously, and I will be at the curve to extract you from the scene. It is critical that you put the car in exactly the right location among the trees in order for this to work as quickly as it must."

"I understand. Is the meeting itself going to result in any action, or is that to be confined to the chase?"

"That largely depends on how aggressive the other two groups are. They will not want to injure you, and your apparent death will cause a great deal of dissension between them. I don't expect any violence at the meeting itself, but be prepared. The responses I have seen from these Chinese 'businessmen' so far are not far short of what I would expect from the Consortium itself."

"Which brings up another question: What's the chance of the Consortium getting wind of this and crashing the meeting with one of their teams?"

"Very unlikely, but I have put safeguards in place to divert them, if necessary. If the Consortium does dispatch a team, it will be misdirected so as to put them at the tail end of the chase. To address your concern about the driving skill you will need, I suggest more time in the simulator that you used earlier today. It has been tuned to respond precisely as the actual vehicle will, and the road conditions are simulated accurately as well."

"I'll take you up on that suggestion. Hello, Grant."

Miles turned as Grant handed him a flash drive. "Here is the first round of experiments. This will get us started on the process and get enough test data to point the team in the right directions."

"Then, I will get this compressed and encoded for transmission. I suggest that you get some rest. I will be gathering samples from you next which, as Ordwyn can attest, it is a somewhat grueling process."

"She told me. After working most of the night, I could use a few hours' sleep, so I'll take you up on that. Wake me when you're ready."

Grant headed back down the hall to his room

as Miles turned back to Ordwyn. "The simulator is ready whenever you are. I suggest that—"

At that word, Miles stopped talking and moving.

"Miles? Miles!"

He recovered as suddenly as he had stopped. "As I said, the simulator is ready when you are. I have been alerted by my surveillance systems of an urgent matter that I must attend to immediately. I will be back in two to three hours."

Miles then spun on his feet in a way that Ordwyn wouldn't even try and virtually disappeared through the door to the exterior tunnel.

"Sure, Miles . . . whatever you say."

"Sam, will you be able to finish up on the initial personnel placements?"

"I think so, Charles. Between what we have already done and the information we got from Thornton's group, we are actually going to be ready to start useful work in a couple of days. Why don't you and Lori go home and get some rest? I have the night watch, and I have an odd comm curiosity to check out."

Dathan stretched and turned away from her console. "That sounds just wonderful. I hear a bed calling my name."

Carver's expression became concerned. "Sam,

what did you see on the comm monitoring tracks that caught your attention?"

"Well, it's actually what I didn't see. There are two Consortium field teams that have gone silent. It is probably nothing but, given how careful we are being about staying out of their way, I want to check on them just in case."

"Mmm, let me know immediately if you find anything of concern."

"I will. See you in the morning."

Baker turned back to his console as Dathan and Carver cycled one after the other through the security door and left the Room. "Now," said Sam, "where have you lads gotten off to?"

Dathan and Carver walked down to the entrance of the tunnel and processed through the security checkpoint. They were halfway through the tunnel when he stopped to pat his pockets. "Go on ahead, Lori, I seem to have left my phone in the Room." She smiled, patting his sleeve, and continued through the tunnel.

Carver went back through the access drill at the tunnel checkpoint and again at the door, surprising Baker as he entered the Room. "Charles, that was a quick night, even for you."

"I just forgot my phone. Ah, there it is." Carver reached over to the console table, and picked up and pocketed the errant device. "Sometimes I think my subconscious tries to get me away from it just so I can actually sleep through an entire night.

"Well, good night . . . again." Carver went through the security lock cycle once again. A short walk down the hall brought him to the security checkpoint where he swiped his card and applied his handprint again. "Good evening, James. See you tomorrow."

"Good evening, Mr. Carver."

Carver strode off into the connecting tunnel toward his apartment and stopped suddenly in his tracks as the armored security doors at each end of the tunnel dropped into place imprisoning him inside the most physically secure location in the entire complex.

Miles had arrived in the alley with barely enough time to plug his portable access controller into the Forester Group's main security network. He had to do this on-site after penetrating an armored wall, as they had been very clever in physically isolating that network from any outside connection. His display screen began working through all the internal surveillance cameras in both the office and apartment buildings.

As soon as he spotted Carver alone in the connection tunnel, Miles killed the power to the tunnel, triggering the doors to drop into place. He began to search through the other surveillance areas and noticed that the connection between the apartment cameras and the security stations in the office building had just been severed. He reprogrammed his connection to find the Consortium strike team that he knew had penetrated the facility and isolated the apartments. He switched to the fourth floor of the apartment building, as that was where Carver's residence was located, and found them set to take down the next person who exited the elevator. Miles knew they had seen Carver and his assistant on the checkpoint camera just before they killed the connection, and they had doubtless assumed that they would be the next two people through the elevator doors.

Even Miles' extraordinary reaction time was not enough to stop the elevator doors from opening. Lori Dathan had only a moment to size up what she saw in front of her. In that moment, she made the decision to which a lifetime of dedication had inexorably led her. With incredible reflexes of her own, she reached into her pocket, snatched out her cell phone and pointed it at the masked team whose guns were trained solely on her.

The Consortium had drawn this particular strike team from a group of ex-special operations soldiers. These men had learned the hard way to make their responses to any dangerous situation instinctive, because taking the time to make a decision about what to do would get them killed. Lori's lone presence without Carver and her quick pointing of the phone like a gun was all it took to spook one of the operatives into firing. In the blink of an eye, Lori Dathan lay crumpled on the floor of the elevator with a bullet in her chest.

Miles implanted a clear image of the Consortium team's vehicle with an un-obscured license plate in the external surveillance record. After he watched the team scramble out of the building, he unplugged his controller and resealed the hole he had created in the wall. He then went to the point where the men had exited and carefully planted two sets of fingerprints and a tuft of fiber.

He took only a moment, though an eternity for him, to salute Lori Dathan's sacrifice.

Chapter 13

Carver and Baker sat facing the shock and pain mirrored back to them by the six faces on the monitors.

Mr. Drake's eyes swept from left to right, obviously looking at the screens in his own location. "I first met Lori when she was still two years from her bachelor's degree. She had written a paper, a monograph actually, on speech analysis for managing high-level negotiations. It was brilliant. Her approach was elegantly simple, yet profound in its implications. She wrote it while preparing for the Los Angeles marathon, which she won over all comers three days after turning in the paper.

"After reviewing that paper with her professor, I asked to meet her with an eye to recruiting her for this organization. She joined us a month after her graduation and has been invaluable for her quick assessment of dangerously agitated situations and her clearheaded plans for coping with them. I congratulated myself on her recruitment every time I saw either her or some task she had accomplished with her usual expert touch.

"I was . . . I am so proud of her."

His last sentence hung in the air like a requiem that left each of them contemplating the deep loss they had all suffered.

Carver stood, looked down for a moment and then back up at the screens with steel in his eyes. "Examination of the exterior surveillance recordings revealed the presence of a vehicle nearby that we were able to trace back to a Consortium strike team. It also showed us the point of access that they used where we found fingerprints of a known Consortium agent with a cloth trace that will likely lead back to them as well.

"We found all this after we regained full control of the system.

"The phone clasped in Lori's outstretched hand speaks for itself. She realized that snatching something out of her pocket and pointing it at the strike team would likely surprise one or more of them into firing. In a moment of total clarity under unimaginable stress and surprise, she did the one thing that stopped the Consortium's obvious plot to kidnap one of . . . to kidnap me in its tracks. I have done the only things I can to secure the result that Lori gave her life for.

"I directed that Lori's purse and cell phone be

removed and destroyed. The police investigation last night noted their absence and made a cursory determination that she had been mugged by someone who had penetrated the apartment's security for just that purpose. We turned the footage of the vehicle over to them, and it will doubtless be ignored.

"As deeply as it galls me to let her murder slide like this, it better serves our larger goals to do so. I think it safe to assume that the Consortium will bury this investigation the same way it did the murder of Ellen Thornton.

"Which brings us to the second aspect of what happened last night. Sam?"

Baker stood as well. "I ran a complete systems check and I found where the Consortium penetrated our internal surveillance cameras. They hacked the feed into the long-term storage system. Their monitoring would have been virtually undetectable had they not directly killed the feed from the cameras in the apartment hallway. They obviously expected to snatch Charles and be gone before we could react. I have taken steps to close off the possibility of a recurrence of this kind of system compromise. The 90-second buffer delay for the image recognition parse is the only reason they didn't see that Charles had gone back to retrieve his phone.

"That said, what happened just before Lori was killed, I have no explanation for.

"The building control system, that aspect of our security that controls physical access to all parts of this facility, has been protected from all known electronic penetration and literally armored against physical access to the system itself. And yet, someone broke into that system and killed the power to the security doors on the tunnel between the office and the apartments, causing them to close immediately. They did this just after Charles stepped into the tunnel and seconds before Lori was shot.

"I have no explanation for this, nor can I imagine how it was done. My staff and I have examined this office building from one end to the other, and we cannot find any breach of that system electronic, physical, or otherwise."

Baker and Carver exchanged a look. Carver turned back to the monitors. "What Sam found, or more to the point didn't find, leaves only one possible conclusion. In addition to the raid by the Consortium strike team last night, we were visited by Thornton's group as well. Someone took control of our access system, secured me in the safest part of this facility . . . and probably tried but failed to save Lori. We have no way to confirm that, but I can't think of any aspect of the situation that would deny it, either.

"More than anything else that has happened, this convinces me that Thornton's team is the contact that has begun working with us on the clandestine research capability. That they have stepped up to actively protect our security is both gratifying and humbling. However, we cannot depend on them to catch us each time we stumble, which means even further increased vigilance on our part.

"Last night, two people made split-second decisions that saved my life. I cannot thank one of them, but I would dearly like to know who the other one is."

———————

"So where is Miles?"

Ordwyn looked up from a large data tablet that displayed a multi-path time line. "I haven't got a simple answer. Last night, he stopped mid-sentence and left here like someone had set him on fire. I didn't see him again until I came out this morning and found him in the kitchen about half an hour ago. He didn't respond when I spoke to him. He's obviously doing much more than just making breakfast for us in there, but I have no idea what."

"I have been emplacing additional monitoring and security precautions," Miles said as he entered the room with a large steaming tray.

"I must be getting used to your creeping up on me, Miles. I didn't even flinch that time," Grant said as he turned toward the kitchen door. "My goodness! That looks like enough breakfast for a small army."

"Grant, you will be spending the day in the

physiological sampling and analysis process. Ord-wyn, you will be devoting your every waking hour to perfecting your control of the variables concerning the upcoming meeting and chase. Nutrition will be elemental to the success of both these endeavors."

Ordwyn nodded to him. "Good morning, Miles; it's nice to have you back among us again. After last night and your non-communication this morning, I was beginning to wonder. What was it that fired you out of here like a shot?"

Miles looked at her for the barest moment. "I under-estimated the desperation that we have sown in the Consortium. They attacked the Forester Group last night. I was able to head off their attempt to abduct Charles Carver. I was not able to prevent their killing one of his associates. I will not be taken by surprise in this area again."

"They killed someone else?"

"Yes, Grant, they killed Lori Dathan. And you should know that, in the last moments of her life, she saw what was happening and acted as courageously as anyone could have. She intentionally died in a way that stopped the Consortium's team in its tracks and left them no choice but to exit the location."

Grant looked like a man who had stared into the pits of hell and seen something he didn't like. "Dam-mit, Miles, they have to be stopped. Why can't you just . . ."

"Kill them, Grant? Simply slay enough of them to make their paramilitary forays ineffective? As Ordwyn so acutely observed, I have considerable powers, but I am not an army . . . or a police force. The only way to stop the Consortium is to defeat their objectives. Killing or imprisoning their agents will only result in more of them being recruited, trained and deployed, with the risk of persuading them to unleash even more destructive hostilities.

"The fruition of your work in nanotechnology will cut the ground out from under many of their most profitable enterprises. That in turn will starve their operations for resources and stop them more thoroughly than any direct confrontation ever could."

"As usual, Miles, your logic is unassailable, but I don't like it and probably never will."

Miles nodded. "Likely not." Ordwyn was intently working on her meal. Miles looked pointedly at her. "I suggest you emulate Ordwyn's sterling example, he told Grant. "We have a great deal to accomplish today, and I will need to divide my attention between your separate efforts and my own preparations. I will return shortly."

Miles stood and left them staring at his broad, disappearing back.

Ordwyn and Grant ate in silence, digesting both their food and the previous evening's turn of events. Grant finally looked up at her. "How are your preparations coming? It sounds like you are going to be a cross between a negotiator, an actress and a movie stuntwoman."

"That's a pretty good summation. I have to actively negotiate with the two groups we expect to show up, fend off a third and then lead everyone on a merry chase that appears to, but doesn't really, get me killed. I didn't realize that I'd signed up to perform in a live, street-theater piece."

"Indeed." Grant looked just a bit sheepish. "Ordwyn, would you mind my asking a personal question?"

His request drew an amused look in return. "Depends on how personal."

"I've had some time to think over the last 24 hours and, silly as it sounds, there is one thing about you that just itches my curiosity."

"My name?"

"How'd you know?"

"Sooner or later, everyone I have ever met and spent any time with just has to ask how I came to be named Ordwyn."

"Is it a sore point?"

"No, not really. Now that I'm about to lose the moniker, I find that I'm becoming oddly attached to it.

"It seems that, in every generation in my mother's family, there has been a woman named Ordwyn. Call it the family curse. I have no idea what language or part of the world it originated in, but our family lore says that it means 'loyal carrier of the spear.' It was my mother's name, my grandmother's sister's name and so on, back through the centuries.

"And, after all that, it is going to end with me."

"To me, it seems both sad and fitting somehow," Grant mused. "I was named Grant after a great-uncle who died years before I was born. Again, for simple curiosity's sake, I would have liked to have known him."

"Well, Grant, if we don't pull this off right, we may both get to meet our ancestors."

"Stevens?

"Yeah, it's Jakowski.

"Not much with Grayson breathin' down everybody's neck."

Jakowski looked around the squad room. Most of the detectives were out working cases leaving him virtually alone. Even so, he bent over closer to the phone and lowered his voice. "Ya still workin' IA?"

He made a face at the phone. "No, I'm not reportn' anybody to Internal Affairs. Look, ya heard about Summers, right?

"Yeah, that's the one. Who's handlin' it at your end?

"She's my partner . . . at least, she was. I want to know what happened to her."

Jakowski's eyebrows jerked up to his hairline. "What?

"No, she didn't take no leave of absence! She walked out the door in the middle of the afternoon four days ago and nobody around here's seen her since.

"That's right, she just disappeared and . . ."

"They did, huh?

"I was just gonna ask what ya were doin' tonight. I'm thinkin' we need ta' talk up close an' personal about this."

Grant was just pushing his plate back when Miles returned. "I still have a question that you really haven't answered, and I think this may be the time to ask it. What does my work in nanotechnology accomplish that you can't already do? Your very existence is the culmination of a level of capability that I won't reach in my lifetime. Why are my beginning steps with nanotech so important to you?"

Leaning back from her own plate, Ordwyn asked, "Even with my limited knowledge of what Grant does and how you function, I've been wondering the same thing. What could modern humanity possibly do that you can't exceed dramatically?

Miles looked from one to the other and took on the thousand-year stare that was his most visible change of facial expression. "I explained to you how I came to be what I am, and how I created certain safeguards to prevent a newly captured awareness from destroying itself within its digital prison. My colleagues took the process much further.

"They realized that they would need to limit the scope of the individual's access to control over his swarm of nano-machines lest he simply command them to disassemble his operating chassis. Once simple insanity was walled off as a possibility, it was necessary to prevent a purely physical approach to ending the horrific situation.

"To do this, they built an analytical component into the nano-swarm that evaluates the results of any action it may take in terms of damage or incapacity of the overall system. So, while I can command my swarm to build the computer Grant is so enamored of or make this residence inside a mountain, I cannot command it to simply stop supporting my awareness.

"Put most simply, the only reason I have been active for 34,000 years is that I cannot truly die. I cannot override the programming that keeps my swarm continuously, indefinitely rebuilding me."

"What? You mean you want me to help you die?"

"Yes."

Grant had thought he was beyond shock. He was wrong. What Miles wanted was to destroy, to disassemble, to end the astounding engineering accomplishment and repository of utterly amazing knowledge that he represented. The very idea took away Grant's power of speech.

On the other hand, Ordwyn's self-expression was not inhibited at all. "Miles, that's insane! How could you ask us to help you do such a thing? What you've seen and what you can do border on the miraculous. How could you possibly want to end all that?"

"How?" Miles stretched out his hand onto the table between them. Then, more disturbing than anything else he had yet done, his voice became almost gentle. "Ordwyn, touch my hand."

Ordwyn's indignant anger at Miles' desire to end himself collapsed into a wary concern that he might actually convince her that it was justified. And, in a moment of crystal inner reflection, she realized that she had become deeply attached to the person who lived inside the machine that Miles had become.

"Touch my hand."

"Miles, I . . ."

"Touch my hand."

Concern slid down into dread as she did so.

"What did you feel?"

"I . . . I felt your hand."

"What precisely did you feel? What did your finger-tips encounter? How did what they felt affect you?"

"I felt the smoothness of the . . . the skin on the back of your hand. It was warm and . . . seemed almost electric to my touch. And . . . and . . . dammit Miles, it stirred the part of me that lives in my heart and feelings!" She looked away, unable to speak further.

"Ordwyn, look at me." Her struggle for inner control would not let her do so.

"Ordwyn . . ." She finally looked back at Miles and Grant realized that he was seeing the Ordwyn who had lost everyone who ever mattered to her . . . mother, father, the police force that had become her family.

Her eyes brimmed with tears she refused to shed as she stared defiantly back into Miles' bottomless gaze.

"Let me tell you what I felt.

"I felt a pressure on the back of my right grasping device that had a maximum force of exactly .127 kilogram meters per second squared. The force was spread over an area of .278 square centimeters and that area was reduced in temperature from 38.1 to 36.8 degrees Celsius. The duration of the contact was 3.9 seconds.

"As I—look—at you, I see a topographic image assembled from and annotated with distances, surface temperatures, variations in emissivity, texture, spectral reflections in the visible light band, the infrared band, and several others. I see acceleration vectors that measure the expansion and contraction of your chest as you breathe. I see changes in the density of the blood flowing through the arteries in your neck that tell me your blood pressure and pulse rate. I see precise measures of the radius of the pupils of your eyes. As a matter of my 'normal' perception I perform a noncontact analysis of you that is more thorough than most physicians would perform for a standard medical examination.

"That is how I perceive the world and everything in it. Twenty-four hours a day, every day without any respite, I sift through an array of data streams and assemble the information into mapped representations that allow me to quickly understand and respond to the world around me. Everything is composed of myriad bits of information that I associate and refine into constructs that I can interact with. As you have observed, it gives me a very detailed and precise appreciation of my surroundings, as well as the ability to make carefully controlled changes in them."

Then Miles' voice became almost a whisper.

"But I cannot see you, Ordwyn.

"I cannot feel the texture of your skin. I cannot smell the natural perfume of the pheromones your body emits as your emotions change. I cannot feel the change in your voice when you speak of those whom you care about.

"I cannot stand on a hill and feel the wind blowing over my body, bringing scents and sounds of the life all around me. I cannot wade into the ocean and feel the water begin to lower my body temperature even as it supports me with buoyancy that feels like gravity itself is being defied.

"It all might be tolerable or even 'normal' if this were all I had ever known.

"But I was once human, just like you.

"I ran through forests, feeling the leaves beneath my feet and hearing the buzz of the insects that lived there. I scooped up handfuls of dirt and marveled at the diversity of tiny creatures that lived in it. I smelled the salt on the breeze blowing off the ocean and heard the music of the crickets chirping at night.

"I shared meals with my family and savored the unique tastes and aromas of the various dishes. I embraced my children as I took pride in their development and accomplishments. I made passionate love to my beautiful wife, whom I cherished far more than my own life.

"And now . . . now I exist in this mechanical prison. A prison with no light, no sound, no taste, no touch and no escape.

"After 34,000 years of this mockery of existence, is it so very difficult to understand that I want an end?"

Grant's own eyes blurred over as he took in the magnitude of what Miles was saying to them. "A few minutes ago, I would have bet anything you cared to name that you couldn't change my mind about your desire to die.

"I should know better by now.

"But even so, what I can and will be able to do in nanotechnology still won't accomplish your . . . goal. I doubt that I will ever be able to reprogram nanomachines that are as advanced as yours.

"No, you won't. But your creation of nanotechnology as a widely implemented engineering discipline will open an arena of endeavor that will focus on developing an endless array of capabilities that use it. And someday someone, with perhaps a little assistance, will finally have the design insights, make the discoveries, link the techniques and complete the experiments that will show the way to attain what I want.

"I've waited 34,000 years. I can wait a little longer."

Ordwyn gave up the fight and began to sob.

Chapter 14

"I understand all that."

Grayson leaned forward in his chair as if he could intimidate the phone he held. "What you need to understand is that the harder I push on findin' Thornton, the more of that kind of blowback you're gonna get.

"No, we haven't even gotten a sniff of 'em, and that ain't natural. By now, somebody shoulda seen or heard something and we should have leads to work. But it's like he just vanished into thin air. And that's not possible.

"I'm already spreading my people into areas they normally wouldn't go and stepping on jurisdictions all over the place. I have an officially 'on leave' missing detective who is not officially being looked for. And, to top it all off, I now have a 'mugging' gone bad into a murder to not investigate.

"There are limits to how much creative incompetence I can use here. If this Forester Group was willing to raise a stink over your hit, I couldn't do much to slow down the process, and you'd have to throw somebody under the bus. As it is, they've been pushin' but only on us, and not the media or the politicians. I can deal with that.

"What I need from you is no more street dustups. Your guys have run into each other and into my cops enough times that I'm startin' to get questions from the command about what's goin' on.

"Well, you're tellin' me that they aren't turnin' up anything, either, so what's the point in havin' an army of 'em on the street?

"Yeah—ratchet the goon squads back, so I don't have to keep fishin' their hides out of the sling! And another thing, two of your geniuses decided they could take command of their dustups with my people. That has gotta stop now, or you are going to blow our whole arrangement here.

"Good. Let the dust settle a bit. Then I'll be able to get more done with less kickin' over the traces to slow us down."

Grayson thumbed the cell phone off and looked at it with disdain, then rubbed his eyes. The more he thought about it, the more he thought that he really should have taken that early retirement.

———

Coming up on the next right was a bump in the pavement that had to be addressed just so. Ah! Past that lay an illusory straight that ended in a rise and a dip followed by a sharp left, which required a tap on the brakes and just the right drift before cresting the rise. Then what was essentially a chicane through a scrub forest ended in a long right sweeper followed by a near right angle left. Accelerating out of the left to see the bridge abutment coming up at the end of another left in 4 . . . 3 . . . 2 . . . 1 . . . now! A hard right to swing past the abutment and out into the field, allowing only a moment to straighten out before hitting the pocket in the stand of trees.

"Whew! How'd I do?"

Miles tapped a spot on the holo-display. "The last two exercises were successful. You could slow about four more miles per hour here to give yourself another second or two to line up for the trees but, other than that, you have learned the course."

"I'll make a couple more passes on the simulator to get it just right. What's the status on the meeting?"

"I have selected the group you are ostensibly to meet with and the second group who will show up uninvited. I have set a process in motion to leak the meeting details to the third, but they will have to pay attention to the data they receive. If they show up as well, so much the better. If they don't, they will certainly be present for Grant's meeting."

"Sounds like it could get crowded. Do I need to hold back if someone doesn't want to play nice?"

"I expect you to defend yourself by whatever means are necessary. Just make sure to leave enough of them alive to report back to their superiors. I have prepared a package that you are to leave at the site that will convince them of Grant's value and availability. I suggest spending some time with the photographs and data on the probable attendees from each group."

"I will, and Miles?"

"Yes."

"Thank you for trusting me with this. I've felt like I fell into all this just because I hung on to Grant so hard. Now, in addition to keeping him alive, this has taken on a whole new value for its meaning to you as well. It feels good to actually do something to help, even though it hurts when I think about what I'm helping you toward."

"Ordwyn, this would be far more difficult without your able assistance."

She reigned in her emotions and smiled up at him then turned back to the simulator controls. "Reset to point 001 and start simulation 3."

As the vibrations of the simulator faded behind him, Miles approached his primary control room and appeared to simply walk through a wall. He came out on the other side standing on the dais surrounded by the not-quite-real holographic displays.

A gesture brought up a series of web surveillance databases in which Miles verified that Grant's nano-tech abilities and desire to escape the Consortium were properly documented and being refreshed and updated by the routines he had implemented. Another screen displayed the traffic among the agents of the three groups of Chinese as they investigated Grant and looked for a way to locate him. This last included a certain amount of conflict with the Consortium's agents as well.

Most important, Mr. Seung was showing considerable interest in Grant, with his minions putting out feelers for a meeting. Miles gestured two messages into existence and sent them on their way. He was just turning to another display concerning the creation of background data for Ordwyn's new identity when a prompt attracted his attention to a different display.

Its contents sent him to a different wall of the room that he also simply walked through exiting into a medical laboratory containing a bizarre array of equipment and an occupied hospital bed.

"Miles, is this thing done yet?"

"Not quite, Grant, but soon. We have several more tests to perform and two more sample sets to collect before I disconnect you from the system."

"Ordwyn said this wasn't going to be fun, but I had no idea."

Miles checked two banks of readings and adjusted three operational entries. "The worst of the process is behind you, both literally and figuratively. The more invasive aspects of the sample gathering will be over in about half an hour and all of it an hour after that."

Miles leaned over Grant's bed to adjust a control, then straightened up and looked down at him. "This is actually going a bit faster than I had expected. You have kept your body in good health, Grant."

"Thanks."

As Miles returned to the "wall" he said over his shoulder, "I'll be back." But, especially considering the current point in the sampling process, he didn't understand why Grant broke out into gales of laughter.

Back in the control room, Miles examined the two displays of the communications and the efforts of the Chinese and initiated a message to Mr. Seung. That individual was definitely interested in setting up a meeting, though he expected Grant to be at it.

Seung accepted Ordwyn as an intermediary only grudgingly. Miles expected him to carefully research her status with the police department. That inquiry could be used to tip off the second group and ensure their unexpected presence at the meeting.

With all proceeding in sequence and in order, Miles walked through yet another wall into a lab where he returned to working on Ordwyn's clone. Its construction would be complete in about an hour, and there were some specific injury details he would implant manually to add the final elements of authenticity to it. The roots of her new identity were in place so it could be activated as soon as required.

The little bistro was not a place Jakowski would normally patronize. In fact, he'd never been there before in his life, which made it perfect. He took a booth that gave him a clear view of the door without being directly visible from it and placed a minimal order with the surly waitress who strolled over. He didn't have long to wait.

At six-foot-four with red hair, Jake Stevens was hard to miss, but Jakowski let him get well into the place before waving him over to the booth.

Jake squinted at him. "That you, Jakowski? This ain't your usual kinda place."

"I'm not here for the food or the atmosphere."

"That's good. This joint don't have much of either one."

Jakowski pointed at the other seat of the booth. "Sit." After Stevens did so, Jakowski got right to the point. "So, Stevens, yer records show Summers is on leave?"

"They're not my records; they're the personnel department's records, an' they show Sergeant

Ordwyn Summers signed out on administrative leave. What'd she do, fill out her paperwork wrong?"

"Who signed in the approval box?"

"Her boss, who else?"

"Grayson?"

"Yeah, Grayson. Grayson put Summers on administrative leave. What's the big deal? Only odd thing was that there was nothin' written in the cause box, an' that's probably just sloppy paperwork. So, what's this about her disappearin'?"

Jakowski paused for a moment.

"What the hell? Who else am I gonna tell?"

"Four days ago, Grayson jumped down her throat about the Thornton case. Told her to drop it in the cold case drawer and move on. She'd been on an' off it for weeks trying ta find an angle that went somewhere, but there was nothin' . . . nothin' at all. So she puts me onto the liquor store robberies, tells me she hasta go take care of some 'personal business,' walks out the station door with the Thornton case file—an' disappears."

"She didn't come back to log off her shift?"

"She just vanished. Didn't come back. Didn't show up for her next shift. Her landlady hasn't seen her. I taped her apartment door, and it hasn't been opened for four days. Two days after she walks out, her desk is cleaned off like somebody knew she wasn't comin' back, an' I find out this morning that her car's been found abandoned.

"Then I see a report about a murder at the Blue Garden apartments. Some mugger is supposed to have disabled their security gear and killed one of the residents to steal her purse and phone. That's a lotta effort for stuff he coulda gotten by taking the vic on the street. But the kicker is that Summers' car was found less than a block away.

"Every piece of the Thornton case was like this. None of it made any sense, like taking down a high-end security system for a mugging. It all just opens up more questions. For just one example, the mugging vic was an employee of the Forester Group. They back technical inventors. People like Thornton.

"Now I got ya tellin' me that Summers, who I know has run into somethin' she couldn't handle, is on administrative leave? Come on!"

"Jakowski, ya do know that Grayson is like the number three or four guy in the whole department, don'tcha? Ya just don't run around accusing him of stuffing one of his own detectives in a hole."

"OK, explain it to me, then. I know Summers is gone missin'. Even her landlady knows she's missin'. How come her boss has signed her out on leave?"

"An' you want me to start sniffin' around to find out what happened to her? If you're even close about this, that might not be healthy."

Jakowski's look would have withered a cactus.

"Ya know, Stevens, I didn't really like Summers all that much. She was a pain in the ass most of the time.

But she was a cop. A cop like me, like you, like the people we both work with and trust with our lives.

"You're IA. Most cops don't like or trust IA. But there's a reason for IA . . . and this is it.

"So tell me, Stevens, do we stick our necks out for one of our own, or do we just pretend that Summers took a long vacation in Florida?"

———————

"I feel like I need a vacation . . . a long vacation."

Grant stumbled through the door into the dining room and dropped into a chair. Ordwyn looked up from the data pad that had become her constant companion. "You look like you need one. I told you that sampling process would hit you like a ton of bricks."

"What time is it, anyway?"

She checked her watch. "A quarter of twelve. You should get some rest." She looked up at him carefully, then added "As though you're going to have any choice about that."

"Yeah. Any chance I could talk you into whipping up some scrambled eggs and bacon in Miles' magic kitchen? Tired as I am, I'm dying for something to eat."

"Sure, it will only take a few minutes to fix you something. I know how the sampling process takes just about everything out of you."

Grant started to get up as Ordwyn rose to go to the kitchen. She smiled back at him. "No, you just sit tight and try to stay awake till I get back. That'll be harder than you think."

Grant realized that she was right about having to struggle to stay awake but, on another level, something was drawing him into acute wakefulness. It made for an oddly opposed set of emotional and physiological feelings. Trying to decipher this curious mental/physical state kept him occupied until Ordwyn came back with a steaming plate and a large glass of milk.

As she walked through the door from the kitchen, the source of his inner conflict became clear. Tired as he was, he really wanted to see her smile again. It was that simple . . . and that complex. She had stirred something in him that he had never expected to feel again. Grant had loved Ellen with his entire being and, looking back on it, he was almost ashamed at how his love for her had turned into grief and rage at her loss. The last three months had been an emotional roller coaster for him, with the last four days being more like a fall off a cliff. His feelings for Ordwyn had felt like betrayal on some level, but on another, the eye-watering velocity that their lives had taken on made him feel like he had known Ordwyn forever.

And there was that wonderful plate of food to give him conversational cover, while he decided how he was going to say what had to be said.

Ordwyn watched him tuck into his meal with

amusement in her eyes. "You might want to slow down just a little. It's really pretty good."

He downed his latest mouthful with a generous sip from the milk glass. "It is, and I feel like I haven't eaten for a week."

He finally put his fork aside and just looked at her for what seemed to her an uncomfortably long time.

"Grant, I feel like I'm being examined like one of your micro-machines. Either say something, or go back to eating."

He pushed the plate aside and looked directly into her eyes. "Ordwyn, when do you head out for your 'fatal' meeting?" Somehow, he wasn't surprised to see the same intensity in her that he was feeling.

She broke eye contact, then stood to turn away from him, and he saw the same Ordwyn who had cried over Miles' desire to die. "I'll leave in about six hours. The meeting will occur tomorrow night. And then . . ."

"And then Ordwyn Summers will be no more," he finished for her.

As she turned back, he realized that he was looking into the depths of her soul. "Miles told me that he would bring me directly back here to start what he calls my 'change.' Apparently it will take about a month and I'll be unconscious through most of it. When it's done . . . I will be someone else. It is one thing to accept that at the level of a survival necessity.

It's a whole other thing to be looking at actually becoming someone completely different, right down to your DNA."

Grant wondered how he was going to phrase his next sentence when she spoke again.

"It would have been so much easier if I hadn't met you."

"Ordwyn, I . . ."

"Please . . . I need to say this . . . to get it all out. I've needed to for some time now but with how quickly everything has happened, there just didn't seem to ever be a good time.

"And now, there really isn't any time at all.

"I have spent my whole life trying not to become too attached to anyone because it hurt too much to lose them. Mom, Dad, and now even the indestructible Miles. As a cop, I continually battled against becoming emotionally involved with the victims. I just kept putting them back into that category of 'cases' so that they couldn't become real people to me. Most of the time, it worked.

"But sometimes, it didn't.

"When I had to break the news to you about your wife, I remember thinking about what a remarkable relationship the two of you must have had and how horribly it must have hurt you to lose her. As I ran headlong into one brick wall after another on the case, I just got more determined to find that one clue that would unravel the whole weird mystery that you had become to me.

"But I wasn't hooked until the night they tried to run you down outside the restaurant. You wanted what happened to your wife made right and were willing to risk . . . to endanger your own life for that. The last man I met with that kind of commitment was my father, and it didn't take a Ouija board to tell me that you would probably meet the same end he did.

"I so wanted to find the answers you needed, so that it wouldn't have to turn out like that.

"Then Miles scooped up the both of us and we began this wild ride through something I still can't quite call reality. I have had my sense of possible versus impossible whipsawed around until the words don't mean anything anymore. And through every wild, impossible thing that has happened to us, you have plunged into it deeper than I could, taken harder hits to your own reality than I would, and kept on coming back . . . every time.

"It just never occurred to me that I would ever meet someone with that resilience, that tenacity, that . . . that ingrained courage. Someone . . . like you.

"Now, this may well be the last time we ever even talk to each other. I want to be so much more to you and with you, but there's just no time left and . . . and . . . would you please say something!"

Grant stood and gave her his lopsided smile. "Thanks."

"Thanks?"

"Thanks for saying what I was about to and saying it so much better than I would have."

"You mean that . . ." She didn't get to finish her sentence because Grant was kissing her with what she could only describe as a tender, massive strength. She had never experienced anything like it before and fiercely pushed away the idea that she never would again.

———————————

Charles Carver had been staring at his bedroom ceiling for at least half an hour when his alarm clock sounded its unnecessary announcement of 6 a.m. He reached for it in irritation then stopped in mid-gesture as he realized that Lori Dathan would never turn off another alarm. He took a deep breath to steady himself mentally as well as physically, got out of bed and went through his morning ritual to prepare for what promised to be a very long day indeed.

He left his apartment and entered the elevator, wondering if he would ever be able to forget the sight of Lori's body sprawled half out of it. Difficult as it had been when men and women he had dispatched to perform dangerous tasks did not return, there was something about Lori's unhesitating sacrifice for him, and for the Group, that made this infinitely more difficult. How could you possibly measure the value of someone who was so clear in presence, so clear in purpose that she could sacrifice her life without even stopping to think about it . . . just because it was the right thing to do?

As the elevator opened on the tunnel entrance, he paused for a moment remembering the last time he had entered it, thought again of Lori, and strode purposefully to the security checkpoint at its other end. The guard watched him go through the verification process, then said, "I have a note from Mr. Baker that he wants to talk to you in the Secure Room. He said it was urgent."

Carver walked up to the secured door, squared his shoulders, repeated the series of identification actions that got him into the building, and stepped through it as it slid aside.

Sam Baker swiveled his chair around from his terminal. "The system notified me that you just cleared the tunnel exit, so I'd guess that you haven't been up to your office yet."

"The guard said it was urgent."

Baker's level gaze held Carver's. "Charles, before we start on today, I want you to know that there was nothing you could have done to save Lori. When you entered the tunnel, we had no idea they were here.

Then they cut the feeds, and she was gone a minute later. Do not blame yourself for this."

For a moment, Carver looked older than Baker had ever seen. "Sam, even with the board's daily meetings and direction, I am in command of this facility. Lori was part of that command and we—I—lost her. I didn't shoot her. I didn't omit some precaution or warning that would have saved her.

"Nonetheless, just as a ship's captain is responsible for his crew, I was responsible for Lori. Just as the captain has to accept casualties and continue with his ship's mission, I will continue the Group's mission. And with all that, Lori's loss will still feel like the loss of my own daughter.

"Please accept that. I have."

Their intense rapport lasted a moment longer in unspoken agreement, then Baker turned back to his monitor array. A flurry of keystrokes brought up a series of lists and text displays. "We received our marching orders from Thornton's group last night. He has assigned specific equipment and tasks to the personnel list he provided earlier. This is all coming from someone who knows nanotechnology and has very specific research goals for pursuing it. If I had any doubt before that this is really Thornton, it is gone now."

"Will there be any problems with implementing his directives?"

"A couple of the equipment placements will need some added subterfuge but, once they are in place, we can proceed with all of it. I have some preliminary estimates that our clandestine research groups should be able to complete most of the initial tasks in about two weeks. Add time for equipment shipment and data retrieval, and we should be sending results back to Thornton in about 20 days."

"What about security for the research techs?"

"Again, Thornton is way ahead of us. His secure communications plan includes providing a very impressive cover for the researchers and for their activities. Honestly, if I didn't know what we were doing, I don't see any way I could uncover it."

"Very well, Sam, confirm our status with Thornton's group. It sounds like you have everything well in hand, so what prompted the 'urgent' flag?"

Baker turned back to his console. "This."

The array of monitors across the far wall began displaying communications logs.

"Something odd is happening among the Consortium agents."

Carver spent a moment reading a few of the logs. "It looks like they are being reorganized or marshaled, possibly."

Baker turned back to Carver. "They are being reorganized into new strike teams and given specific action orders. We haven't been able to decrypt the orders completely, but I think they are being briefed for a tightly coordinated and very massive strike.

"It's the kind of effort we saw when they were about to attack the warehouse that was supposed to be Thornton's hideout. And one more thing . . . notice the headers on the encrypted orders."

Carver went back to studying the log displays. "Yes . . . this is unusual. None of the comm channels or encryption tags match up with those commonly used by their teams." He turned back to Baker. "What do you make of this?"

"I think that someone is getting ready to mount a maximum strike effort using Consortium resources that the Consortium's high command doesn't know about. Given their near-frantic and thus far unsuccessful search for Grant Thornton, I would bet that George Osterman has been pushed so hard and so far that he has taken matters into his own hands."

Carver felt his insides go cold as Baker continued. "All indications are that they still don't have any idea where Thornton is, so I don't think that this is aimed at him. That leaves only one target worthy of this kind of effort.

"Us."

Standing in the midst of his array of holographic displays, Miles noted the ready-to-proceed response from the Forester group and the concern expressed about the Consortium's activities. He cross-referenced their intercepts with his own and verified that they did not contradict his analysis of the Consortium's intentions. He responded to the Forester Group and then sent off three missives to the Chinese entrepreneurial groups that Ordwyn would shortly confront.

The responses from the Chinese were about what he had expected.

Miles then made three more remote adjustments to the system that was putting the final touches on Ordwyn's clone and pushed through the wall that led back to the elevator and the living area. He walked into the common area and then to the dining room, where Ordwyn was checking the gear she had laid out on the table. He added one item to her assortment.

"Miles, my sidearm! I certainly wouldn't want to go to this kind of a parley without it." She placed it next to a pair of throwing knives and looked over the array of equipment. "I think you've got me as well-equipped as I can be for this without giving the game away."

"I would still prefer that you wear the vest."

"Thank you, but no. If one of them sees me in a micro-thin vest that can stop bullets from a .50 caliber machinegun, I'm not going to be very credible as a rogue cop on the run.

"Trust my skills. I do."

"Very well, the two contact packages are in the car.

Call the number as soon as you drop the first one, and the system will alert our friends. Again, be certain to 'lose' the second at the meeting. As we have discussed, I will be waiting for you in the trees and will be unable to intervene once you enter the meeting.

"Stay with the script."

"Why, Miles, if I didn't know better, I'd say you were worried about me. And before you bother to tell me that we are just making sure Grant's part in this strange play is completely believable, I'm going to tell you that I think your concern is sweet."

"Your car is ready and you already know the route. Is there anything you need before you leave?"

Ordwyn looked down for a moment, took hold of her emotions and looked back at Miles. "Grant and I said our goodbyes. I'm as ready as I'm going to get. Let's do this."

"What the hell are you doin' out there?

"His name is Grant Thornton. You've had his picture and description for five days now and come up with exactly nothin'."

Grayson ran his hand through his rapidly thinning hair. "Yeah, yeah, I know all about that. I'm takin' my own heat. But ya know what? That's why we've been gettin' all that cash. This is where you start actually earnin' it.

"Now get back out there and find a lead, a sighting . . . something that ties to Thornton!"

He wished he were using the desk phone so he could slam it back onto the hook. After a deep breath, he tapped another number into the cell.

"Morrie, what have you heard from the traffic cam and face-recognition crews?

"Yeah I'm askin' about Thornton. Has anybody watchin' that over-priced TV show seen anything that even remotely looks like him?

"Well, what have ya seen?

"Summers? What about her?

"They are, are they? Well, tell 'em we are still lookin' for her, Morrie. If we find her, there's a good chance of finding Thornton.

"Yeah, you guys watch this city like a swarm of ghosts, so it's time one of your guys spotted either her or Thornton.

"Or I'll be callin' you!"

He pushed the disconnect button and, once again, thought really hard about throwing the phone across his office. Then he dialed one more number.

"It's Grayson.

"Ya think? Tell me somethin'; what did your guys find out about that apartment mugging where they broke past security to steal a woman's purse and cell?

"That's right, they shot the vic.

"How come they didn't hit more targets?

"So, she was talking to the building security when they killed her?

"No, no, I just had an idea about another case I'm workin' on in the same area. Can you send me a copy of the surveillance footage from around the building? I want to run out a hunch.

"You can do that huh? OK, just send it to my computer.

"Yeah, thanks."

Maybe, just maybe, Summers and Thornton were right where nobody would look for 'em. All he needed was an image close enough to Summers to troll through that entire section of the city.

Chapter 15

Ordwyn hadn't really known where she was until Miles laid out her route for the meeting. She had been on the road for over three hours and was just now closing in on the first drop site. After being cooped up in Miles' hideout, it felt a little odd to be out driving again.

This next part was a bit tricky. While the car's windows were tinted enough that she wouldn't be easily recognizable while in it, she would have to get out in order to drop the first package. The risk if she was spotted and connected with the car was that the police and the Consortium would be after her like packs of wolves. So she had to carefully keep the hoodie she was wearing adjusted to conceal her face and hair.

There was a pay phone on the right side of the street and, yes, it was about half a block from the convenience store on the same side of the street. This was the place. She had an odd realization that pay phones had become rare enough to qualify as land-marks now.

She pulled over to the side of the street just opposite the phone, got out of the car and walked around to it. She was wearing gloves and was careful to hold the receiver away from her ear when she picked it up. While she pretended to place a call, she attached a small adhesive-wrapped package to the bottom of the shelf that would have held the phone directory, had it not been ripped out some time ago.

Her task completed, Ordwyn placed the receiver back on the hook, went back to the car, got in and drove away. As she did so, she opened the disposable cell phone that had been in her right jacket pocket and pressed the redial button. She watched the display just long enough to verify the number it called, did a slow count to five, hit the disconnect button and put the phone back in her pocket.

Given the appallingly indirect route she would follow to the meeting site, she had a bit over six hours of driving still ahead of her.

————————————

Ordwyn's cell call triggered a relay that sent a coded message to Miles' data net. That message triggered another to be sent to two of the three Chinese groups and placed a certain data file where it should be discovered shortly by the third. The message described the approximate location and the exact terms of the meeting.

Miles noted that Ordwyn's segment of the operation was proceeding in sequence and order. He then returned his attention to monitoring the Consortium's strike team activity. They were indeed preparing for a strike in considerable strength against the Forester Group's building. He had intended to be present for that event, but it appeared that the strike team had moved its schedule up to tonight, and he had another higher-priority engagement.

An alert from one of his systems directed him to a data transfer within the police department, for which one Thomas Grayson was the designated recipient. Miles' system deftly redirected the transmission through its own processors, where a series of carefully selected images of Ordwyn Summers was inserted into a specific part of the data.

Another missive arrived from the Forester Group with further status of the clandestine nanotechnology research group. Grant's communications and cover story were being implemented with singular efficiency so that the researchers would be able to get started several days ahead of schedule. The Group had noticed the ever-increasing comm activity between the Consortium's strike groups and expressed concern that it represented a threat they were unprepared to deal with. After a few milliseconds of consideration,

Miles replied that the Forester Group should increase its physical security measures and stay focused on managing the research team.

All in all, it was turning into a very productive morning.

Nearly ten hours of sleep had restored much of Grant's acuity and energy after yesterday's medical procedures and last night's goodbye to Ordwyn. What he had come to think of as "the parting" had been surprisingly difficult. After so short a time and under such trying circumstances, he had come to care for her a great deal more than he would have expected that he could. And this sense of loss had become far too familiar.

As he had told Ordwyn, his best tonic for stress and loss was work. So he dived back into planning the nanotechnology research project. After thinking about the research plans he had put in place, he had realized that he could map out the second tier of investigation simply by writing contingencies into it based on the outcomes of the first tier. Since he would be out of commission for roughly the next month, this would give him a nearly complete picture of what he needed to proceed to tier three when he came back to consciousness again.

This third tier was where the excitement would

begin. Here he would begin pulling the successes from the researchers into a coherent methodology of nanotech design. He would begin building his first prototype devices as well as honing the design and internal evolution parameters of the systems which, in turn, would begin making real nano-devices. From there, he just had to tell them what to make. Assuming, of course, that he survived to do anything at all.

"A sound plan, Grant. I will forward it to the research group as soon as you have it ready."

Grant looked over his shoulder to see Miles standing in the doorway to his computer room. "Now I know that I have been around you for far too long. That came as a total surprise, and I didn't even think about flinching when you pulled one of your 'magic' appearances."

"You are beginning to expect the unexpected. That is a survival skill that will serve you in good stead." Miles walked over to the desk and inserted a flash drive into the computer. "Mentioning survival, here are the details of your new identity."

Grant accessed the drive and began opening files. "Interesting: Very nearly the same background and education; but absolutely all the details are changed. I can step directly into this persona with a minimum of effort beyond memorizing a completely different set of names, dates and places. Impressive as usual

Miles, but one question: Doesn't this sound just a bit too much like me?"

"Without the physical changes, yes, it would. However, your appearance will be radically different. It will, in fact, be sufficiently altered so that anyone who is tempted to connect this identity back to Grant Thornton will take one look at your physical parameters and immediately decide that the backgrounds are strictly coincidental."

"Yes, that is something to reckon with. I will be sufficiently changed that no one would ever connect the new me with the old me. I'm still trying to wrap my head around that."

"For now, I suggest that you put your new identity aside and focus on your upcoming meeting with the Chinese. The details you will need for that exercise are in the directory named 'selling,' for that is precisely what you will be doing . . . selling yourself as a frightened, fleeing, highly desirable nanotechnology design engineer who is willing to sell himself to the highest bidder capable of rescuing him from the Consortium.

"Pay particular attention to the negotiation script. None of these individuals can be trusted. They are in this for money only and will turn on anyone if they see a benefit to themselves in doing so. You will ultimately strike a deal with Mr. Seung because he heads the most powerful of the syndicates and will do whatever needs to be done in order to keep the other two away from you.

"He has already begun making arrangements to transport you to China and, unbeknownst to him, I am helping him directly with those arrangements. When the time comes, we will make the necessary moves to convince him that he has you safely in his custody when, in fact, he does not. It will be rather like one of your staged magic acts."

"Great, Miles—just don't cast me as the lady who gets sawed in half."

Grant said it before he thought about the fact that Miles simply didn't have a sense of humor. Then he thought about living without the ability to laugh for 34,000 years and recognized another very poignant reason why Miles was ready to die.

———————

Grayson had been watching the surveillance footage from around the Blue Garden apartments and the Forester Group office building for the last two-and-a-half hours. It was not his idea of entertainment. Unfortunately, he didn't know anyone else he trusted to do it and keep his mouth shut afterward.

He had just about decided that this was a waste of time when he saw a figure hurry down the sidewalk and disappear between the two buildings. It looked like a woman of about the right height and build. Now he had to figure out how the damned enhancement controls worked. He finally isolated a clear frame of the figure and zoomed in on the face.

"Well I'll be . . . It is her."

There in his carefully selected closeup was clearly the face of Ordwyn Summers.

The question was, what was she doing there the morning that—what was her name—? Oh, yeah— Lori Dathan was killed? And, most especially, how did those two events connect to Mr. Grant Thornton?

Given the stink that the Forester Group had raised about Dathan's murder, he couldn't simply barge in and demand to search the place. What he could do, however, was to put up a perimeter around it to make sure that he knew everyone who went in or out. And just maybe . . .

One of his too many phones would ring . . . like it was doing now.

"Grayson.

"Of course my people are still lookin' for Thornton. And, yes, I took all the clean cops off it and put just my own people out.

"Why is that good?

"Look, I have been able to cover a lot more territory since you pulled your guys off the streets and . . .

"No, they haven't found anything yet.

"You go turnin' 'em loose again, and it's all gonna go back in the toilet. You want that?

"Your puttin' the whole crowd under Phillips and Hall?

"Yeah, I know 'em. They're acoupla hotshots who need a dictionary to figure out what 'low profile' means.

"Uh-huh. Where are they gonna hit?

"Whaddaya mean I don't need to know?

"Well my guys are all goin' to . . .

"You don't, huh?

"OK, let me know when ya find Thornton. I'll just keep lookin' till then."

Grayson stuck the phone back in his pocket, thought about it for a minute, then pulled it back out and turned it off.

———————

Jakowski almost jumped out of his skin when his cell phone rang.

He swore, pulled the ear bud to his bug in Grayson's office out of his ear and answered the cell call.

"Jakowski.

"Stevens, ya scared the hell outa me.

"Never mind. What's up?

"Yeah, I been keepin' close tabs on him and I don't like what I'm findin' out.

"Well, for starters, he's got about half the precinct on his own personal payroll. An' then he has conversations with somebody called George where it sounds like he's takin' orders from the guy. There's just a whole lot about Grayson that's startin' to smell really rotten.

"Who's he?

"Yeah, I heard his name a few times. So?

"Ya don't say. Well, that explains a couple of things.

"If he's in another precinct, I wouldn't come across him, but Grayson might.

"Ya mean there's a whole network of cops workin' for these guys?

"Sheesh, now whadda we do?

"Yeah, I know he's been steppin' on a lotta toes in the other precincts huntin' for Thornton.

"Stevens, if the rest of IA doesn't wanna mess with these guys, what are we gonna do?

"Well, it sure sounded like that's what ya said.

"Oh crap, Springer? He's right next to the Chief. You pull him into this and we're gonna have a lotta explainin' ta do!

"Ya shouldn'ta done that without talkin' to me first.

"Why? 'Cause my butt's in the sling right next to yours if this blows up in our faces, that's why.

"Grayson's sending anyone who's not under his personal control out of the office this afternoon. I can meet with you and whoever else then.

"Yeah, I guess I shoulda thought about that before I pulled the trigger with ya, huh?

Carver looked out of his office window at the park below. Again, he was amazed at how tranquil it could look while they were on the edge of a virtual war just across the street. Predictably, the computer chimed at just that moment with a notification from Baker that the board meeting was about to start.

He stood, squared his shoulders and walked into his outer office. "Marion, I expect to be in the Room for the remainder of the day. Why don't you take the rest of the day off and go home?"

She was amazed at how easy he was to read sometimes. Then again, he had no reason to put up his defenses against her. "Charles, I'm not going to be any safer there than I am here and, if it comes to that, I'll be quite a bit better off here. Besides, you're all going to need a lot of coffee tonight."

She was right, as usual. "Yes, I suppose we will."

He proceeded to the stairs, started down, stopped, and turned back to her. She read his question before it got out of his mouth. "No, I don't think there was anything you could have done about Lori. Sometimes, what we do simply isn't safe."

He just looked at her for a moment, smiled tiredly, and started back down the stairs.

The other directors were starting to appear on the wall monitors as Carver entered the Room. He waited for all of them to appear and then started.

"I have copied all of you with the communications

we have been receiving from Thornton's group. They have been detailed and appropriate to what we are trying to accomplish. The precise work assignments will make results correlation and reporting a quick and accurate process that will leave much less data reduction to be done at the other end. I sincerely believe that these instructions originate with Thornton himself, even though we haven't communicated directly with him, nor have we identified whom we are actually dealing with.

"The people and equipment that will comprise our clandestine nanotechnology research group are either already in place or will be by this time tomorrow. Sam—and Lori's—early actions with the dismissed NanoStar employees have allowed us to get a running start on this project, which has resulted in a vastly accelerated startup schedule.

"I wish I could report that we are doing as well with our security against the Consortium's efforts as we are doing with establishing the research group. We have monitored the comm channels being used by the various operations teams on the Consortium's side and those used by identified rogue officers on the police force. It is our belief that both groups are concentrating and staging for a coordinated assault on this office."

Carver looked around at the monitors and noted the reactions.

"Thornton's group has suggested that we stiffen our perimeter defenses and move our operations personnel to a secure room within the building—probably this one. While they attempted to assist and defend us from the Consortium attack that resulted in the recent death of Lori Dathan, they were only partially successful. We do not see any indication that they have the resources to mount an armed defense of this location.

"From what we have been able to glean from intercepted communications, we believe that the attack will come tonight. We are doing what we can to prepare, but this building was never intended as a fortress for fighting off groups of armed operatives.

"This may be our last communication."

Silence filled the Room like invisible sand while they all looked at each other . . . possibly for the last time.

"Charles, if you are . . . lost, what will become of the research groups?"

"We have anticipated the necessity of handing off both control and communications with them. We have three auxiliary communications centers prepared to pick up on both coordination of the researchers and communications with Thornton's group."

"Can they maintain the necessary security?"

"Yes, Mr. Drake, we believe they can. They are maintaining the secure comm channels that we are using for this conference."

"What about dispersing the operations personnel . . . even if it's just sending them home?"

"We considered that, Marcella. But if the Consortium has decided to eradicate the Group from this location, dispersing our personnel would just make them individual targets, leaving us powerless to do anything for them. Here they have at least some chance."

The man who looked for all the world like a pirate was one of the most shocked. "My God, how did it come to this?"

Amy spoke up from the end screen. "Gerard, I think the answer to your question is that, sooner or later, it had to. We have been on a collision course with the Consortium since the Group was started. We have had a number of violent encounters with them, even to the point of the entire nuclear propulsion team being killed. Charles lost his father in that battle.

"While different in scale, this is still another battle in that same war. It is yet another case of the Consortium saying that they will take what they want because they can, and a desperately small group of us telling them no, they can't.

"Charles, is there anything that any of us, or the remote teams, can do?"

"No, Amy, I don't think so, but I thank you from the bottom of my soul for asking.

"Are there any further questions or comments?"

Again, the silence was instantly oppressive.

"In that case, we will put continuous status and surveillance monitor data on stream to all of you and communicate in more detail when we can.

"While they are clearly coming for us tonight, that doesn't necessarily mean that the rest of you are safe. Please see to tightening your own security to the maximum.

"Good night, and may God watch over us all."

"Damn, but this has a lot of places where it can go wrong."

"An unfortunately accurate observation."

"Miles, that entrance didn't even surprise me. I must really be getting used to you."

Grant leaned back in his chair at the dining room table, stretched and pointed at the data pad. "I've gone through this plan from one end to the other. Even with you orchestrating the whole process from end to end, I still see too many holes. The biggest of which is how to make sure the Chinese follow the script when it comes to smuggling me out of the country."

"That, I have some indirect control over. Part of what they are planning will fall through at the last minute. I will then be able to direct them to a fallback of my own preparation."

"OK, but what about the clone? It will likely have

to fool an autopsy conducted by someone with the Consortium breathing down their neck."

"Oddly enough, your clone is considerably easier to create than Ordwyn's. Hers had to be precisely damaged to replicate massive injuries, where yours will be an exact replica requiring only one direct adjustment. When the medical inspector delves into it, he or she will find you . . . dead, but you."

"So, what aspect of this plot does worry you?"

"Mostly my indirect control of the Chinese syndicates. I have to interest them in you without whipping up a frenzy of greed that makes them excessively violent in their pursuit of it. While I can control the Consortium teams to a degree due to my penetration of their communications, the Chinese operate in near independent cells. Control is a matter of indirect influence rather than command checks and balances that I can directly affect."

The silence stretched while Grant got his nerve up to ask his next question. "How is Ordwyn doing so far?"

Miles locked Grant in his thousand-year gaze and said, "Grant, Ordwyn is doing fine, and I will be there to guide her if she needs it. You need to focus on your own coming encounter with the Chinese. I thought you understood that you may never see Ordwyn again—certainly not as she is now.

"Once nanotechnology begins to have its irreversible

impact and the Consortium starts to dissolve, it will tend to fly apart in dangerous pieces. Some of those pieces will have angry memories of a man and a woman who have caused them a great deal of grief. It simply won't be safe for you to be near each other, even with your new identities.

"Ordwyn's death needs to be as real for you as it will be for everyone else."

"Stiles?

"Grayson. What's the status?

"*No!* You guys are not out there to kill anybody. That's too close for team 2. Pull 'em back across the street. I want coverage in layers . . . not standin' in each other's pockets.

"Because that's where they get the best look at the end of the alley.

"One more time . . . I want to know *exactly* who goes in and out of those two buildings and I want to know it *when* it happens. If I need one of 'em collared, I'll tell ya.

"Why? You seen any of 'em?

"Good. They're all supposed to be off on some job, so you don't have to look out for 'em.

"Yeah. Just stay coordinated with the other teams, keep your eyes open and tell me just as soon as you see anybody. Got it?

Grayson punched the disconnect button and sighed. It seemed like they got dumber every year. Which reminded him, he picked up the phone again and punched in another number.

"Yeah, it's me.

"Uh-huh. You remember that problem we talked about? I want it solved.

"The sooner the better.

"Detective Sergeant Fred Jakowski.

"That's the one. Make it look like he was done by an informant or a perp. And I don't want the body found for at least 24 hours.

"Yeah, the usual.

"Good.

He punched the disconnect, dropped the phone on his desk and just stared at it.

What was the line from that old song? Oh, yeah: 'You gotta know when to hold 'em, know when to fold 'em' . . ."

Grayson nodded, swiveled his chair around to his desk safe and ran through the combination. He reached inside and pulled out three passports and an envelope. He checked the envelope's contents. It was stuffed full of hundred-dollar bills.

"Nice."

Ordwyn had parked her car in the spot Miles specified. It gave her an excellent view of the meeting location, a small, single-floor office set in the middle of a fenced-in heavy equipment yard. The little building was obvious and visible from all angles. The yard full of giant machines could hide an army.

She pulled the cell phone out of her left pocket and pressed its redial button. She watched the display to verify the dialed number and slowly counted off five seconds. She then pressed the disconnect button and fished the other cell phone out of her right pocket. Both went into a zipper-secured pocket inside the hoodie.

She had purposefully arrived at the site early to reconnoiter. First she would watch to see if the Chinese had already determined the location. Barring that unlikely event, she would make a fast sweep of the yard on foot to check for hides and any possible problems with her planned exit routes.

She paused for a moment to check her own well-being. She was comforted to discover that she wasn't nervous about, or overly hyped for, this encounter. After being at the effect of too many events outside her control, she was ready to take direct substantial action.

She felt good. She felt ready.

———————

Ordwyn's call triggered an alert on Miles' monitoring system that in turn triggered a timer. The expiration of that timer would send a message to the Chinese, who had already accepted the terms contained in Ordwyn's earlier package, and would give them the exact location and time of their meeting with her.

Miles, who was already on his way to the meeting location, noted Ordwyn's message, and the fact that the time delay allotted for the confirmation message was very nearly perfect for its purpose. He checked the surveillance feeds from the Forester Group's office building and noted that the Consortium's agent teams were rapidly approaching. Grayson's teams were already in place and had been there long enough to become bored with waiting for something to happen.

As the Consortium teams crossed an invisible line that Miles had established, he cut their communications with their command group and the suborned police team's communications with Grayson. His own comm system then signaled the Consortium troops that they were about to encounter Forester Group guards stationed around their office building and dressed as police SWAT officers. These "guards" were to be routed to clear their way into the building. Their objective of taking the building was reinforced.

Though not in the detail that his control room would have provided, Miles watched the surveillance feeds to see the Consortium squads move into place behind Grayson's teams.

He expected a confrontation, but nothing like what happened next.

The Consortium hit squads simply opened fire on the unsuspecting police teams without any warning. The police teams returned fire but were very nearly overwhelmed. Their only advantage was that they had taken up positions that offered them good cover as soon as they realized they needed it. With now inferior numbers, the police were slowing the advance of the Consortium agents but not stopping them.

Miles triggered another prearranged communication that summoned backup for the beleaguered police and watched the carnage continue for a long fifteen minutes until reinforcements began to arrive. He then restored communications between the Consortium, Grayson and their respective units.

Even with reinforcements, the battle continued for another ten minutes. Finally, the Consortium agents ripped off a heavy volley of fire at the combined police units and withdrew as their leadership and Grayson struggled frantically to contain the fallout from this catastrophe. Miles continued to observe the situation at the Forester Group's building until the backup police units had asserted firm control.

He triggered a timed message to Grayson that, in half an hour, would tell him that Ordwyn was at a heavy equipment storage facility west of the city. It would arrive at a time when Grayson would be totally unable to do anything about it. Miles then continued on to Ordwyn's meeting location, fully aware that much still hung in the balance.

———————

Charles Carver and the Forester Group staff had very little warning of the firefight that erupted outside their offices and homes. Baker noticed odd movements on the external surveillance cameras and had barely time enough to hit the alarm button before all hell broke loose.

The staff who were still in the office were all gathered into the Secure Room. Those in the apartments went to the connection tunnel. They could all hear the battle raging as they ran for shelter, and they all realized that they were the prize being fought over.

The group in the Secure Room watched the external monitors as men seemed to shoot at each other endlessly. Though it lasted for a little over 30 minutes, it seemed to go on forever. Once the police appeared to have established control over the streets, an officer presented his credentials at the main entryway's access station. After considerable conversation and two calls to precinct stations, the officer established that his group was indeed the "real" police and that the fighting was over.

The Group's personnel slowly began to leave their safe rooms as the police interrogators dismissed them. Out on the sidewalk, most of them were somewhat shocked to still be alive. What they saw looked like war footage from Iraq. There were bodies everywhere.

Carver was dazed. He walked over to his favorite park and was stunned to see what looked like a battlefield. Most of one of Grayson's teams had taken positions there and been attacked first by the Consortium's hit squads. There were dead men everywhere, caught in the curious poses of instant, violent death. He was sickened to see that the fountain he used to take solace from was pumping water stained red with blood from the bodies of two men floating in its pool.

The police attempted to question him and the others, but they didn't get much past everyone's shock at what had happened in a place where such things weren't supposed to happen.

———————

It was time.

The darkness was as complete as it was going to get. Ordwyn checked her gun, knives and tracking beacon; she took a deep breath, a firm grip on the briefcase, and got out of her car. It was parked at the edge of the equipment yard fence, behind a sign that obscured it from either the road or the yard.

She had seen the first group of Chinese arrive and watched their bodyguards check out the yard and the office. She waited until the second group arrived and was fully engaged in a loud, hand-waving argument with the first. With a little luck, the third group should arrive in about five to ten minutes—just when things were getting interesting.

"It's showtime . . ."

Ordwyn stepped out of the shadows and began walking into the yard toward the office. Halfway to the group of arguing men, she stopped.

"Good evening, gentlemen. I believe I'm expected."

The shouting stopped as they all turned to look at her. She held up the briefcase.

"We have a business deal to discuss. I brought my proof of value. Where's yours?"

Another short bout of Chinese shouting erupted from the group in front of the office, which one of them silenced. This more assertive individual turned back to Ordwyn.

"My apologies, Sergeant Summers. Some of my colleagues don't understand the finer points of conducting business negotiations. I am Mr. Seung. I assume that your briefcase contains the proofs of both your contact with Mr. Thornton and his knowledge that we requested.

"Bring it to me, please."

This wouldn't do. She needed them closer to her.

"This," she held up the briefcase, "has a great deal in it. May I suggest that we spread it out on a table in the office?"

Seung gave his opposite number from the rival group a withering look. "That won't be necessary. We can take it with us."

"I beg to differ, Mr. Seung. Our conditions, to which you agreed, require immediate inspection and agreement on certain arrangements.

"No inspection, no agreement, no deal. Now, shall we retire to the office?"

This resulted in another heated exchange between the two Chinese principals, which ended as abruptly as it began.

Seung turned back to Ordwyn. "Very well, we will examine the documents in the office—after you surrender your weapon to one of my men."

Ordwyn reached behind her back and handed her 9mm over as Seung's statement brought another short burst of Chinese from the other principal.

Seung sighed audibly. "Mr. Chong will accompany us."

Ordwyn, the two Chinese principals, and one each of their bodyguards formed an unlikely parade through its door and into the office. The two groups of remaining bodyguards were left outside, eyeing each other nervously.

Much better.

Ordwyn walked between the four men in the tight

quarters of the office to a table pushed up against a wall. She put the briefcase on the table, dialed in its combination, and opened it. As she reached into the box, the two bodyguards both drew guns.

She paused, hand still inside, and said, "Will you tell your goons to relax? If they try to use those things in here they are just as likely to shoot you or each other as they are me." The two principals gestured, and the bodyguards lowered their weapons. She then slowly removed a sheaf of papers from the briefcase and held it up for all to see.

A short burst of Chinese from each principal got guns back into holsters. Ordwyn spread the pages of the file out on the table.

"As promised, here are the results of preliminary testing performed on Mr. Thornton's designs. While they may not be overly meaningful to you, I direct your attention to the assessments performed by three different venture capital organizations. As you can see, they were very impressed."

Seung and Chong stepped to the table and, after hard looks at each other, actually took *turns* examining the reports. They muttered in Chinese under their breath as they read.

If her time sense was still on track, Ordwyn expected to hear from group three just about . . .

Gunfire erupted outside the office. Ordwyn's elbow went immediately into the chin of the bodyguard standing next to her. She stepped around under the arm of the stunned man, who was twice her size, pivoting him directly into the bullets fired by his compatriot from the other side.

She ducked and came back up with a throwing knife, which she used to take out the man who had just fired. Then she snatched her gun out of the first dead guard's belt and spun around to cover the two surprised principals, who had tried to get to the door.

"You know, I really wasn't expecting you two to try something like this. You are supposed to be businessmen. Well, I have other offers."

With that, she turned and executed a running dive through a very small window above the table that she had opened earlier. At least one of the principals was armed and she heard bullets crashing into the wall after her.

She hit the ground rolling and came to her feet running. The opening she had made in the fence earlier should be right about . . . there! She ducked through that gap and quickly made her way back to her car. There was considerable gunfire in the yard, so she was going to have to get their attention.

She pulled up toward the yard gate, cranked the wheel hard left, and stood on the gas. The rear wheels broke loose with a satisfyingly loud squeal as she took off down the road like a shot. A quick check of the rearview mirror showed cars being backed and turned around to follow her.

Excellent!

Now she had to be away, down the straight to the road that teed in from the left. Not too fast; they had to be able to follow this turn. On to the farm road and look in the mirror for . . . there they were, headlights had just turned onto the road behind her. Now she had the opportunity for some speed. Through the low hills, they were still there, onto a harder surface road with better traction. Then, on the next right, there's the bump in the pavement that always had to be addressed just so. Good! Past that lay the illusory straight that ended in a rise and a dip followed by a sharp left, which always required a tap on the brakes and a right drift before cresting the rise.

For a moment she was thrown because the chicane through the scrub forest went through tree stumps instead. She recovered and drove hard through it. The long right sweeper was coming, followed by the near right angle left. She accelerated out of the left to see the bridge abutment coming up just at the end of another left. It was time to slow slightly and in 4 . . . 3 . . . 2 . . . 1 . . . She made a hard right to swing past the abutment and out into the field. Now she would need to straighten out before hitting the pocket in the stand of trees.

Only someone had flooded the field.

Ordwyn had studied driving at insane speeds over a wide variety of road surfaces intently. It was an integral part of her job, and she had become very good at it. Driving, however, is an exercise in physics. The equations of friction, inertia and momentum are stern masters and most unforgiving of those who attempt to violate them.

The flooded field was now a marsh, with no traction to speak of. Ordwyn had become a passenger in a slowly spinning car that was sliding toward a stand of trees.

It seemed as though everything had slowed down. The headlights seemed to swing lazily across the landscape as, with each pass, the trees got nearer. Then on one pass she saw Miles running toward the car with a large bundle slung over his shoulder.

Her last thought before hitting the trees was . . .

"I wonder if we'll need the clone."

Chapter 16

Charles Carver's night was not restful.

The conflagration that had occurred virtually on his front doorstep had shaken him deeply. That, on top of Lori's recent death, had ripped away the comforting illusion that the Group was simply working to create a better world, making it brutally obvious that they were engaged in a war. It had also thrown the ruthlessness of the Consortium into stark relief.

He knew the Consortium had been badly wounded the previous night. By his own rough count, they had lost at least thirty agents, either killed, or wounded and captured. But how long would it take for them to replace those losses? Probably not long enough.

The one bright spot in the whole sorry mess was the PR it had generated. The news crews had been all over this one, and that would be a major detriment to the Consortium's attempts to manipulate events from behind the scenes. As a result, they would have to keep their further operations as covert as possible.

That, at least, offered some hope of slowing this spiral of violence.

He went directly from the tunnel entrance to the Room. "Sam, what do we know?"

Baker hadn't slept at all. "We know it was more than just the Consortium trying to blot us out."

Carver sat down. "What have you learned?"

Baker turned back to his console. "The beginning of the Olive Street Battle was . . ."

"The what?"

"The Olive Street Battle. That's what the media are calling what happened last night. At the beginning of the fight, it appears that the police had already been in place around the office and apartments for over two hours. Putting twenty-eight officers out around our facilities was authorized by one Thomas Grayson. There is considerable debate going on—both publicly and no doubt privately—as to whether Grayson himself had any authority or real reason to do this.

"No one has named the Consortium as the source of the second force to be deployed in our neighborhood, but it is obvious that they came in after the police had set up their perimeter and attacked the cops with no warning. Now, while the department is not releasing names of the dead pending notification, I was able to get a preliminary list of the casualties off the comm link between the morgue and Grayson's precinct."

"Sam, I have the distinct feeling that this rendition is about to get to its punch line."

"Just so. All but two of the twenty names on the casualty list are officers known to have been suborned by the Consortium."

Carver had thought he was finally beyond shock. He was wrong.

"They had a pitched street battle between their own people and killed nearly fifty of them?"

"Basically, yes. A backup SWAT team was called in shortly after the battle started, but no one can figure out who called them. They probably accounted for about a third of the Consortium's strike team casualties. From what we can pick up off the police comm channels, there are a lot of hard questions being asked about why this odd lot of officers from all over town came to be hunkered down in positions around these two buildings. Meanwhile, the news services are howling about the gang of terrorists that shot it out with them."

"What attention have we drawn because of all this?"

"So far, not much. The police quizzed most of the staff. I spent an hour with them explaining that we heard the shooting and went to the lowest rooms in the two buildings, and that we were not expecting a shootout in front of our buildings. That last is a bit of a stretch but technically accurate. What did they ask you?"

"Quite honestly, I was very rattled, and I suspect that I didn't make much sense. So after about ten minutes of questioning, they gave up on me.

"Sam, what sort of security plan do we put in place to deal with this?"

"The one we have worked fairly well. We aren't ever going to be able to fend off that kind of attack. Herding everyone below street level and hitting a panic button to make an auto call to the police is about the best we can do. Anything beyond that would involve having our own strike team on site. Given the acute attention this has brought, I can't see us being able to mount that kind of response force even if we wanted to."

"Well, I guess it's back to as close to business as usual as we can get after something like this."

"Maybe not."

"Sam, I hate it when you do that."

"Sorry, but we got some more information about Thornton from our intercepts of the Consortium's comm channels. They think he is trying to flee to China."

"What could have given them that idea?"

"I'm not sure. And I don't think they are, either. They are, however, mobilizing some of their operatives to look into it. Given last night's losses, they must put some credibility on the report to commit anyone to investigating it."

"Put a query into his group about this. I know they haven't even claimed that they know him, but it is fairly obvious he has some connection there."

"And that brings up another interesting item . . . Don't look at me that way; it's been a hell of a night. We got another message from Thornton's group with more work instructions for the research team. This is a decision tree that specifies which work to perform based on results of prior experiments. It appears that they want us to run the research group on autopilot for roughly a month."

"And we get that on top of a rumor that he's running for China."

Carver looked into the distance while he considered their options.

"I don't see where we have enough information to do anything different. Let's continue to work with the group and operate the research teams accordingly. Keep monitoring as much comm traffic as you can to see if you can come up with anything that confirms or denies the rumor about Thornton going to China.

"It's a good thing I am comfortable with the uncertainty principle."

———

"Yeah, that's right. I'm not in my office because bein' Tom Grayson is not exactly a good plan right now.

"Actually Osterman, I don't even know why I'm

talking to you. I tried to tell you we had a lead at the Forester Group offices, but would you listen? Of course not! Would you tell me you planned to hit the Forester Group offices last night? Oh, hell, no! Result, our teams shot each other to hell and gone.

"You think you got problems? I'm dodging the chief, three precinct captains and IA over this. More cops died last night than for the last 50 years of this department. And all of 'em, every single one was one of my bought people.

"Oh? And why was that?

"Yeah, your guys jumped all three of my teams and started killin' everybody in sight. Are you tryin' to tell me you didn't send 'em out to do that?

"Well somebody did.

"Look, I got one last piece of information for ya. One of my guys had an informant . . . Yeah, *had*—he's dead now. Anyhow, this CI works with one of the Chinese body shoppers and told him that his boss was just about to buy a guy and ship him off to China. The guy's name was Thornton.

"That's right, Thornton. Apparently, he's tired of hidin' under a rock and is trying to get out of the country. Oh, and one other little item. My missing cop Summers; she turned up dead about four miles from an equipment yard where a bunch of Chinese shot it out with each other.

"Yeah, it was a real busy night.

"You want me to what?

"Maybe you didn't hear me. My guys are all dead, in the hospital or on the hot seat with IA. Right now, I couldn't investigate somebody stealin' a school kid's lunch money.

"Get serious, Osterman. We are done, finished, over with. I'm not even sure that I can save my own butt at this point.

"Look, you want to try snatchin' Thornton from the Chinese, you go right ahead.

"You already have!"

Grayson saw no reason to resist the impulse any longer. He threw the cell phone across the room where it hit a doorframe and shattered with a very satisfying crash.

Miles pushed through the wall into his control room and mounted the dais at its center. The array of displays responded to his gestures and showed him the current status and communications of all the major players in the drama of Grant Thornton.

The police were actively searching for Thomas Grayson. The Consortium had pulled its remaining strike teams into safe houses. The Forester Group was still forwarding necessary communications back and forth with the clandestine nanotechnology research group, even though the Group had gotten hold of the

Chinese flight story. Mr. Seung and Mr. Chong were apparently reducing a Mr. Han's export business to a shadow of its former self, in more ways than one.

Miles decided that the situation had simmered long enough. It was time to stir the Chinese pot.

Miles sent a message to Mr. Seung, castigating him for killing the messenger who was to negotiate Grant's flight to China and telling him how very much more difficult this made everything. He wasn't surprised to receive an immediate reply asking for another meeting and guaranteeing that this one would be very different. At a guess, Seung had received verification of the contents of the briefcase describing Grant's capabilities.

He decided to let Seung stew while he checked on the progress of Grant's clone. It was almost done and would be ready shortly after noon. Grant himself had been diligent in preparing for his meeting with the Chinese and was ready as well. While Miles had intended the meeting to be the following day, perhaps the additional pressure on the Chinese to meet that night would knock them off their game just that much more.

Miles thought about the schedule change and decided the legitimate police should probably be distracted while this most delicate operation was in play. He checked on Grayson's movements, sent off two messages, and verified their receipt. He found another communication from Grayson to one of his few still-active minions, ordering him to kill one Fred Jakowski. Miles redirected that assassin into the hands of the uncompromised police. He then set up three more active data correlations that would automatically notify him if specific conditions occurred; then he stepped off the dais and walked through the wall again.

———————————

This time, Grant was seated where he could watch through the door into the common room. He saw Miles exit the far door and walk toward the dining room, where Grant was working on his own data pad. "What news from the outside world, Miles?"

"Our Chinese associates are performing about as expected. They have simplified the equation by destroying one of their rival groups, which had tactlessly intruded upon Ordwyn's meeting with them."

At the sound of her name, Grant stifled a nearly overpowering urge to ask about her. That was partly because he knew he had to stay focused and partly because he knew that his mentor/rescuer wouldn't tell him anything. Miles had mastered compartmentalization.

"Are you prepared to talk to them about the meeting?"

Grant looked at his data pad again. "I'm as ready as

I'm going to get. I won't have any trouble conjuring up the necessary desperation. I know the players, and I gather that Han's organization is the one that is being eradicated. Does that change anything about the call?"

"No, but another situation does. A combined Consortium hit squad tried to attack the Forester Group's headquarters last night."

"Over *me?*"

"It came about partly because you continue to elude them and partly out of their frustration with my intercession. Most of them have come to believe that the Forester Group is behind the long list of unaccustomed failures they have suffered over the past week. It appears that the individual in charge of their now not-so- covert operations thought that the Group had you or knew where you were."

"Miles, this has got to stop. I won't have people killing each other over me. I won't!"

Miles looked at Grant for what was for him a long time without speaking. "The fastest way to stop all this is the path we are now on."

"But, the Forester Group? They're a collection of investors and scientists. I can't believe they are prepared for this kind of street warfare. How many of them were killed?"

"Last night, none were. As I mentioned earlier, they lost one of their security people to an armed probe by the Consortium."

"One died night before last and none last night? How is that possible? Unless . . . What happened to last night's 'attempted' attack?"

"The Consortium's agents wound up shooting at each other. Two groups of them, each unaware of the other's presence, collided in front of the Forester Group's office building. Both groups suffered substantial casualties."

"How substantial?"

"Enough so that I think we can expect a move against the Chinese as they attempt to ship you off to their homeland. I have monitored communications that indicate a level of desperation on the part of the operations manager I mentioned. He very likely sees extracting you from the Chinese as his last chance . . . and he is very likely correct."

Grant looked and felt sick. "More killing. There has to be more killing?"

"These people think only in terms of taking what they want and killing or disabling anyone who gets in their way. Your wife was killed because you got in their way. If all had gone as planned, they would have killed you as well. I have learned an oft repeated and bitter lesson that men such as these have to be fought at every turn. Let them have their way, and their rapaciousness knows no bounds."

For a moment Grant thought of Ellen and then of Ordwyn—who, as far as he knew, might also be dead.

He felt very, very tired. "So it's up to me to make all of this mean something. To make it worth the lives that were and will be lost."

All the events of the last six days came crashing into his consciousness. He had been too busy, too scared or too tired to sort out the grand scheme of it all while it was happening. Now it lay before him like a picture map painted on a wall: clear, plain, and inescapable.

He had become a prize to be killed or captured, depending on what was wanted of him. To have any chance at all of balancing his own scales of integrity and justice, he was going to have to elude a host of determined—and, in some cases murderous—people in order to use his talents to remake the world. In that moment, he saw *why* he would have to do *what* he would have to do. And for the first time, he truly accepted it—all of it.

He saw something else as well.

He looked deep into Miles' bottomless eyes and spoke his truth. "Miles, when I was a boy, I loved to read. Many, if not most, children's books are the simplest form of escapism. But a surprising number are philosophical morality tales for all of us.

"One in particular told of a man who came from another place and another culture. He was a man who could see and do things others could not. He was alone. There were no others like him. And yet, even in his absolute uniqueness, he felt a connection to the multitude of ordinary humans around him. So much so that he used his singular abilities to help them when and where he could. His name became a synonym for the best that any of us could ever hope to achieve.

"You sat here at this table and told me that you want to finally die and end your imprisonment in your android body. You want release from your memories of what it was like to be simply human.

"And yet, you have walked through the ages of mankind. You have seen both the best and the worst we can be. You have seen how even our most splendid intentions can go horribly wrong and the price we are willing to pay to set it all right again. You alone among all of us can stand in the shadows and tip the scales ever so slightly. You can add that one change of circumstance or situation that makes all the difference to the outcome of this amazing experiment we call humanity.

"I will do what I need to do. I ask in return that you consider what I have said and allow at least the possibility that you might be able to endure your own pain and help the rest of us along our way."

He thought he saw something flicker behind the eyes whose gaze he held . . . and then the moment was over.

Grant took a deep breath. "Oh, and Miles, if you

want to read that story I mentioned, look up Jerry Siegel and Joe Shuster in your archives. I think you might find some very interesting parallels with their most famous character.

"Now, what exactly do I need to say to Mr. Seung to cinch his unwavering attention and greed?"

———————————

Thomas Grayson was many things. Most of them were thoroughly reprehensible, but stupid wasn't anywhere on the list.

He had laid backup plans for his escape, evasion and comfortable survival just in case this whole influence-for-hire sideline came apart. In reality, it had blown up in his face, which would make his strategic withdrawal a lot more difficult, but still doable.

He had his passports. He had stashed money in accounts across the country and outside of it as well. He had as much cash on him as he could use at this point. There was just one last item to take care of. He had needed some assistance in making all these preparations. Osterman had provided a number of the contacts who made them possible. The contacts and the details of those arrangements were all in a notebook. In addition to containing his only access to much of what had been prepared, that notebook also tied him to everything that went down last night and more besides.

The notebook was in a safety deposit box in the First National branch next to the airport. It would be his last stop on his way out of town. He had plane tickets to three other cities under the false names on the passports and connecting flights to distant countries without extradition treaties. One more thing to do and he would be rid of this whole, sorry mess.

He drove his rented car along a route that avoided surveillance cameras as much as possible, but he had to get on the freeway for the last three miles to the airport. Once he had that notebook, he could leave the car in the bank's parking lot and walk the rest of the way to the airport. He might even get to the terminal early enough to browse a newsstand for a book to read on the flights. His car easily negotiated the interchange ramp from the freeway to the airport entrance and exited from the entry road into the bank parking lot.

Grayson felt the heavy summer heat the instant he left his air-conditioned car and the blissful relief from it as he entered the bank's cool, climate-controlled interior. One thing he wouldn't miss was the weather in this place.

As usual, the teller in charge of the deposit boxes was on the phone with somebody. He saw her motion to one of the floor managers, write something down for him, and then start to discuss it. His first inclination was to flash his badge and demand special treatment. But, given that he had tossed the badge right after leaving the precinct for the last time, that would be as difficult as it would be unwise. Best just to wait. The teller finally looked up, saw him waiting, and walked over.

"How may I help you?"

Grayson fished the box key out of his pocket and held it out by its key ring at the end of one finger without saying a word.

The teller examined it, noted the number, then looked back up at him with her professional courtesy smile. There was something in her eyes, but Grayson couldn't tell what. "I see you want to access your safety deposit box. Please follow me to the vault."

She stopped at a logbook on a pedestal beside the massive steel door and made an entry. Then she motioned to Grayson to sign next to it. Once he did so, she compared his signature to the card from her file. She then led him into the vault, where she used his key and her master to open the thick, armored door, slide the box out of its recess in the wall, and lay it on the table in the center of the room.

"When you are done, let me know, and I will re-secure the box and give you your key."

He watched her leave the room and turned to the box. There was nothing in it but the notebook, which he retrieved and slipped into an inside coat pocket. He thought about the teller's apparent nervousness for a moment. Then he decided he just needed to calm down and focus.

He was about to leave when he saw a notepad on the table with a pen next to it. He thought a moment, grinned, wrote a note on the pad, removed the top sheet of paper, and placed it in the box.

"Wouldn't you like to know what was in here?"

Grayson chuckled as he closed the lid, summoned the nervous teller, collected his key, and left. He'd thought about just leaving without the key, since he would never be coming back here, but it was best that he do nothing out of the ordinary at this stage.

The floor manager gave him what looked like a strained smile as he opened the door for Grayson to exit. The heat beat on him as he left the building and walked to his car. After retrieving his roll-around suitcase from the car's trunk, he looked at the key, tossed it into the trunk, and shut the lid. He then turned toward the sidewalk that arched up over the street and ended at the airport's main terminal.

Not twenty feet away, Fred Jakowski stood with half a dozen uniformed cops, who walked up to surround him. There was an expression on Jakowski's face that Grayson had never seen before, and he was holding a set of handcuffs.

"Hello, Captain. Goin' somewhere?"

Chapter 17

"I don't think I've ever made this much preparation for such a short trip."

Grant looked up at Miles from his data pad. "And I know I've never been as nervous about one."

"We have reviewed your route from here to the small airport where the Chinese house and maintain their locally based plane. You know the details, sequence and timing of each event once you arrive. You are as ready as you are going to get."

"Yes, I guess I am.

"Miles, as little as it probably means to you, I want to thank you for all you've done. Without your help I'd be dead now, and nanotechnology would be well on its way to being just a footnote in scientific history.

"Aside from our short meeting a month ago, I've known you for about a week. It seems such a short span of time for so much to have happened." Grant paused and gathered his emotions. "In case this all goes bad tonight, I want you to know how much I have come to respect you. As poorly as you think it turned out, your artificial human project was more than worthy of the success and rewards it should have received.

"I know you have your own reasons for what you've done. You have made that clear. But please hear my heartfelt thanks for what you have done for me and for Ordwyn. However briefly, you gave us a second chance when, without you, there would have been none."

Grant held out his hand and, for the first time, Miles reached out and shook it.

The commuter airpark lay at the base of the foothills that skirted the mountains west of the city. Before the latest economic distress, it had been busy with corporate movers and shakers flying to distant, urgent appointments. Grant noted the sparse traffic as his car wound up the scenic road to the plateau where the airport was located.

There were only three cars in the lot next to the hangar with the large, white Sky Services sign on its roof. They were all black SUVs with heavily tinted windows. It looked like his hosts had been busy preparing his reception. Grant checked his watch.

"I guess it's time for the guest of honor to arrive."

He climbed out of his car, retrieved the carry case

from the trunk, and proceeded to the only door into the hangar from the parking lot.

He opened that door and stepped into a tableau straight out of a movie. Four armed Asians stood in a semicircle ten feet from the door with assault rifles trained on Grant's chest. A twin-engine turboprop stood in the hangar behind them.

"I thought I was expected, but I never imagined . . ."

One of the men stepped forward and pressed the muzzle of his weapon against Grant's neck. He then proceeded to pat down every place on Grant's body where he could possibly have hidden a weapon of any sort. Strangely, the experience triggered the odd memory of a comedian's punch line: "The last time I got that physical with someone, I had to buy her dinner first."

The man handed Grant's carry case to another, who looked into its every pouch and corner before handing it back to Grant. A barked report from the man in what Grant assumed was Chinese brought someone he recognized out of the small office enclosure to the right of the door.

"Mr. Seung. How nice to see you. As your man has assured you, I am not armed in any way. Please have your guards lower their rifles."

Seung was old. Even being a member of a race that carries its age extremely well, he looked old. He snapped out an order to his men, who took up guard stances facing away from Grant and Seung. "Your associate was armed and quite skillful with her tools. We are taking no chances that what happened to her might also happen to you."

Grant gave him a pained look that was only partially pretense. "She was into guns and knives. I'm not. Can we talk in that office over there?"

Seung turned and Grant followed him into the small dispatcher's office. Two more guards, armed just as their colleagues had been, were waiting for them.

Grant gave them perfunctory glances, walked over to the dispatcher's desk, put his well-examined case on it and sat on its edge. He and Seung glared at each other for a long moment.

Then Seung smiled broadly and said, "Welcome, Mr. Thornton. We have gone to a great deal of trouble to arrange this meeting."

"And I have gone to a great deal of trouble to attend it. Mentioning which, this," Grant pointed at the case, "was very difficult to come by on such short notice. I have a feeling I'm not going to like the answer, but tell me why it is necessary anyhow."

"Ah, yes, the re-breather." Seung craned his neck to look at the case. "And you got exactly the specified make and model. Very good."

"The reason for it?"

"It is a basic issue of location. This small airfield will not allow one of our jets to land or take off. That means that we have to fly you to a larger airport and then transfer you to another plane for your journey. Given the other interests who are pursuing you, there must, of necessity, be only one such transfer.

"The transfer itself presents another problem. Since our flight plan will take us out of this country to one that yours thinks ill of, the airplane we use and its contents will be thoroughly inspected by your government before we can leave. That means that either we have to indulge in considerable bribery or hide you in a manner that precludes your discovery.

"The former of those two options would doubtless attract the attention of those interests whom we wish to avoid. The latter, however, comes with its own challenges. Our solution to them was to file and expedite the necessary paperwork to send one of our fallen comrades back to his homeland for his final rest.

"We do this rather more commonly than you might think, as it is often necessary to send, shall we say, sensitive equipment back to our homeland. Fortunately, with a casket that has been prepared and sealed by a duly authorized funeral establishment, this is quite possible. You people have such strange sensitivities.

"We will simply substitute you for the equipment that was going to be transported. You will be moved from one plane to the other with no one the wiser."

Grant gave him a mirthless smile. "And the

re-breather is to keep me alive so that the 'goods' arrive at their destination undamaged. That could be a really long plane ride."

"The re-breather will outlast any compressed air—what do you call it? . . . ah, SCUBA—equipment by orders of magnitude and assure you of breathable air for many hours. However, our crew would of course open the casket once we were safely over international waters so that you could enjoy your trip to your new home. I understand that you find this distasteful, but you have been paid quite well for what will be only a few hours of discomfort."

"Yes. Understand that I verified the arrival of your deposit in my offshore account or I wouldn't be here."

Grant picked up his case, walked around Seung to the door, and turned. "OK, show me this casket I'm supposed to travel in."

Mr. Seung actually looked a bit embarrassed. "There has been a . . . delay in its arrival. We are investigating this."

Grant's face twisted into a defensive scowl. "What kind of delay?"

"We are attempting to determine that as we speak. We should . . ." The near guard's cell phone rang. He exchanged two brief bursts of conversation with his caller. The guard then said much the same thing, even though Grant couldn't understand a word, to Seung.

"That is unfortunate."

"Seung . . ."

The old man talked over what Grant was going to say. "It seems that the interests I mentioned earlier have intercepted the delivery of our casket."

"*Intercepted!* What . . . where . . . when did this happen? What are you going to . . ."

"Mr. Thornton, calm yourself."

"Calm myself? You don't have these guys trying to kill you. Calm does not enter into this! How are you going to make this work without that casket?"

Seung gave Grant the look of a father dealing with an unruly, spoiled child. "We do have an alternative plan."

"Which is what?"

"Come with me, please." Seung walked out of the office and around its corner toward the plane. He stopped at an aluminum container that looked like a part of the plane itself. It was cradled on the forks of a forklift and half full of boxes.

"This is the cargo pod that is normally attached to the underside of the airplane. It has to be kept pressurized and heated in order to preserve the condition of its contents. We will remove this equipment and place you in it instead."

"*What!* Even if I survive the ride, what happens when we get to the international airport?"

"We will taxi the plane to our maintenance facility at that location and summon another casket from our supplier to meet us there. You will be transferred to it for the inspection phase of your escape. This is not an optimal alteration to our plan, but we should be able to conceal your presence long enough to get you past the inspection and into the air again."

Grant took a long look at the cargo pod. "Seung, this is not even close to what I signed up for. I am six feet tall and, while I'm not fat, I am going to make one hell of a tight fit in that thing. If . . ."

Grant was interrupted by three bursts of gunfire and turned back to Seung. "How long ago was that casket intercepted?"

"About five minutes ago. Mr. Thornton, you have run out of other options. Get in the pod so that we can get you out of here!"

The guards had already emptied the pod and laid a moving blanket in the bottom of it. Grant gave Seung a hard look, then took out the re-breather, put it on and started it. He stepped up to the pod and clambered over its side. One of the guards immediately started driving the forklift with the pod resting on its forks over to the plane. The forks pushed the pod up against its mating points on the plane's fuselage. The guard jumped off the lift to secure the half-dozen fasteners that anchored it and sealed it to the underside of the aircraft's fuselage.

The large hangar doors leading to the runway began to slide open then stopped as gunfire erupted directly outside the hangar. The guards ran to the door and began firing as Seung and his personal escort hastily retreated to one of the SUVs.

The pilot was already aboard the plane starting the engines when a particularly violent exchange of gunfire took down two of the four remaining guards. One of the survivors took a small cylinder from his pocket, adjusted it, and threw it through the gap between the doors. A powerful explosion rattled the whole building. The other guard ran to the control box and commanded the doors to open again. The controls took a bit longer to engage the door than they had the last time he used them, and he swore at the balky system in Chinese until they finally began to move again.

The pilot was fully focused on those doors because they were his only escape from this rapidly deteriorating situation. He didn't notice the dark figure that approached the back of his plane with a large bag over its shoulder.

As the gap between the doors widened to just past the wing span of the plane, the pilot gunned the engines and began to move toward the runway. This drew another volley of gunfire that the guards rushed outside to suppress.

The pilot braked until the gunfire subsided, then advanced the throttles again. The plane gathered speed and exited the hangar. The pilot noted that the guards were fully engaged with shooters crouched among a stack of shipping crates. Without any further delay, he taxied the plane quickly to the end of the landing strip, shoved the throttles to the firewall and sent the plane roaring down the runway.

Seung called the pilot on the car's radio while his SUV was swaying drunkenly around the curves as it sped down the airport approach road.

Once again, the wall shimmered, deformed and parted to admit Miles into his monitoring and control room. He went directly to the dais and began to summon data, images and communication intercepts to his holographic arrays. He parsed channels and data streams until he found what he was looking for.

The radio that Seung used to call his pilot was encrypted, but that barely slowed Miles' systems down. In milliseconds, he was listening to a recording of the entire exchange between them. The pilot reported that he had taken off and successfully climbed to 20,000 feet. He noticed a temporary, but slight, loss in cabin pressure as he passed through 12,000 feet, but it stopped and all was well with the plane's hull and controls.

He accessed a recording from a different monitoring array and was shortly listening to Seung's men report that they had routed the group that attacked the hangar. The Chinese had five casualties, including those lost during the attack on the delivery truck. The attackers, who were believed to be from the Consortium, lost four. Miles also learned that a backup contingent of Chinese had arrived at the airport and were cleaning up all evidence of the vicious firefight that had occurred there.

Another batch of recorded, decrypted messages indicated that Thomas Grayson had been apprehended near the airport and was being extremely informative about his recent activities. There was no indication on any of the monitored police channels that there had been any disturbance at the commuter airport west of the city. They were mainly concerned with the aftermath of last night's firefight between their officers and an unknown group of operatives.

A quick switch over to a set of single sideband channels yielded the news that the Consortium's agents were on alert for one George Osterman, who was to be captured alive if at all possible, and warned anyone with ties to Grayson to go to ground. They were also tracking a light plane that should be landing at O'Hare airport in Chicago momentarily. Miles accessed two different systems and set four bogus reports of violent activity at an O'Hare hangar to be sent to the Chicago police in about ten minutes.

Grant's unique set of comm links was forwarding information that the Forester Group was directing and monitoring the results of the clandestine nano-technology research group. Grant's parsing tree for using results to direct further research efforts was working out quite efficiently.

After a thorough review of the research results, which took about four minutes, Miles went back to the Consortium channels. He homed in on the activity surrounding a twin-engine light plane that had just taxied into the Sky Service hangar at O'Hare. Another channel reported that the plane's pilot had radioed Seung that he was being attacked. Seung's local Chinese security seemed to think it had everything under control and would be done with the intrusion shortly. Apparently police were responding to a number of calls reporting gunfire at this hangar.

Miles continued to monitor the data and communications radiating from the O'Hare hangar and finally received the information he had been looking for. The police had killed or captured four Chinese who fired on them, a contract pilot and two unidentified men who appeared to be part of an operations team of some sort. Most of that team had escaped, but they left behind a dead male who apparently had been a stowaway in the plane's cargo pod. A bullet hole was found in the pod that had been partially closed with frozen blood.

Charles Carver sat at the oblong conference table and tried very hard to put the empty chair next to him out of his mind. Even after the horrendous events of the last 48 hours, Lori's death still weighed heavily on him.

One by one the monitors filled with the familiar faces of those Charles had begun to think of as his family. He looked around at them and said a silent prayer that none of the monitors would be blank at some future board meeting.

As the last screen came to life with its virtual occupant, Charles sighed and started.

"I have tried to keep everyone up to speed and informed but, with the events of the last few days, it has been difficult in the extreme. I have called this meeting primarily for two reasons. The first is to update everyone with our current estimate of the situation regarding Grant Thornton. The second is to make sure that the information we do have, and our educated suppositions, are distributed to all of you as well.

"We will start with item number two, as number one is likely to entail protracted discussion. Sam, what is our current security status?"

Baker stood slowly. He was bone weary and had gotten virtually no sleep since the battle outside their offices. "There have been no further incursions or actions against either the office or the apartment buildings. We have overhauled the monitoring, control, and alarm systems completely, and sincerely believe that the Consortium will not be able to compromise them . . . again.

"We have created an emergency control station in the tunnel connecting the apartments and the offices. If we are attacked again, the tunnel will be the most secure area available to us. We will be able to control our access systems and surveillance cameras from this station. Short of an armed conflict with the Consortium's agents, this is the best we can do to assure the safety of our people.

"It has been said that the best defense is a good offense. In our case, our best defense is a good knowledge of what our opponents are up to. Unfortunately, our knowledge of the plans and activities of the Consortium at this point is chaotic.

"We know that they suffered extreme losses in the street battle outside our offices. Between their compromised police personnel and their special operations agents, we estimate that the street battle alone cost them at least fifty casualties, with most killed and only a few captured. Beyond that, we have only fragments of information that are puzzling at best and contradictory at worst.

"For instance, we have comm intercepts that indicate some kind of armed conflict at the little commuter airport outside of the city. But there is no police confirmation of this, nor have our agents been able to find any corroboration. We know that a major operation was mounted in Chicago last night. Then we intercepted comm that sounds like the Consortium is actively hunting George Osterman, the head of their own covert activities group.

"The local police forces are in an uproar after they discovered that Captain Thomas Grayson and most of the police killed in the street battle were working for one George Osterman. They are sufficiently distracted with cleaning up their own house and rounding up the rest of Grayson's men that they are all but ignoring nonviolent local crime, so we probably won't see anything of value from them for a while.

"This brings us to the situation with Grant Thornton. Charles, I'll hand the explanation of that one over to you." Baker sat down like a stone dropped on wet sod.

"Sam, you are too kind . . . and too exhausted. Please get some rest as soon as you can.

"The news about Thornton comes in three flavors: the good, the weird, and the bad.

"The good news is that the structured research guidance system appears already to be working. We are beginning to get results from some of the research efforts that are pointing the way to the next experimental direction. Our original estimate that this current structure could keep us going for a month may be conservative. So, nanotechnology research is proceeding apace.

"The bad news is that we have reports that Thornton has been killed. As Sam mentioned, there was a gun battle at an O'Hare airport hangar in Chicago last night. One of the casualties is a man who, from a police photo we obtained, looks like Grant Thornton's identical twin. The police are running a DNA analysis. If it's him, we should have confirmation in a few days. This comes on the heels of confirmation that Sergeant Ordwyn Summers was killed as part of a falling out between Chinese technology pirates— the same pirates who just shot it out with the Consortium at O'Hare.

"The weird news is that we are still getting what looks to be guidance for the researchers that is coming from Thornton or from someone who knows as much about nanotechnology as he does—and there isn't anyone like that. We have received two messages this morning that redirect major portions of the research to really promising ideas.

"To summarize, we don't appear to be in imminent danger, the nanotechnology research is proceeding better than expected, Grant Thornton may or may not be dead, and we may or may not have been dealing with him through the group that is guiding the research.

"Questions?"

"How will we ever know who we have directing our nanotechnology effort?"

Carver looked at Baker for a moment and back at the screen at the end of the array. "Amy, I have no good answer for you. As near as I can tell, we need to go with what we are getting from the people we've been calling the Thornton group until we have reason to suspect its quality. So far, there has been nothing to discredit their input in any way."

"So," came the response from one of the monitors, "we just keep feeling our way along and hope we don't put our hands into a nest of snakes."

"Yes, Mr. Drake, that's about it.

"Any other comments?

"Very well, the one good outcome from all this is that the Consortium has been thrown into utter disarray. If we are thrashing about in uncertainty, they are drowning in it. All of our intercepted communications among their agents indicate that they are pulling back from all covert operations. The whole Grayson mess has put them in a position of such extreme public exposure that they have to retreat as rapidly as possible.

"For the first time since the Forester Group was founded, we have an opportunity to work very nearly unfettered by the actions of the Consortium."

———

Grant looked around. What a remarkable place.

This was where Miles had gathered his samples and where he had built Grant's clone. Grant himself examined the room that would be his home for the next month. He lay in bed with an IV dripping into his arm and tried to imagine how different he was going to look.

Miles was focused on adjusting an array of infusion pumps and plugging them into the IV one at a time. "These solutions will assist my nano-machine swarms by providing some 'raw materials' for the transformations they will perform on your body. I will start your anesthetic shortly."

Grant just watched him for a few minutes. "Miles, I can't tell you how relieved I was when you pulled that pod off the airplane and replaced me with the clone. I really didn't think you were going to be able to pull that one off."

"As I said earlier, it was basically a stage magician's trick. The battle kept Seung's men busy and away from the plane, and the pilot couldn't see the rear of his craft. I simply unlatched the pod, removed you, inserted the clone and then re-attached the pod. My unique abilities allowed me to do all this in a very short time, and that meant Seung never had any reason to suspect the switch."

"I am extremely grateful, nonetheless. One thing I don't understand, though. How did you manage to shoot a bullet into the pod at just the right time and just the right angle to make it look like the clone had been shot during the fight?"

"I did not do any such thing."

"Explain, please?"

"The nano swarms that were maintaining the clone to keep it 'dead' but not decomposing served a dual purpose. I sent them a command that activated a secondary program. That program made them leave the clone body, causing it to begin to lose blood. They then augured a hole in the side of the cargo pod that would appear to be a bullet hole. When the dead clone was examined, it would be found to have been 'killed' by the bullet I had placed at the end of the wound channel I originally constructed into the clone."

"But, wouldn't an autopsy have discovered at least some trace of the nano-machines?"

"Not at all, Grant. They left the pod through the hole they made in it."

Grant shook his head. "And the clone's blood flowed to the hole and partially sealed it when the plane gained enough altitude. Amazing."

"Like any good magician's trick, the assistant provided the necessary distractions while I simply operated the preset mechanism to perform its designed tasks."

Grant took one last look around as Grant Thornton. "Well, Miles, I guess I'm ready."

Miles inserted a syringe into the IV juncture and squeezed a clear liquid into the saline stream that was flowing into Grant's body.

"You will begin to feel drowsy in a few minutes, and then you will sleep. You will come back to a semi-conscious state on two occasions to allow for process adjustments, but you won't remember them. When you awake 33 days from now, you will be Jason Keller in all but your memories.

"Jason Keller. I like that name"

"Good. I have built an entire history and identity around it."

The sedative was already beginning to take effect. "Miles, please tell me if Odrwyn made it. I really need to know."

Miles looked down directly into Grant's eyes. "No; you want to know. As I have already explained, for the foreseeable future there will still be far too much uncertainty in this situation and with the Consortium in particular for you to be concerned about her.

"It is time for you to sleep now. In what will seem like the blink of an eye, a month will pass and you will wake up as a completely new person. Many would give everything for that opportunity. And, indeed, you already have."

The last thing that Grant Thornton saw was Miles' face looking down at him.

He could have sworn he saw a faint trace of a smile.

Jakowski hated cemeteries.

He hated them mostly because he knew too many of their residents. His visit today was no exception.

The plastic wrapped around the small cluster of flowers felt odd in his hands as he walked past row after row of markers. So many people who probably didn't know how soon they would wind up here were laid out side by side over acres of manicured ground. He found the row he was looking for and, five plots in, he stopped to look down at the marker that announced its occupant.

"I got Grayson for ya. I know he wasn't the one who killed ya, but he was in it up to his neck."

He laid the flowers on the stone just below the name:

"Ordwyn Summers—Sergeant CPD"

Chapter 18

It was almost evening.

The shadows had merged. The lights around the Crestview Cemetery sign were switched on by the system that detected the onset of night. The quiet was almost like the thick silence that accompanied new-fallen snow. Everyone had left for the day.

Almost everyone had left.

A lone figure stood in front of a marker in a corner of the newest part of the cemetery. The man was medium height, barrel-chested and obviously very strong. In the past of a century ago, he might have been a blacksmith. He brushed a shock of blonde hair out of his eyes and knelt to place a single white rose on the marker.

"I'm sorry it took me so long. I know I shouldn't be here now. But today . . . today I finally had to come.

"It's been a year. A whole year, and you wouldn't believe what has happened, how much has changed. I knew that nothing would be left untouched, but it's just

astounding. You always said that I underestimated what would happen, and you were right.

"Because of what we did, the nanotechnology work was able to come out of the closet, and it is changing the whole world. I wonder what the Forester Group would think if they knew all that had actually happened? If they knew that the technology they released into the world really did come from me. I bet they guessed some of what happened.

"I never did get to meet Charles Carver. It's one of my few regrets.

"The Forester Group set up an institute in Grant's name to continue the work and place every new nanotechnology discovery they created in the public domain."

He looked at the grave marker just to the right of the one he knelt at. It read simply "Grant Thornton—RIP."

"Grant Thornton is well and truly dead. When Miles revived me, I looked in the mirror and saw that I was half a foot shorter, with broader shoulders and blond hair instead of black and, well, literally everything had changed. My new body not only looked different, it felt different. I felt completely lost at first, but I finally knew I was Jason Keller. I knew it down in my very bones. All the background and constructed memories became my own. As he helped me gain control over my new body, I could feel the differences—and the amazing strength he built into it!

"I just wish you could have seen it.

"Goodbye."

The man stood, turned, and walked away. The grave marker that bore the white rose read:

"Ellen Thornton—my friend, my love, my wife"

———————————

Jason approached the ornate fence that enclosed the entire cemetery and stopped for a moment to disengage the latch. He walked through the gate, closed it, re-latched it and walked back to his car two blocks away.

As he bent to unlock and open the door, he heard a whisper of a voice.

"I've got a gun on you, so you will do what I say. Unlock the passenger side door."

He looked over the roof of the car, only partially surprised, and found a vaguely familiar face looking at him over a gun. He pushed the button, allowing the man with the gun to open the door on his side.

"Get in and drive."

"It might help if I knew where we are going."

"It's not far. Now shut up. Drive to the corner and turn left."

Jason did so, Then, a bare minute later, "Turn right and slow down."

The man pulled a garage door remote control out of his pocket and pushed the button. A door in the middle of the building on the right obediently began to roll up. "Turn in here."

The door led into a large warehouse with a floor covered in packing crates. Jason steered the car around them to a space with a table covered in chemical lab equipment and a cot set off to one side. Jason drove up to the table and stopped. His passenger pushed the controller button again and the roll up door rolled back down. "Turn it off and get out."

Jason carefully opened the door and stood up. His uninvited passenger did the same. The man stepped over to the table, pulled out a chair and motioned to Jason with the gun. "Sit down."

After Jason took his seat, the man stepped back so that he was between Jason and his car. "Who are you?" the man asked.

"Wait a minute. You kidnapped me, and you don't even know who I am?"

"No, and I kinda figured I'd know who came to visit Ellen Thornton's grave. But I don't know you. I set up a video bug to watch that stone nearly a year ago. I've seen everybody who came. I knew all of them. But I don't know you."

"And why would you watch Ellen Thornton's grave?"

"Why not? Look around. This is my life now. Anybody could tell from looking at that table that I cut and sell drugs. It's not much, but it keeps me going. After I finally killed Grant Thornton, her husband, I thought I could go back to the commit-tee and pick up where I left off. With him dead—and I was sure he was dead because all the DNA and the other crap they tested said so—nanotech should have been dead.

"But somebody, or some bunch of people, picked up right where he left off; didn't even miss a beat. Next thing I know, I'm on the run from the same people who used to pay me, and pay me well, to clean up their messes. An' the only link I've got left to a life that used to be damned good is that rock with her name carved in it. So I put a bug on it. And now I've got you.

"So, yeah, I want to know who you are. I want to know who bollixed up everything I did to stop Thornton. I want to know who could send me and my guys runnin' every which way. I want to know . . ."

Jason never did find out what else he wanted to know.

At that moment a figure came flying over Jason's car, placed an elbow in his captor's right ear, knocked the gun out of his hand, stepped under his arm and pivoted him up into the air and back down flat on his back onto a cold cement floor.

"We were wondering when you'd surface again, George."

The deep, throaty voice shocked Jason into the realization that George had been taken down by one very impressive woman. She was tall, muscular, blonde, and proportioned like a movie star. It also brought back the reason he should recognize George.

"Well I'll be . . . that's George Osterman isn't it?"

"In the putrid flesh."

"I'd seen pictures of him, but apparently life hasn't gone well for George. I almost didn't recognize him. And, speaking of recognition, who are you?"

"We can discuss that later. Right now we need to get out of here. The police have been alerted that a dealer they have been trying to run down for months has just been spotted right here in this building."

She looked at the table. "And I'd guess the contents of that table will account for George's free time for the next twenty or thirty years." She fished the control for the roll-up door out of George's pocket and activated it. "Shall we?

"Let's go in yours," she said, as she headed for Jason's car. "Leaving it here will cause unwanted official questions, and I can retrieve mine later. The good news is that George disabled the surveillance cameras for two blocks around this place."

"This seems to be my night for strange passengers."

They got in the car. Jason started it and asked the obvious question: "OK, where are we going?"

"I've seen your place and, trust me, mine's much nicer. Drive over to Broadway and 9th."

———

Jason followed the directions. She kept her silence until they reached the specified corner where she pointed him to an underground parking lot with an elevator that accessed the apartment building above it. She was right. Her place was much nicer.

"All right, I've been kidnapped by a thug from my sordid past and then by a gorgeous blonde with a knack for martial arts. Now would you please tell me who you are and what's going on? You could start with how you knew that George grabbed me."

She smiled, and Jason felt his knees weaken. "That was the easy part. We knew that someone had bugged Ellen's grave."

"You did? How?"

"Because we had already done so, and we saw George place his hardware. What we didn't know was the location he was watching it from. We were also watching you and figured tonight would be the night you would finally show up in George's crosshairs. You did, I followed you and George back to the warehouse, and you know the rest."

"OK, let's broaden the topic. Who's 'we'?"

Jason pulled out a chair and took a seat at her kitchen table while she got out a cup and walked over to the most elaborate coffeemaker he had ever seen. She poured the cup full, walked around the table, and put it down next to him. She then sat on his lap, put her arm around his massive shoulders and looked into his eyes from an uncomfortably close and definitely stimulating distance.

"'We' are me and our mutual friend. He's even bigger than you are, walks kind of funny, and he's really old."

"You know M . . ." She put her finger over his lips.

"Yes. I do . . . odd jobs for him."

Jason was finding it difficult to avoid being completely mesmerized by her somehow oddly familiar deep blue eyes, but he struggled back for one last question. "So, back to number one. Who are you?"

"My name now is Samantha Everett. But he told me to tell you that I am the answer to the last question you asked him when your name was Grant."

It struck him like a lightning bolt. "Ord . . ." She stopped him with a deep, powerful kiss that brought back a cherished memory.

"It's really you?" he asked when they broke for air.

"It is most definitely me—not short, dark-haired and wiry any more, huh?"

"Damn, but he does nice work!"

"Doesn't he just."

She pulled the zipper down the front of her jumpsuit and, with absolutely no resistance from Jason, got busy with something she had put on hold for entirely too long.

Miles stood on the dais and released a monitoring array for re-tasking. The array had been collecting data on one of the Consortium's more nefarious financial schemes and the damage it was doing to a company whose management didn't know what it was up against. The data had no bearing on nano-technology and did not directly concern him. It was merely another instance of the Consortium's unbridled greed.

For a moment that lasted millennia, Miles paused and looked back through the centuries.

"Ridwyn, you are the best person I have ever known. I loved you the day we met, and I always knew I wanted to be by your side. You are kind, generous and just. If something is wrong, you will make it right."

He turned back to the display arrays and began setting monitors, adjusting data records, intercepting and emitting messages. It was past time for the Consortium to have a general run of bad luck—very bad luck indeed.

A Note from John

Try to imagine something doubling its capability every two years.

That is what has happened with the integrated circuit chips that operate our computers. Those chips have doubled their power and capability 25 times over the past half-century. That means that today's computing machinery is roughly 33 million times more powerful than what was built into the Apollo moon rocket. In two more years it will be 66 million times more powerful. Shortly after that, a computer with the processing power and complexity to directly emulate the human brain will exist, and it's a fair bet that the software to create a genuine, human-level AI will not be far behind.

That first AI has been designated AGI, Artificial General Intelligence, by the community of computer and logic engineers who are laboring to create it. You see, while the media may have consigned AI as the dumping ground for silly ideas, an entire generation of technical wizards has taken it on as a personal challenge. This community of AI developers is currently debating how long it will take AGI, once it is created and aware, to become ASI—Artificial Super Intelligence. That ASI would be a greater-than-human-level intelligence.

Think about that for a moment.

An Artificial General Intelligence would have the same intellectual skills as you and me. However, it would be able to exercise those skills at about 2,000 times the speed available to us, and it would have access to instant recall of all the knowledge the human race has accumulated over the last 6,000 years. Estimates of the time that it will take AGI to evolve into ASI range from a few years to a few seconds.

What would an ASI be like? What would it think, what would it do? No one can answer those questions. But setting those musings aside, here's the real question: What use would an ASI have for us slow, stumble-minded humans?

The sciences of nanotechnology, robotics and genetics are in headlong races very similar to that of computer hardware and software. A system with the same abilities I have attributed to Miles is not very far in the future. One that vastly exceeds his abilities is not much beyond that.

And yet, the media that is supposed to be reporting developments that have high-impact potential for our lives is strangely silent on AI. It's almost as if their decision to ignore the subject some forty years ago has become irreversible. We are exposed to a daily barrage of matters legal, economic and political, but AI is rarely mentioned at all.

The *Escape the Machine Trilogy* is my effort to stimulate a public conversation about Artificial Intelligence. Miles will be back in *Promises to Keep* and *Before I Sleep*. You can also visit me at johnclunsford.com and connect with Miles at EscapeTheMachineBlog.com.

I strongly recommend the references listed on the next page to get a grip on what has been happening with AI. I am making this recommendation out of a deep desire to foster this public discourse on a subject that is shortly going to affect us all, profoundly.

Read, investigate, contemplate and keep going back to the existential questions of "Who am I?" and, out of who I really am, "What do I want?" The future is happening now—and probably a lot faster than we expect.

References

Our Final Invention. James Barrat. New York, New York: Thomas Dune Books, 2013.

The Singularity is Near. Ray Kurtzweil. New York, New York: Penguin Group, 2005.

Superintelligence: Paths, Dangers, Strategies. Nick Bostrom. Oxford: Oxford University Press, 2014.

"Why the Future Doesn't Need Us." Bill Joy. *Wired Magazine,* Issue 8.04, Apr 2000. http://archive. wired.com/wired/archive/8.04/joy.html

About the Author

John Lunsford was born in Fort Worth, Texas, at the outset of the baby boom generation. The culture of the time was wide-eyed with wonder and optimism. Imbued with that sense of wonder, he set himself a grand adventure: to learn how to read. Once he mastered that, he read everything he could get his hands on—which led him to his interests in and questions on just about everything. He wanted to know the how and why of all of existence. His fascination with 20th-century history in grade school led directly to the questions that have become compass points in his life: What if? And then what?

The monstrous, ridiculously complex computer he encountered at Texas A&M during his freshman year lit a bonfire under him and his questions. Over the next 40 years he made a profession out of working with software engineers to make their code as error-free as possible. Incredibly challenging, his work is a source of immense satisfaction for him.

His work encompasses an array of accomplishments. He designed and worked on the data links that send information to and from satellites. During the first fifteen years of the personal computer revolution, he taught people who had never seen a computer how to use one. Then he co-created and taught to engineers a class on how to build fax machines from the ground up, which consumed the next fifteen years. That effort has carried him around the world several times.

He has watched and been a part of the exponential acceleration in the development of computing technology. His lifelong experience with it has cultivated in him a feel, a vision for the growth that led to his *Escape the Machine* trilogy. It presents us with a "what if" that is fraught with both possibility and peril. It is quite possible that the human race will see more change in the next twenty years than it has seen in the last thousand.

John's grandmother went from Tennessee to Texas in a covered wagon and lived long enough to watch men walk on the moon broadcast on her television set. John has watched computers go from devices that absorbed vast hours of human thought to, very possibly, beginning to think about us.

It's going to be fascinating to see what happens next.

To connect with Miles, go to
www.EscapeTheMachineBlog.com
and to learn more visit us at
www.johnclunsford.com